CARBIDE

by ANDRIY LYUBKA

Translated from the Ukrainian by
Reilly Costigan-Humes and
Isaac Stackhouse Wheeler

JANTAR PUBLISHING

London 2020

The following Patrons contributed to
the costs of publishing this book

Victoria Amelina

Natalia Bruslanova

Deborah Costigan

Jimi Cullen

Britta Ellwanger

Maria Genkin

Konstantin Grytsan

Yaroslava Hlynska

Igor

J&S

Ania Jacyniak

Nataliya Kabatsiy

Leonard Kizman

Oleh Kotsyuba

Oleksandr Kyryliuk

Iryna Lozynska

Mab

Natasha Mansour

Olha Moroz

Volodymyr Novosad

Sergiy Panko

Oleksandra Saienko

Taras Sich

Eco Volt

Erik Wheeler

Shelley Wheeler

Giorgio Zeljkovic

The Friends of Jantar

First published in Great Britain in 2020 by
Jantar Publishing Ltd
www.jantarpublishing.com

First published in 2015 in Chernivtsi as *Карбід*

A CIP catalogue record for this book is available from the British Library
ISBN 978-0-9934467-4-0

This book has been published with the support
of the *Translate Ukraine* Translation Grant Program

The Contents

Introduction by MICHAEL TATE:

       Carbide versus *Candide* and the notion of Eastern Europe 9

CARBIDE by ANDRIY LYUBKA   11

Chapter 1: *In Which Tys Appears and Then Disappears Underground* ... 15

Chapter 2: *In Which Tys Rushes Over to Icarus's* 21

Chapter 3: *In Which the Plot Would Have Ground to a Halt if Not*

       for the Genius of the Carpathians 39

Chapter 4: *In Which Our Heroes Reach a Disquieting Impasse* 49

Chapter 5: *In Which the Mayor Pours and Probes* 59

Chapter 6: *In Which Tys Finally Announces His Idea* 69

Chapter 7: *In Which Work Commences and Then Suddenly Ceases* ... 81

Chapter 8: *In Which There's Grief and Nothing But Grief* 91

Chapter 9: *In Which the Femme Fatale Finally Makes an Appearance* 115

Chapter 10: *Scrambling for a Solution* 131

Chapter 11: *In Which the Tunnel is Revived!* 143

Chapter 12: *In Which all the Extras Exit the Stage* 155

Chapter 13: *In Which Reality Intertwines With Illusion* 175

Chapter 14: *In Which the Action Unfolds a Week Before the Unveiling*

       of the Fountain of Unity 189

Chapter 15: *In Which the Protagonist Hears Something He Shouldn't*

       Have, and the Protagonist Is Transformed into a Coward 201

Chapter 16: *In Which Tys Saves Himself or Doesn't* 215

Chapter 17: *In Which the Part of the Story That Takes Place in the Best*

       of all Possible Worlds Comes to an End 229

Author's and Translators' Biographies 249

Carbide versus *Candide* and the notion of Eastern Europe

The author, Andriy Lyubka, was born in Riga in 1987, in those days when Riga represented the far northern Baltic border between the Soviet Union and 'the west'. These days, he lives and works in his 'hometown of Uzhhorod', another border town. That particular border has a number of meanings. It separates contemporary Ukraine with contemporary Slovakia and is both administrative and quite physical: Uzhhorod's western city limits form the Ukraine/ Slovak border. Both Ukraine and Slovakia are 'new countries' formed since the fall of the Berlin Wall in 1989. That border on the western side of Uzhhorod also divides the EU from 'East Europe' or more whimsically, that land border divides West Europe from East Europe. These borders cannot be viewed as historically permanent but do represent a wall of ignorance between perceptions of Eastern and Western Europe and how that is expressed in literary culture. Finally, it is worth pointing out that in the time between writing and publishing *Carbide*, Ukraine's eastern border with Russia changed violently. Borders are more than abstract notions.

Lyubka maintains that before Voltaire, 'Western Europe was largely ignorant of Eastern Europe. It was at once undiscovered, rich, romantic, documented and threatening. Unknown armies invaded from 'the East' but 'the East' also possessed the golden hoard. The East was a contradiction, both a powerful neighbour and a setting for fairytales'.

In Lyubka's *Carbide*, Voltaire's 'Bulgarians' return as a group of criminals inspired to smuggle a whole country into the EU. It is a hilarious satire using one of Europe's greatest satirical texts to update a notion of a nation. Where Candide is an optimist, Carbide is pessimist. Where Candide's philosophy has the intellectual foundation of Spinoza, Carbide is a delusional drunk who just makes things up as he goes along.

Enjoy!

Michael Tate
London, October 2020

CARBIDE

by ANDRIY LYUBKA

BRATISLAVA (Reuters) – A smuggling tunnel the length of seven soccer pitches complete with its own train has been found running beneath the border between Slovakia and Ukraine along with more than 2.5 million contraband cigarettes, the Slovak government said on Thursday. Police said the tunnel had possibly also been used to smuggle people into…

July 19th, 2012

Chapter 1:

In Which Tys Appears and Then Disappears Underground

Someday, there'll be nobody left around here.

But for now, there are 30-odd thousand people living here, below the mountain and above the river. They'd really like to move away, but that's frankly a bizarre thing to want. Vedmediv's a perfect place to live. This ancient city's original name says it all – Mediv, a variation on the Ukrainian word for 'honey'. It's a sweet spot, and that didn't escape the attention of would-be conquerors. The name changed to Vedmediv, a variation on 'bear,' literally a 'honey-finder,' when the mighty hordes of the Bear Empire swept westward. The locals didn't change the name back after the Empire broke up, though; that's how lazy and apathetic the Vedmedivites were. The people residing in the neighboring villages would always say that Vedmediv should've been named after a snake, the only animal that can move while lying on its belly.

There was one guy who wasn't a typical lazy Vedmedivite, though; he was a real go-getter, a leader, a man who got his countrymen's spirits vibrating again – a spirit vibrator. He must have been born under a blue moon. He went by the name Tys, while his students (he taught history at a school in town) would call him Mr. Chvak to his face, and Carbide behind his back. Malicious gossip had it that the teacher was prone to breaking wind in the classroom, leaving students dizzy with his noxious fumes – which smelled just like calcium carbide.

Tys's wife Marichka was lazy, like a true Vedmedivite. She always made her henpecked husband do everything, which just made her lazier. For instance, she'd say, 'dinner is served, come on in!' But Tys was no fool. We're talking about a guy who attended an institution of higher learning – and he graduated and everything! – he wasn't about to let his wife boss him around. He'd retort with something like 'no, you're served, you come on in!' He was always absorbed with his books and maps, always studying and annotating them, as if the vanished world he found there was where he actually lived. Marichka would get bored and ask her husband to come out of his study so they could chat. But he stuck to his guns: 'Tys is busy.' One day, curiosity got the better of his wife and she asked:

'Why do you go by Tys?'

'Ugh, you should just go back to your own business, woman, you wouldn't get it anyway. It all started with Rome. Emperor Tiberius did a lot of good for his people. He got the name Tiberius from the Tiber, the river Rome was built on. We have the Tysa River, so I went with Tys.'

'Well, why do you go by Tys instead of Tyserius, huh? Because nobody would take you that serious? Remember that time I asked you to pick up some soap? You just assumed I meant bath soap, so you went ahead and got some birch branches to massage me with in the sauna, and you kept going on and on about how studies have shown that it's more efficient and good for your circulation. You were so pleased with yourself. But I just needed some damn soap to do the dishes!'

'Marichka, my love, don't get so worked up. I just want to do some good for our beloved Transcarpathia – and all of Ukraine. I put the interests of society and the state above my own. Only our descendants will truly appreciate the value of my work.'

'Why don't you make a few descendants of your own? We haven't gone to bed together for a year! You're always sleeping in your study. It's like you're afraid of your own wife! Some champion of the people you are! More like a fucking chumpion!'

It wasn't easy for Tys to live among workaday philistines incapable of thinking beyond their own immediate self-interest. He valued the happiness and prosperity of his native Transcarpathia, not mere money, titles, or comfort. Tys could always find the time to visit his local tavern, throw a few back, and tell hoi polloi about the glorious history that transpired in these parts, but he couldn't find the time to fix the door of his own outhouse. So you had to hold it shut with one hand the whole time you were doing your business, which would greatly inconvenience visitors whenever they tried to wipe themselves or pull up their pants. The door would often screech open and the neighborhood kids would see Carbide squatting there, eyes bulging with surprise.

Tys may not have been able to realize all his ambitions, but that hardly mattered. He had a grand project to give his life meaning, an idea that would compensate for all his slip-ups and failures and allow him to make his mark on Ukrainian history. Humanity has always failed to honor its champions. There haven't been a lot of them to speak of. The people are philistines, and no prophet is accepted in his own country. Since time immemorial, champions have been mocked – Tys knew that perfectly well. He was a historian, after all. Knowing that kept him from losing faith. It was only recently that he'd found his true mission in life, though.

Some people spend their whole lives waiting for a big break that never comes. Generally, it's something we're afforded purely by chance, so we have to be able to spot it and cling to it, grip it tightly and never let go. Tys's chance fell right into his lap, much like the apple fell right on Newton's head. The apple did a number on the physicist's noggin, while our hero did a number on himself without any outside assistance. Marichka screamed at him when it happened, half deranged, 'you worthless alcoholic, you can't even drag your sorry ass home from the bar!' Tys was happy, though. Fate had finally given him his chance. Some may believe his wife's version of the story – her husband was walking home from the bar, ungodly drunk, and he fell into an open manhole and slopped around in sewage for a while. Yes, all of that was true, but there was more to it than met the eye.

Only Tys had an insider's perspective on what had really happened. Sure, he did fall into a pool of filth, but it was in that moment that an idea flashed through his mind and filled his life with meaning. Into the depths, that's the ticket! It was down there that he would find the path to a brighter future for his hapless kinsmen. Underground Ukraine! He had to do something nobody had ever thought of before. His whole path through life was a symbol for this plunge – the study of history entails digging, scouring, and unearthing. As a young man, his intuition had led him in the right direction, down into the depths. Now he'd finally arrived – in the municipal sewer system!

Tys came home trailing a wake of aromas that stung Marichka's eyes, but a demented smile adorned his face. That may account for why his wife thought he was still hammered. But that wasn't the case – he'd only drunk one bottle of vodka, two, max, and it's not like he'd even really wanted to. It's just that there was no other way to reach the working class. For instance, he'd order a shot, take a seat next to some construction workers, and propose a toast to Svyatoslav, the famous Kyivan count, which he would supplement with a brief history lesson – twenty minutes, tops. That's how national consciousness is shaped – one toast at a time. So, Tys was doing it all for Ukraine, not himself – not that Marichka would know anything about that.

Once he'd gotten out of the tub and wrapped himself in a down blanket, he was unreservedly happy. He had torrents of alcohol in his head to embolden and exhilarate him. Tys fell into a deep sleep as though he were dropping into an open manhole, but it was fame, stars, the Ukrainian guelder rose, and the respect of his kinsmen awaiting him down there, not sewage. He saw himself passing between rows of happy Ukrainians, all applauding in admiration and singing the folk song 'Many Years.' He's walking along with a smile on his face. There's something glorious at the end of his path, a banquet table heaped with food and drink. There's vodka – pepper-flavored, plum-flavored, and plain – and beer, too – basically, everything a national hero could want. The Ukrainian coat of arms adorns one side of every glass and the EU stars shine on the other. Tys's name is inscribed on the bottom. The name of a person who accomplished his great mission and finally ended the suffering of Ukraine and united it with Mother Europe. That's how it was going to be, no doubt about it. He'd make it happen. How good of fate to give him his chance now, at forty-four years young, still brimming with energy and fortitude. Now he'd found his vocation. All he had to do was assemble a team that would help make this ingenious plan a reality. He'd put together a team of loyal compadres who'd never think of betraying him. He'd pay Icarus a visit tomorrow, and his friend would light up when he heard Tys's idea. He'd get all his friends together, forming a team of spiritual giants, patriots, and Ukrainians. Everything would come together. Glory to God, for He sent Tys into the sewer, giving him a profound clue! As he was falling asleep, Tys kept falling underground, where challenges and accomplishments, fame and triumph awaited him. He was mumbling something in his sleep, smiling, squirming, digging his hands into the earth, diving into it, plunging deeper and deeper.

Chapter 2:

In Which Tys Rushes Over to Icarus's

Tys woke up and couldn't figure out where he was for the longest time. He'd spent the whole night underground, digging, burrowing, and gnawing his way through the soil; now there was a naked light-bulb dangling above him by a wire attached to the ceiling. The light grew brighter and then dimmer – something was on the fritz. Tys imagined that a flashlight piercing the darkness and illuminating the bottom of the shaft where he and his team of friends were digging would look just like that.

A distinct, yet barely perceptible smell hovered in the room – the unmistakable stench of sewage. Tys didn't scrub it all off yester-day. Naturally, he couldn't smell it – people can't smell their own fragrance, just as they can't see their own shortcomings. Marichka, on the other hand, stepped into his room and made a sour face like her bare foot had just landed in a still-warm cow plop.

'Oh Lord, you should at least crack a window if you don't even have the decency to wash up properly! Or sleep outside, next to the dog! Actually, you'd probably drive the dog away, too, ya hapless boozehound, ya worthless tippler! I don't know how the kids in your class put up with it! How are you expecting them to listen to you if your own dog wants nothing to do with you? Take a look at your study, you slob: the fixture's broken, now there's just a lightbulb dangling from the ceiling, like this is a barn or something, the books are thrown all over the place like a tornado just touched down, the bones from the borsch I made two damn days ago are all over your map, and the smell – everything smells like shit! What did I ever marry you for? Why didn't I listen to my mom? She said it'd be better to marry a corpse than a historian. Better yet, I should've married a cripple, at least I'd get some government money! Anyone but a history teacher!' his wife raged.

'Well, my late father warned me, too – don't choose a sow from Sasovo or a wife from Korolevo! But I didn't listen. I married you – all those damn wedding toasts about how Kingolevo is the village of kings and you're its queen! You're a cow, that's what you are! A cow that's poisoned my life, always stamping her hoofs and distracting me. Now get lost! I can't hear myself think.'

At first, Marichka wanted to spit right on the floor, but then she realized she'd be the one cleaning it up, so she simply gave her husband the most disdainful look she could manage and walked out. At that moment, he looked absolutely pathetic, all sprawled out on a tattered old chair missing one leg. It tilted downward slightly, just like the Titanic before it went under. Tys was only wearing his checkered boxers and high black socks – his dirty big toe had poked a rather large hole in the left one – pulled almost all the way up to his knees. His greasy salt and pepper hair was sticking out every which way. The long, static-filled hair on his skinny, rickety legs, interwoven with a dark web of veins, was standing as high as an elephant's eye. A long moustache – one end sticking up like an antenna and the other glued to his cheek with saliva – completed his look.

Tys's appearance that morning was in stark contrast to the grandeur of his design. His spirits rose immediately when he thought of the epoch-making idea he had conceived the previous night. He even cracked a smile, exposing the gold tooth in place of his top right incisor. Tys tried twirling his moustache, but it was just too wet and slimy, so he merely wiped his hand on the chair in disgust. It was as though some invisible mechanism, some motor, had started up somewhere inside our champion's body, making his movements quicker and his posture more expansive. In the medical field, the feeling you have when you awaken after a night of heavy drinking and you're still drunk is called the morning euphoria effect. You're abnormally active, happy, and energetic. Tys hadn't heard of this phenomenon, so he interpreted the chemistry playing out in his body as a mere testament to the brilliance and power of his design.

Now every moment had become vitally important. He had no right to delay. He had to hustle, get across town to see his best friend, the man who would help him realize his plans. Tys hopped into his pants – they were two sizes too big, so they would have slid right off his slender waist if not for his belt. They were so tight at the top and flared out so wide at the bottom, he looked like he was wearing a dress. Our champion then had to undo his belt, since he'd forgotten to put a shirt on. He pulled it over his head, tucked it in, slipped into his black, pointed dress shoes, now caked in mud, like a salamander's skin, looked himself over in the mirror out on the enclosed porch one more time, grabbed his jacket, donned a black hat, extracted an old digital watch from his jacket pocket and put it on his right wrist, regarding this as an incredibly original touch – something only a man fated to complete a grand historic mission could pull off. There was a bottle of his wife's cheap perfume by the mirror. Tys's intuition told him that a few spritzes definitely wouldn't hurt. For some reason, Vedmedivites believed that going heavy on the perfume and cologne made them smell just great, so bathing was strictly optional.

Meanwhile, the motor inside Tys persisted, pumping his legs with reckless energy, so he nearly sprinted across the yard, ducked into the barn, and then rolled out of there a split second later on his ancient bicycle. He flung his leg over the frame and heard a ripping sound – it was the back of his pants coming apart, but he simply didn't have the time to change his outfit now. I mean, it's not like anybody could even see a hole in a bicyclist's pants. At least that's what Tys figured, and he should know – we're talking about a guy with a college degree. He didn't get all that far at first, no farther than the edge of his property, actually – because the bike chain ate his pant leg and bit his skin too. The clumsy cyclist lost control, and, much like Don Quixote, fell from his metal steed and crashed to the ground with a thud. Tys had to fiddle around for a few minutes before he could extricate himself from the chain. He pulled up his pant leg. Then he took two clothespins out of his breast pocket and used them to hold his pants in place, rose to his feet, spat, hopped back on his bike, and tore down the streets of Vedmediv like a third-grader – taking dangerously sharp turns, kicking up dust, and scattering the packs of stray dogs dozing in the sun.

Icarus was an influential and well-known figure in town. He and Tys had been friends since grade school. At first, it was Icarus who sought out Tys's company, but now it was the other way around. It all started when their teacher Mrs. Pavlivna assigned them seats next to each other. They were like two peas in a pod. They really enjoyed making mischief, like ditching class together, deflating the wheels on their classmates' bikes or peeing in the flower plots of rival homerooms. Icarus and Tys complemented each other quite well, so it's probably no coincidence that fate brought them together. Back then, the kids called Icarus Istvan, his real Hungarian name, or Stepan, the Ukrainianized version. He'd copy off Tys, who was a much better student. Their paths diverged after graduation. Icarus went to the local trade school to receive training as a mechanic, while Tys enrolled at Uzhhorod University to study history. Tys returned to

Vedmediv after completing his studies to teach, thereby affording Icarus the opportunity to express his sincere gratitude for letting him copy all those homework assignments and tests. By that time, Icarus had become a businessman (that's the title his proud neighbors and family had given him) or smuggler (that's the title the local newspaper and police had given him), so he was flush with cash – which he'd often loan to Tys, even back in the 90s, when the economy was wretched, knowing full well that the impoverished teacher would never even be able to think about paying him back.

Icarus's business got off the ground on his 18th birthday, the moment he could travel abroad without his parents' permission. Back then, he was taking classes at the trade school and working part-time at a local auto shop. That evening, he stuck around after work, waited for the head mechanic to go home, and then took one of the customers' cars for a little ride. It was in the shop so they could enlarge its gas tank with a welder and air compressor the next day. The auto technicians would heat up the metal of the prehistoric Audi's fifteen-gallon tank and resize it to hold nearly 25, so the owner could haul one and a half times more diesel fuel across the border to Hungary, where it cost three times as much. The shrewd businessman would syphon it into customers' tanks, or 'dump it off on the Magyars,' as they used to say in Vedmediv, meaning sell it to the locals – leaving just enough for the return trip – and then head back to Transcarpathia. Naturally, he'd have to share his spoils with the customs officers, who'd take the exorbitant cut of four hryvnias a gallon. The kicker was they thought the Audi had a standard, fifteen-gallon tank, so they'd only shake the cunning smuggler down for fifty-eight hryvnias (he'd burn a hryvnia getting there and a hryvnia going back). The owner of that Audi taught Icarus the phrase —'fuck em' over or get fucked' – and it promptly became his personal creed.

So, on the night of his eighteenth birthday, Icarus stuck around the auto shop until his boss went home, tossed five bottles of vodka and two cartons of cigarettes in the back of the Audi, filled it up, and set off for Hungary, where he delivered the diesel, sold the vodka and cigarettes at twice their original price, and loaded up on mandarin oranges – which were scarce in Ukraine at that time – as well chocolate and gum. Kids would go crazy for those foreign wrappers and nag their parents around the clock to buy them more. Icarus gave the customs officers their cut, sold the rare goods to some local hawkers, returned the car to the auto shop, and hit the sack right around four a.m. He made 45 bucks in one night. It'd take a couple Ukrainian schoolteachers to make that much in a month.

Icarus enjoyed his business, so he kept working at the auto shop for peanuts just so he could make his smuggling runs with other people's cars. He was a guy with ambition; he didn't just blow the money he earned. No, he was planning his next move – he'd save up and buy his own car the following year, which would put an end to his pseudo-job at the auto shop. This commitment to his goals was his defining character trait; once Icarus got consumed with an idea, he couldn't rest until he'd followed through. By the age of 20, he'd earned quite the reputation as a sharp businessman, and not just in Vedmediv – they knew him in all the border towns. He could boast of sizable capital, a fleet of cars with gas tanks the size of a submarine's, a great wife, and a seat on the Vedmediv City Council.

Fifteen years had trickled by since then, and the whole fuel-smuggling scheme had lost its viability. Hungary had joined the European Union, and the weighted cost of gas and diesel had levelled out all across Europe. Yes, there still was a slight difference in prices between Ukraine and the EU, but it was barely enough to feed one marginal smuggler, at best. The customs officers had started writing down your car's mileage and gas level at the border, so you'd get slapped with a huge fine if you went through the same checkpoint a half hour later with your gas tank nearly empty after driving just a few miles. Smugglers would cross the border, sell their gas, head to some parking lot, and sit there for five or six hours. They'd hook up a special device that looked like a meat grinder to the odometer and spin the handle. They'd crank up the mileage in just a few short minutes and then head back. The customs officers would see they'd crossed the border seven hours ago and driven over four hundred miles in that time, so yeah, obviously they were going to be running on empty. They could get around paying big fines that way, but they'd make a measly 20 bucks or so for a run that could take up to 10 hours.

Naturally, that kind of small-time operation didn't appeal to Icarus, who'd already become a smuggling magnate, the king of the border. He was pretty sharp – we're talking about a guy who finished trade school here. He had the skills to design vehicles that could transport contraband in the most efficient and convenient way possible.

His fleet grew, yet became ever more chimerical with each passing year. Icarus had been building up his fleet ever since he purchased his first car, an old Opel. He'd buy up vehicles whose rightful place was most certainly the junkyard and overhaul them into smuggler dragons. He eventually got his hands on an old Lada Niva, with a tank that looked like a huge pillow underneath the body of the car and could hold about fifty gallons. Later on, he purchased an Icarus model bus and pretended to be a charter driver, though it was only his relatives that ever rode the thing. It had an obscenely large tank, unmatched along the entire western border of Ukraine, with a capacity of nearly a hundred and forty gallons. That's not why Vedmedivites dubbed him Icarus, though.

Another nickname would have suited him better at the time, like Ichthyander, the fish/man hero of Belyaev's *The Amphibian*. The locals were calling him Kursk for a while there, because of what he was up to at the beginning of the 2000s – right when the eponymous Russian submarine sank. It was all because fuel was only negligibly cheaper in Ukraine relative to Hungary, Romania, or Slovakia at the turn of the century, so hauling it across the border wasn't so profitable anymore. From then on, fuel ceded its place to cigarettes, as tobacco excise taxes were nearly ten times higher in the European Union. Icarus, recognising that the tides of history had changed for Ukraine, made a gradual transition to a cigarette-centered smuggling model. The restrictions he had to deal with were a lot tougher, though; an individual could not carry more than one carton into the EU, and within a few years the maximum allowance dropped to two packs. During Icarus's transitional period, he kept driving his bus and making a few bucks off selling diesel. It was packed to capacity – 65 passengers – and they all were carrying a full set of alcohol and cigarettes, which enabled Icarus to make some halfway decent cash for a bit, but everyone realized the customs officers would be cracking down on them soon.

Much to Icarus's credit, he kept with the times and adjusted to his new circumstances swiftly. He went back to the basics, remembered his training as a mechanic, and sketched out all kinds of plans. His new idea was grounded in his new situation. He'd be allowed to carry fewer and fewer goods through customs checkpoints, so his business would go belly up in no time. On the other hand, it wasn't looking like Ukraine would be joining the family of European peoples in the foreseeable future, which meant the price differentials due to excise and other taxes would persist for years to come, and he'd be able to keep making pretty decent money. But how could he get past customs and deliver his goods? The easiest path lay through the woods, where the border was strictly a formality – a six-foot chain-link fence topped with barbed-wire. It was a simple matter to make a hole and wiggle on through. Hell, Icarus could have moved the Carpathian Mountains and the whole damn Transcarpathian Region through one little hole in that fence, just like threading a needle. The only trouble was that he wasn't the first guy to think of it. Much more notable figures were wheeling and dealing in Uzhhorod, Mukachevo, and the surrounding areas, sending their caravans through the woods before anyone else could. Local politicians and customs officers became newly minted smuggling barons, and eventually even the big bosses in Kyiv joined their ranks, once they caught a whiff of the profit to be made. They created an Emergency Anti-Smuggling Committee, came to Transcarpathia, and threatened to punish the local politicians and customs officers to the fullest extent of the law. Naturally, they agreed that the best way to interdict smuggling was to give the higher-ups a cut of their profits. The business continued to flourish. The long and the short of it is that there were some real predators skulking around the Transcarpathian woods and Icarus wouldn't dare cross them.

He kept his chin up, though, and soon he hit upon a brilliant idea – smuggling by water! After all, the Tysa flows into Hungary, right into the European Union! So, all he had to do was pack the cigarettes in watertight containers and drop them in, and his business associates would fish them out on the other side of the border. Icarus conducted a few experiments, which convinced him that sending cartons one at a time just wasn't viable – only 20 per cent of them reached their final destination. Some of them got caught on branches and reeds, and the current washed a good portion of them up on the riverbanks, so Icarus needed a boat, one the border guards wouldn't be able to spot but that he could track all the way.

In other words, he needed a radio-controlled submarine. But how was a trade school-trained auto mechanic supposed to build one in Vedmediv, where the most advanced piece of technology was the coffee machine in the lobby of the tax office? Simple – Icarus took a 25-gallon plastic barrel – the kind the locals would use to sour cabbage for the winter – stuffed nearly four hundred cartons of cigarettes in it, and dropped it into a pond on the outskirts of town. The barrel submerged pretty quickly. Then he made three rings out of foam plastic and two out of wood and wrapped them around the barrel, which was now floating confidently on the surface like a bobber. That was no good, so he stripped off one plastic foam ring and one wooden one, so his amphibious craft would run nearly a foot underwater – just deep enough to go unnoticed by the border guards, yet avoid the danger of snagging on the river's bottom in the shallow areas. The local Gypsies always said the Tysa was the perfect river for Jesus, since you could walk across it without getting your balls wet.

Now all he had to do was fit it with a little motor to control its speed and direction, and a transponder to track the location of the goods at any given moment. It took Icarus two months to complete all the prep work and experiments, then he dispensed with all his jeeps and buses and focused exclusively on developing his fleet of amphibious barrels. Within six months, he had 15 of them floating down into Hungary twice a day, bringing him astronomical profits in stable foreign currency. Icarus's employees would fish them out of the water just over the border, break the seals, sell the cigarettes, place the rings and motors inside the barrels, cover them with plastic, and then cover that with a foot-thick layer of sauerkraut. Then they'd load them into a truck and send them back to Icarus in Ukraine – the miniature motors were pretty powerful, but there was no way they could push the huge barrels upstream to Vedmediv. The Hungarian and Ukrainian customs officers couldn't figure out what Icarus was up to for the longest time, since hauling Hungarian sauerkraut, which cost twice as much as it did in Ukraine, couldn't possibly be profitable. The smuggler claimed he just liked the taste of Hungarian sauerkraut – it's got a nice, salty kick to it.

That couldn't last forever, though. The customs officers on both sides realised he was making a killing right under their noses without giving them a cut, so they started checking everything more carefully. A Hungarian customs officer probed the mound of sauerkraut in one of the barrels with a long knife, and its tip struck something hard. Then the whole mystery unraveled. Articles about the sizable submarine fleet cruising between Ukraine and Hungary kept appearing in the local papers. The discovery of his scheme didn't land Icarus in prison, though. Kolya, the truck driver, was a simple guy – he made a good stooge. The authorities pinned the whole cunning and technically flawless scheme on him. Icarus wasn't a heartless bastard, so he paid the driver's wife a tidy sum to thank him for taking the fall – $5,000 for each year of his three-year sentence. In the end, everyone was happy – Kolya and his wife, the tireless guardians of justice on both sides of the border, and the local columnists, who discussed the incident ad nauseam for the next few months. They even tried to calculate the smuggler's profit on each trip. One student at Uzhhorod University who'd taken it upon herself to write an article about the whole affair mentioned that an ocean had once covered the area where the Carpathians now stood, so sailing was in Transcarpathians' blood and it was only a matter of time until someone heeded their ancestors' call.

Yes, everyone was happy – except for Icarus, obviously. He'd lost his source of income. He even got to thinking about starting some sort of legitimate business. He had the startup capital, thank God. He didn't think about that for very long, though. Go straight in a country with a legal system that encourages shady dealings, chicanery, and off-the-books transactions? Nah, he was no sucker. So, what other options did he have?

That's when it became clear he was always going to be Icarus – not Ichtyander, Kursk, or the Amphibian – his business was rising from the water to the heavens. The border was closed – the Magyars put a net across the Tysa that not even fish could get through, provoking indignation from environmental activists all across Europe, and the mightiest crooks of all – the politicians – were already moving their wares through the woods, so his only option was taking to the skies. One day, Hollywood will make a movie out of this, like the ones about Henry Ford and Bill Gates, two other great businessmen. His grand success story had a hook that would stir the hearts of audiences everywhere. Here's how it all played out – Icarus was lying in his hammock out in the backyard, swatting the flies away, slurping his beer, and listening to 'Celebrating with a Song,' a program on a local radio station. Just then, a little paper airplane his son had thrown from the upstairs window flew right over him. He sprang out of his hammock, knocked over his beer, stomped on his radio, and started running around like a madman, nearly tripping and breaking his leg in the process.

'Mum, Mum,' hollered the kid, quite entertained by his dad zooming around the backyard. 'Come over here, quick. A bee just stung dad in the bum!'

It was no bee, though. It was something bigger and sharper – it was an idea. At that very moment, his son's paper airplane helped Icarus realise that stiff competition and strict laws couldn't kill his business. After all, God had made man free; he could walk and swim, and even fly. All he had to do was get his hands on a plane. Not anything fancy, like a Boeing, or even an Antonov An-24. Icarus could make do with an Antonov An-2. No, even that primitive crop duster was too big for his operation. He had to be inconspicuous, invisible. Yes, the Antonov An-2 could transport a million cigarettes at once, but it needed aviation fuel and landing strips – though short ones would do – on both sides of the border. The president was just about the only person who could entertain dreams of a business with that kind of infrastructure, so Icarus decided to curb his appetite and investigate the various hang gliders available on the market.

It turned out that none of them were suitable for Icarus's purposes. First off, you needed a special license, which would bring down a squall of questions in a quiet little city like Vedmediv. Secondly, all the hang gliders for sale had insufficient carrying capacity – besides the pilot, they could only transport two boxes of cigarettes, and all you could make on one run was a measly two hundred bucks – chump change. And what if they caught him and confiscated the hang glider? Big losses, bankruptcy, and a hungry debtor's death.

So, Icarus decided to build his very own aircraft. In addition to hang gliders, he considered kites and airplanes. If he went with the latter, the fuselage would have to be light, made out of aluminum, probably, the wings would have to be wide enough to stay airborne, and the engine would have to be lightweight, yet very powerful. That's when the rudimentary knowledge he'd acquired during his tenure at the auto shop came in handy. Icarus bought a few aviation magazines, poked around on the Internet, and then got to work on his aircraft. He even came up with a preliminary name for it – B-2004, with the 'B' meaning 'border' and '2004' standing for the next year, when the inventor was planning on launching his celestial business.

This undertaking wasn't as easy as it may seem, and nimble as Icarus was, dozens of problems, both great and small, tripped him up on the way to his goal. Numerous defeats, and, more mundanely, the lack of necessary materials, stifled his enthusiasm. Nevertheless, his trans-border B-2004 was ready to set off on its maiden voyage on May 1st, 2004. This date wasn't chosen at random – on that day, the EU expanded once again. A few Central European countries, including Hungary, became full-fledged members. Grand celebrations – with fireworks, singing, and speeches by politicians – had been scheduled for May 1st. Basically, the utter pandemonium at the border would enable Icarus to complete his first experimental flight – a risky business – risk-free.

Actually, it wasn't exactly his first one. He attempted to conquer the skies back in February, out in a pasture behind an old farmhouse. The B-2004 could pick up enough speed within 40 yards to rise roughly six feet off the ground. That wasn't close to high enough, though, especially considering he'd have to load the little aircraft up with cigarettes, so the crafty designer replaced the metal wings with plywood ones and the jeep engine with a light and more powerful one from a brand new Japanese motorcycle. After that, the aircraft should have been able to reach at least 25 feet. Icarus did a few test flights at the farm that April to make sure. After a little tinkering, it was ready for take-off on the long-awaited day, May 1st.

Icarus chose a flat, deserted area of the border, roughly ten miles away from Vedmediv, for his first run. He brought the B-2004 out there on a truck, made all the final preparations, and waited for nightfall. Everything should have gone smoothly, but greed spoiled his plan. The smuggler intended to limit himself to two boxes of cigarettes for the first flight, but his confidence mounted with each of those four long hours waiting out in that field. So, he attached six boxes, instead. After all, the aircraft was designed to hold nine or ten, so it wasn't as though he was pushing his luck or anything. The B-2004 had to pick up enough speed along a straight forty- to fifty-yard stretch, take off, and gradually ascend to roughly twenty-five feet, which would be enough to clear the fence that marked the border and the trees in the neutral territory, then land on flat ground over on the Hungarian side. Radar wouldn't be able to detect the aircraft at that altitude, either.

All his calculations were well-reasoned and precise, but the amateur aircraft engineer didn't factor in wind resistance. So, the little craft took off all right, but then it started to wobble and failed to gain enough altitude. Icarus clipped the tops of the first Hungarian trees and lost control. The engine sputtered out and the B-2004 crashed into a tree. Now it was hanging between the sky and the ground like a dead duck. This was a total disaster. Customs officers from both sides of the border, a bit tipsy after all the festivities, drove towards the smoke and racket. At first, they couldn't believe their eyes – some kind of crudely-made monster strapped with boxes labelled 'Marlboro' hung in mid-air with a portly man wearing a motorcycle helmet and big rhinestone sunglasses dangling, head down, from the center of the frame.

Icarus was defiant during the first interrogation, firmly denying any connection with smuggling activities, refusing to cooperate with the investigation, and threatening to have them all fired. The conqueror of the skies had gotten pretty sloshed while he waited for the onset of twilight, so he was brimming with audacity. He kept claiming he'd designed the aircraft for his own amusement, because he just really liked flying, and he wasn't planning on crossing any borders. It was just that a strong gust of wind had blown him over into Hungary. When asked why on earth he needed to rig six boxes of Marlboros, which amounted to no fewer than 60,000 cigarettes, to his aircraft, Icarus answered imperturbably: 'I just really like smoking, and I'm afraid the world is just going to run out of cigarettes someday, so I took 60,000 along with me, you know, just in case.'

One Ukrainian newspaper dedicated a whole page to this incident, simply calling the story, 'The Icarus of Vedmediv.' Everyone appreciated the scathing nickname, so that's what they started to call him from that day on. He did a three-year sentence and then walked free, but the idea of developing the best smuggling scheme ever stayed in his mind, and he kept at it, albeit on a much more modest scale.

Anyhow, Tys was right to turn to Icarus, because if there was anyone in this God-forsaken town who would believe in his grand design, it'd be him. Moreover, unlike the history teacher, he had the money to make the idea a reality – and not just the money, he had the connections, too. In October 2010, three years after he got out, the Vedmedivites elected him as deputy of the regional government. His criminal record didn't discourage voters from supporting a candidate who swore to uphold the law and raise their standard of living in no time flat. After all, the Ukrainian people had elected an ex-con as president earlier that year, so Icarus had no difficulty integrating himself into the new elite.

The brakes on Tys's bike didn't work, and he just couldn't get around to fixing them, so although he did stop pedaling like a madman, he didn't manage to slow down enough to hop off without hurting himself. As he was careening towards Icarus's gate, he realized that he wouldn't be able to stop in time, so he started braking by dragging his foot. His shoe snagged on the ground, causing him to lose his balance and hit his balls on the bike beam. He yowled like a cat and then crashed into the metal fence running around Icarus's property. The smuggler heard the commotion and dashed across the yard to see Tys, still lying underneath his bike, moaning and holding his crotch with both hands. The front wheel had been bent into the shape of an eight and the back one was spinning over the teacher's head, making his bike look like a unicycle. It knocked Tys's hat off his head and into a little ditch when he looked up to acknowledge his friend.

Icarus had every reason to believe Tys had come to ask for money, yet again, to be repaid God knows when, and he figured that he'd have to buy his loser friend a new bike wheel, too, but this wasn't the case. For the first time ever during their many years of friendship, he hadn't come to ask a favour. He hadn't come empty-handed. Well, maybe technically his hands were empty, but his head was full of ideas. Two minutes later, he was explaining everything to Icarus, his eyes wild. His childhood friend looked at him mistrustfully at first – then shifted his gaze to Tys's hat, still lying on the ground near the gate, now occupied by one of Icarus's hens, and, finally, began staring right into his guest's eyes. Icarus's sympathetic expression turned mocking, then intrigued. Roughly 10 minutes into Tys's monologue, Icarus latched onto his friend's arm and led him swiftly towards his car.

'Hop in. Let's take a ride. That way we'll have some privacy. Keep talking, though. It seems like your idea isn't actually that dumb,' Icarus said.

The two of them hopped in the car and drove out towards the country, as gawking passersby watched them crawl down the street as slow as a turtle. The driver sat there, unable to take his bewitched eyes off the man in the passenger seat, who was acting like a crazy person, flailing his arms and trying to shout over the roaring engine that drowned out his words like the ocean drowning a shipwrecked sailor.

Chapter 3:

In Which the Plot Would Have Ground to a Halt
if Not for the Genius of the Carpathians

'Hmm,' went Icarus, smacking his lips. Engrossed in thought, he completely lost touch with his surroundings for a second, rested his head on the wheel, and went quiet. The car was parked on the side of the road, just outside of Vedmediv, where it wouldn't attract any outside attention. Tys looked straight ahead, at the thick patch of bushes that separated the field from the woods, and then shifted his gaze to the unmoving Icarus. It was as if the history teacher's battery had died – his ardor, enthusiasm, and frenzied gesticulation were gone. There he sat, disappointed and exhausted. Maybe he'd just started to sober up and the charm was wearing off. His head was buzzing, his heart pounding, his hands trembling. Suddenly, Icarus's head snapped up. He looked Tys straight in the eye and declared:

'You've really got something here. Yeah, you're on to something. This is a red-hot idea, I'm tellin' ya!'

'We can definitely pull it off!' It was like Tys had just woken up. He felt another burst of energy down at the bottom of his soul. 'We'll get to work right away and have everything running like clock-work by next spring.'

'I have my own work to do – you know, some things I still have to take care of. Also, the two of us won't be able to handle this alone.

I think we need to bring in at least a few more people. It's a monumental project that'll be of great importance for all of Europe, not just the two of us, or even Transcarpathia. This just isn't a two-man job.'

'But, Icarus – what we're talking about isn't exactly legal. We can't be hiring people off the street. The more people who know about it, the less chance we have of making it happen.'

'Well, yeah, obviously. That's why we'll only hire people we can count on. I already have a few in mind, people I got through prison, the terrible nineties, and the woods on the border with. It's a good idea, they'll definitely bite.'

'Well, but… ' Tys's eyes started darting fearfully, and his voice quavered. The idea used to be his, but now he could feel it slipping away from him, becoming a common endeavor. Actually, it could easily be stolen from him. '… still, it's a project for the elite, not hoi polloi. We could get our wives in on it. That way, there'd be four of us, which is already eight hands. We'll get the job done all by ourselves eventually.'

'Eight hands he says! As if you can do anything with those hands of yours. Work with your head. Good job on offering up the idea, but we don't need you tryin' to dig. Do you seriously think my wife's going to waddle around with a shovel? And I find it hard to picture Marichka ten feet underground, miner's hat and all. Let's leave that to the professionals. We'll be the ones managing the process. That's how things are done, Tys. Anyway, there's one guy we're gonna have to bring on, no matter what, and that's Mirca. First off, nobody knows the border like him. Second, we need to make sure he's on our side. He might throw a monkey-wrench into the works if he finds out that his competitors have launched a large-scale project. It's better to get him on board now – and we'll be a stronger team for it.'

'Mirca? Who's that?' Tys asked, swallowing wetly, notes of jealousy and fear rising in his voice.

'The Romanian guy who lives by the cemetery, big-time smuggler, the guy they call the Genius of the Carpathians. You must know who I'm talking about.'

'Ahhh, the Genius of the Carpathians,' Tys drawled. 'Yeah, yeah, I know him, obviously I do.'

'Well, that's great. If you know him, then you realize we can't do without him. Nobody knows the land like him. He can move through those mountains like a beast, on safe trails only he knows about. So, you okay with him coming on board then? Let's go over to his place for a chat.'

'Well, if you think that we can't get by without him, then let's go. I don't really trust Romanians, though.'

'Nobody trusts anybody. This is just business – we're just trying to make a buck, as the Americans say. A common interest and reverence for our holy book will keep us together.'

'What book's that?'

'The criminal code.'

They turned around and headed toward Vedmediv. They had to stop by Icarus's place first, on the other side of town, because Tys insisted that they couldn't show up at the Genius of the Carpathians' empty-handed. They needed to seal their compact with a bottle, to establish a trusting relationship. It was obvious that Tys just wanted to throw a few back, but his argument about building trust worked.

The Genius of the Carpathians didn't have the best reputation; he was considered a cruel recluse, which wasn't entirely fair. He was actually just a tough, taciturn guy who didn't like blabbing about his business to strangers. He had red hair, a square face with clearly defined features, and a large birthmark by his right ear. He was a man of few words, no doubt about that. It was a habit he'd gotten into when he first set off down the smuggler's path. Two borders – one with Hungary, the other with Romania – run right past Vedmediv. The Slovakian border is a one-hour drive away, and you can get to Poland in two. The Hungarian border was the most popular with more reckless types. First off, it was the easiest to navigate, because it went across flat country, open fields, and the Tysa. Secondly, back in the Soviet days you could bring nice clothing and food products that were hard to come by in the USSR back from relatively-wealthy Hungary. Goulash communism, as Kadar's regime in the Hungarian People's Republic was often called, hinged on a simple agreement between Party and people – the government wouldn't really repress them or hassle them too much about all that communism jazz and would provide everyone with more than enough food and money, while the people, in turn, wouldn't protest all that much against the undemocratic system that had basically occupied the country. So, those favoured by fortune traded with Hungary; they'd go there and bring back products that were incredible luxuries as far as the average Soviet person was concerned.

Things looked a little different when it came to Romania, which Ceausescu had turned into a poor and hungry nature preserve. After his public falling-out with the USSR – when Romania refused to deploy tanks to recalcitrant Prague in '68, Ceausescu decided to create something like an island in the middle of a dry valley, to build a country that wouldn't depend on its neighbours – the USSR and Hungary, in particular – for anything whatsoever. When the Romanian despot's idiocy reached its peak in the early eighties – right around the time he decided to pay back all the loans he'd racked up from all sorts of international organizations – life in Romania had turned into a real hell: food had disappeared from store shelves, the TV stations would only broadcast for two hours a day, public transportation wasn't running, and the secret police had begun catching and killing more and more 'enemies of the people.'

It's no wonder Transcarpathians had little interest in Romania. Back then, people used to joke that all you could bring back from Romania was cement... but the trouble was it had already hardened. In other words, there was no extensive communication or commerce between the USSR and Romania; however, there was always a way for one guy to make some decent cash. That's how Mirca, an ethnic Romanian from Transcarpathia, saw it. In the mid-eighties, he took to visiting his relatives on the other side of the border. He saw for himself that there was nothing to take back with you, but you could bring just about anything – matches, vodka, sausage, jam, shoes, light fixtures, nails – and the Romanians would snap it up. There was just nothing in Romania; people were willing to hand over all the money they had for anything of value. That's where Mirca set out on his long road from pimply candy smuggler to underground millionaire and crime lord on both sides of the border.

He didn't much care for his nickname – the Genius of the Carpathians. It was people's way of mocking him. He was a real daredevil, so he'd found a way to make a living in a hungry desert – which is what Romania was in the late eighties. After all, Ceausescu had been dubbed the Genius of the Carpathians, and later the Sun of the Carpathians. When the despot, corrupted by absolute power he shared with no one but his wife Elena, started gradually losing touch with reality, all kinds of arse-kissing bureaucrats began competing to see who could glorify his name the most. They created a cult of personality and everything that entails: countless portraits, academic degrees and titles for Ceausescu the Genius, letters of appreciation from the people, and crap like that. The General Secretary of the Romanian Communist Party had two unique traits: a terrible phobia of being invaded and gigantomania, caused by his superiority complex. Anyone could invade at any moment – the duplicitous capitalist West or the belligerent imperialist USSR, so

Ceausescu allocated the lion's share of the budget to arming the country and building fortifications. He spent the rest on rebuilding Romania, which entailed flooding it with concrete – whole cities and especially structures built during previous eras, which Ceausescu despised, were levelled, and socialist high-rise monstrosities sprouted all over the place. One of the unstable dictator's dreams was to make Romania a purely urban environment – without any villages or villagers – a country in which everyone would work at factories and live in towering apartment blocks.

Building the Transfagarsan Highway, which was set to run right through the highest peaks in the Carpathian mountain range, was one of Ceausescu's most insane projects. Engineers everywhere thought it couldn't be done, that building a concrete road that high up in the mountains was an absurd, unjustifiably expensive folly, but Ceausescu, much like the Russian despots before him, threw all the country's energy into this project, treating human lives, money, and nature with equal profligacy. Right around that time, the local press bestowed the nicknames 'Genius' and 'Sun' of the Carpathians upon him, equating him with God, whose will could remake the face of the Earth. In Transcarpathia, people knew about the hunger and poverty in Romania, so they said 'the Genius of the Carpathians' with cutting sarcasm in their voices. So, Mirca, a man with no sense of humor who was absolutely indifferent to jokes of any kind, obviously didn't exactly relish that nickname. He couldn't do anything about it, though – once something gets stuck on people's tongues, it's damn near impossible to forbid them from saying it.

The nickname 'the Genius of the Carpathians' did have a mocking ring to it, especially considering it referred to a person who would run five pounds of candy and five pairs of nylon stockings across the border. Nevertheless, the scale of Mirca's activities expanded from year to year. It was as though that needling nickname had begun to direct his fate. Mirca studied the area around the border thoroughly. Then he started crossing at official checkpoints less and less often, because it'd become easier and easier for him to hide out in the Carpathian highlands, taking the same routes as the wolves, where no border guard could catch him. So, his profits rose – if you went through the mountains, you could traffic anything you wanted, in unlimited quantities.

By the early nineties, the Genius of the Carpathians had whole crews of workers and carriers. Mirca's carts and caravans filled up the twilight borderlands. Shortly thereafter, however, his business model was no longer viable, since communism had fallen, and now Romania could get better-quality goods from the more prosperous Turkey instead of impoverished post-Soviet Ukraine. With his source of smuggling income running dry, Mirca began seriously considering a shift to the potentially juicier Hungarian border. But suddenly, there was a new game in town – drugs. The Gypsies had cornered the market on every border Ukraine shared with Europe. Their services came cheap – they willingly risked their lives and weren't afraid of anything. Generally, drugs were transported through the woods on dark nights, but there were some real virtuosos who would swallow a bag of coke or stuff it in their anal cavity and then cross the border, brashly looking the corrupt customs officers' right in the eye. Later on, most drug trafficking shifted back to the woods, since the human stomach and anus are, in fact, limited in size. You can carry a lot more *on* you, than you can *in* you. Plus, a couple of Gypsies had bags burst in their stomachs, and they died of overdoses, going into furious euphoria right there in front of the passport window. After that, the situation got much tenser – the customs officers even toyed with the idea of setting up x-ray machines at the border. In short, all that was left was the woods.

In the woods, the Genius of the Carpathians was in a league of his own. Only he knew the forgotten trails, the ravines where you could wait until patrols passed, the shortest route to the first Romanian road (where hawkers waited in jeeps), spots where you could sleep along the way, and springs where thirsty travelers could get fresh water. Pretty soon, the Gypsies tracked Mirca down and suggested he become a guide of sorts for them. He agreed, and for the next few years, they paid a pretty penny for his services – he was cautious, he knew everything there was to know, and he was as precise as a compass.

Things continued that way until the geopolitical situation changed and Romania hastened into the embrace of the European Union. In the mid-2000s, the Genius of the Carpathians severed all ties with the Gypsies – deep down inside, he was actually afraid of them – and undertook his own business. He started trafficking illegal immigrants. Although if we're being perfectly honest, he wouldn't take just anyone. Initially, more established market players would bring him Pakistani and Chinese people in the back of their trucks. Mirca would lead them through the Carpathian woods toward a bright European future. Within a few months, he made direct contact with the immigrant suppliers, but, in that case, not all of his runs could be successful, since he had to share with the border guards. Trafficking 10 kilograms of drugs through the mountains is one thing but leading a 100-strong herd that you could see from space is a different matter. One time the border guards caught the Genius of the Carpathians and made him cut a deal – he would have to share the immigrants with them along with the money.

After all, they had to report the number of offenders they'd caught to the higher-ups. So, roughly once every two weeks, the Genius of the Carpathians would take a group of twenty or thirty Chinese people into the gloom of the primeval forest, where he'd lead them on a meandering path around Vedmediv, wearing them out and leaving them disoriented. On the second or third day, when everyone, including the guide, was on their last legs, their food was running out, and it seemed as though they'd covered hundreds of miles and Paris, or, at the very worst, Vienna, must be just beyond those trees, the Genius of the Carpathians would round up his group and announce that they'd arrived in Romania and were now in a safe place far away from the border. The Chinese people would reward him generously, and Mirca would disappear into the dense forest. The vigilant Ukrainian border guards would come across the potential immigrants a few hours later. That way, the wolves would be full and the sheep whole – well, except the Chinese people, of course. Mirca made a good living, and the border guards improved their statistics. He was the real genius of the Carpathians, wouldn't you say?

Anyhow, Icarus had his reasons – a large cross-border project in Vedmediv had no chance of succeeding without Mirca. He was such a big player that it wasn't just about securing his assistance. The most important thing was just to make sure he was on their side. He was just too powerful, they couldn't snub him. Heaven forbid they'd have to compete against him or make an enemy of him. Given the risk and questionable legality – to put it mildly – of Tys's design, they might wind up needing some connections in law enforcement, border patrol, or smuggling circles – which were often actually the same circle. All they could hope for was that the Genius of the Carpathians would bite when he heard their monumental idea and join the team.

Mirca lived in Vedmediv, on Partisan Street. The street got that name back in the days of the Bear Empire. It led to the city cemetery, so folks would always joke that yet another corpse had 'departed for the land of the partisans,' thereby expressing their attitude toward the occupiers. This quiet and sinister place suited Mirca and his reputation. It was a dead zone everyone tried to steer clear of, so it was perfect for secret business negotiations. Tys, whom Icarus had entrusted with holding the litre-bottle of homemade 105-proof plum-flavoured moonshine, had managed to suck down nearly a third part of it within the five minutes it took to get there: he was all tongue-tied, euphoria was flaring in his eyes, and his gestures were buoyant and hysterical. This made Icarus decide he'd talk to the Genius of the Carpathians himself, so the Romanian wouldn't think this was all some drunken delusion.

The car slowly rolled up to the property. Icarus got out and walked through the gate, while Tys kept sitting there, holding the bottle – 'building trust' through the medium of alcohol would have to wait until they'd reached a preliminary agreement with the Genius of Carpathians.

An hour later, when Mirca and Icarus came out to the car, Tys was sound asleep, his cheek pressed up against the glass. Saliva ran down his chin, and the drained bottle lay at his feet.

Icarus scornfully took stock of his associate and said to himself quietly: 'Yeah, we don't need anyone. We'll get the job done all by ourselves.'

Chapter 4:

In Which Our Heroes Reach a Disquieting Impasse

Tys woke from a heavy and sticky alcohol slumber when the car stopped by an abandoned building at the site of a defunct collective farm. The Genius of the Carpathians sat in the back seat, scowling silently. Night had fallen; the headlights pulled a small dwelling and a doghouse – its occupant barked furiously – out of the darkness. Icarus honked the horn, and a dark figure came out the front door.

When the headlights struck its face, Tys recognised Ychi. The three conspirators got out of the car. Icarus and Mirca walked towards the master of the house, while the history teacher vanished from the strip of light rather briskly. A split second later, they could hear tinkling and a loud sigh of satisfaction. His prostate had clearly made its presence felt. Then Tys headed back to the others, adjusting his pants and zipping up as he walked.

'Good evening, lord of the manor!' The teacher proffered his hand to Ychi, grinning so widely that his gold tooth glimmered in the light.

'Go wash your hands first,' the stocky owner said bluntly. Tys wiped his hand on his jacket, still smiling, and proffered it once again. Ychi wouldn't budge. 'I said wash your hands, not wipe them off on your filthy jacket. There's a spigot over there, to the right of the door.'

Tys submissively slid his hand into his pocket and slinked off towards the house, as if nothing had happened. They were mid-conversation by the time he returned.

'How much you gonna pay?' Ychi was giving the Genius of the Carpathians a mistrustful look.

'Pay? Well, I don't know. As much as for a regular workday. We haven't really thought about that part yet. Actually, we're inviting you to become a partner, a stakeholder. Tys cooked up this whole thing – that's his contribution. Icarus'll procure the equipment: all those shovels, helmets, wheelbarrows, and stuff.' Mirca gave Icarus a meaningful look, and he turned beet red and swallowed hard, resentment flaring up on his face. Meanwhile, the Romanian continued. 'I'll procure some stuff, too, and make sure the cops don't stick their noses in our business. As for you, Ychi, you can invest your labour, and then you'll make money, a steady percentage, once we start bringing in a profit. It's like a joint-stock company. Everyone has equity in the business.'

'Fuck that joint-stock and steady percentage bullshit. Just pay me by the hour. Nothing's going to come of all this anyway. I'll take a feather in the hand over two in the pigsty.'

'Hey, hey, cool it!' Icarus interjected. 'Everything'll be just fine. Nobody's gonna take you for a ride. We're here because we respect you and believe in you.'

'Well, I believe in money. I'm talking an advance.'

'You'll get your money, Ychi, and your advance. So, are you in? Are you gonna see the project through? It's crucial that only you be involved. One person doing the whole job, that's it. We don't need any more eyes and ears.'

'I'll do it. Why not? That's if you pay me. Come on in already, you can't be talking about important things like this standing around outside.'

Tys listened hard to their negotiations, realizing that Ychi had already been brought up to speed. He didn't like that one bit; why should they enlist a hunchback for a monumental undertaking that could change the fate of a whole continent? Couldn't the three of them – Tys, Icarus, and the Genius of the Carpathians – just take turns digging? Why did they need repulsive old Ychi, who could usually be found digging a grave on Partisan Street and then drinking a bottle in honour of the dearly departed soul? That was his life, day in and day out. Those millionaires didn't want to get their snow-white hands dirty, but every new pair of calloused mitts threatened to expose them and wreck the project.

The crew went inside. The modest decor consisted of an old television on a nightstand – a makeshift antenna slanted to one side – a box-spring bed, like the ones at summer camps, a wooden table with a stool on each side, an old wardrobe, and a wash basin in the corner. A remarkably nice light fixture – too nice for this room – hung up above. A bunch of dangling crystal decorations and tiny mirrors refracted the light. It looked familiar to Tys, but he couldn't recall where he'd seen it before.

Ychi was simple, stupid, unskilled labour: hands to do all the dirty work for Icarus and the Genius of the Carpathians. He appeared well suited for it, since digging was all he knew. Stocky, strong, and frightening, Ychi looked exactly like the archetypical gravedigger in a small city like Vedmediv should. His physical shortcoming – the enormous hump on his back – scared people away and made him the butt of devastating jokes from the local children. Each new class would start calling him Quasimodo once they got to the unit on *The Hunchback of Notre Dame*. Well, Tys faced something similar when the high school students started reading Voltaire and pronouncing his nickname as 'Carbead' to rhyme with 'Candide.' Ychi had gotten used to these insults at a young age, so now they didn't make him mad. He wouldn't even turn around when yet another pack of brats started yelling at him:

'Quasimodo! Hey Quasimodo, where's your Esmeralda? Did you bury her?'

He didn't get angry. Instead, he waited patiently. Despite his deformity, God had given him the strength of an ox, so although he was pushing 60, he still felt young, invincible even. Over the course of his long life, he'd buried his fair share of the people who once mercilessly ridiculed him and, shameful as it is to admit, felt prodigious pleasure when the first shovelful of dense, damp earth slammed down on yet another funnyman's coffin.

The history teacher never called him Quasimodo, though. In the teacher's lounge, the gravedigger was exclusively known as Ychi-Itchy-Bitch. This was all because, a good 20 years ago, at the dawn of the country's independence, one student raised his hand to ask if Ukrainian really didn't have any words with a 'y' and a 'c' next to each other, as an emigre linguist had recently claimed. The teacher, Mrs. Budnippyr, God rest her soul, was about to start holding forth, but the student's thoughts outpaced his teacher's.

'I don't think it's true. What about Ychi-Itchy-Bitch? My daddy's as Ukrainian as anybody, and he said that last night. It has a 'y' next to a 'c.'' The class roared with laughter, while Mrs. Budnippyr turned blue with rage and smacked the kid in the face with a ruler so hard his lip split. The student burst into tears, and the class started laughing even harder. Hearing all the commotion, the principal entered the classroom. Mrs. Budnippyr explained the whole situation to him. As is usually the case in Ukraine, justice favoured the person who threw the first punch – and had a little administrative pull. The principal walked over to the student, whacked him upside the head, and summed up his stance on the issue.

'First off, Ychi is a Hungarian name, not a Ukrainian one. Secondly, 'itchy' and 'bitch' don't even rhyme. Thirdly, have your parents come to school with you tomorrow. We'll have a nice chat about your talent for poetry, you smart aleck. Now be quiet and get back to work!'

The next day, the kid came to school with his parents, who, instead of sticking up for their son and making a stink about him getting hit, brought the principal a box of chocolates and a bottle of cognac. His father apologised profusely for his son's behaviour, groveled before the principal and went on and on about how great the school was. Even once his apologies had been accepted, he kept falling all over himself.

'Actually, I'm the one to blame. We had company over a few weeks back, and we were reminiscing about a classmate of ours who'd just passed. Well, naturally, Quasimodo and his deformity came up. Everyone's kind of afraid of him – they all dread ending up under his shovel. You know, I was talking about how me and my buddies used to yell 'Ychi-Itchy-Bitch!' at him. I guess my little menace overheard, and he committed that phrase to memory. That's how it always goes, the worst stuff sticks with kids.'

They were able to sweep that little incident under the rug, but it remained etched in the boy's mind for a long time, probably because of the public humiliation he faced when the whole class laughed at him. So, the student – his name was Svyatoslav Konar – was determined to prove that he really could rhyme. That's how it always goes with poets. All their poems emerge from an inexhaustible spring of childhood trauma, humiliation, and insecurities. Svyatoslav started writing for every special occasion. He was actually pretty good, too, which came as a real surprise to his parents and teachers, so good that his elders would often ask him to dash off some cute little poems for an assistant principal's birthday party or the school's Victory Day celebration. The conniving, spiteful hack was really plotting his revenge, obviously. Revenge for his humiliation, and then fame. After all, that's what all poets really crave.

Three years after the incident with the gravedigger's nickname, Svyatoslav Konar approached Mrs. Budnippyr in the hallway and presented her with a sheet of paper folded in four.

'This is a poem I've dedicated to you. Once again, I'm sorry for everything bad that happened between us. I'd like to affirm my boundless respect and my gratitude for all you've done, since you were the one who sowed a love of language in my soul. It was you, Mrs. Budnippyr, who once discovered my modest talent that now blossoms in the Elysian fields of Ukrainian language and literature.' An unfeigned flame of kindness burned in the student's eyes, and a young man's meagre tear rolled down his cheek. Svyatoslav, like every professional poet, was a hypocrite and a liar. His teacher only found out about that later, though. First, she rushed into the teacher's lounge, beaming with joy.

'Listen up everyone, listen to this!' she exclaimed, then read the poem to her colleagues. Everyone was deeply moved, and they started praising the student, who, according to them, had been reached by a life-changing educator. The teachers unanimously foretold fame and immortality in the hot womb of Ukrainian poetry personified by Mrs. Budnippyr.

As it turned out, that womb metaphor proved miraculously precise; however, that fact was only spotted later, by the readers of *Transcarpathian Youth*, where the proud teacher sent her grateful student's poem. The regional newspaper published the precocious poet's work under the heading 'To a life-changing educator – Stepanyda Budnippyr – from her grateful student, poet, and native of the abundantly talented region of Transcarpathia, Svyatoslav Konar.' This is how the poem went:

Driven by your love for the pure Word,
Under your wise tutelage,
My teacher, did I see not the chaff of our language,
But golden, pure, and eternal words.

Come I do into this harsh, wide world;
Up until my final days, I'll remember your lessons woven with
wisdom,
Now that strange and immortal strumming on my soul
Tingles with our people's songs and poems!

Nobody knows which *Transcarpathian Youth* reader first realised that the poet was a disciple of Ivan Velychkovsky and that the poem was an acrostic. This was a moment of sweet and exquisite revenge; the poet hadn't even hoped that the teacher would get it into her head to publish his masterpiece in a newspaper distributed to the whole region. He would've simply relished having Mrs. Budnippyr decipher his message, and even if she hadn't, he would have contented himself with enjoying her extreme denseness and his own ingenuity. The extent of his success stunned even him, though. For the next few months, it was particularly nice to hear stories about his teacher – maddened, disheveled, distraught – running from newsstand to newsstand, trying to buy up every copy. That was all for naught, obviously, and the story of a hot-tempered young poet who'd become a local celebrity after his first publication kept circulating for quite some time. Naturally, Svyatoslav Konar took some flak, but his parents weren't actually too hard on him, because all their family friends, the whole town, actually, openly admired the kid, despite the public shaming. He had to transfer to a different school, but he didn't quit writing poems and eventually did become a famous poet. As often happens with gifted youths, however,

Konar died young from alcoholism and disillusionment regarding the future of humanity. Mrs. Budnippyr outlived her tormentor and even showed herself to be a model Christian when she came to his funeral. A while later, Ychi's shovel bade her farewell, too. People all over town wouldn't stop talking about the incident for a while after that, and everyone at the school still remembered it.

The clinking of glasses at the gravedigger's table tore Tys away from his meandering reminiscences. All at once, the teacher livened up and started listening intently to their conversation.

'Well, alright, this idea of yours really is interesting, and it seems doable, but where exactly do you want to dig?' Ychi asked, pouring a round of reeking moonshine. They looked at each other in silence for a moment.

'Thing is, we don't have a spot yet.' Icarus was the first to raise his wrist. After that, he grabbed a pickle, sniffed it loudly, and then crunched down on it just as loudly. Tys, seeing that he was falling behind, downed his drink, eyes rolling back with pleasure. 'We should all talk it over. It has to be quiet and close to the border. It seems like digging at the cemetery, by Mirca's place, would be good, since nobody would be surprised to see Ychi going there every day. There aren't too many prying eyes back there. Mirca lives nearby, so we could keep all the tools and machinery in his barn.'

'Nah, the cemetery's no good. Yeah, it's quiet and all, but it's too far away from the border. The project would drag on for years,' Mirca said and drank.

'Oof... yeah, as much bad about it as good... ' Ychi drawled pensively, pouring Tys another. The teacher interpreted that as a call to action, so he promptly downed his glass again. The host looked at him reproachfully but poured him yet another. 'The cemetery's nice and quiet, but I'm not sure we even need to do this in a quiet spot. It's hard to hide a project of this scale. Like, where are we going to put all the dirt? I say we don't hide. Let's go the other way on this.'

'What's that supposed to mean?' Tys interjected.

'My experience shows that you should do secret things right out in the open. That way, there's a better chance nobody'll figure out what you're up to. For instance, I worked as a security guard at our city's House of Culture, before the fall of the Bear Empire,' the gravedigger said, gulping down another glass. Tys lifted his head, looked at the light fixture, and suddenly remembered where he'd seen it before. It had once hung in the House of Culture, imparting a solemn atmosphere. Solving this mystery warmed the teacher's heart, and he drank.

'So,' Ychi continued, 'I remember the KGB spooks scurrying around town, trying to figure out where the People's Movement of Ukraine could be holding their constituent assembly. They scoured every anti-Soviet person's apartment, combed every barn and garage in town, checked all the collective farm buildings, and even inspected every school gym, but it never crossed their minds that the assembly could be held in the largest, most central hall in town, at the House of Culture.'

'Well, yeah,' said the Genius of the Carpathians. 'Who would have the gall to do that? It's just like that old yarn about the smuggler crossing the border on his bike – I bet that actually happened. It was summer, so he'd only be wearing sandals, shorts, and a t-shirt, and the maximum allowable number of cigarettes – two packs – would be attached to the rear basket with a metal spring. The customs officers couldn't figure out what was going on, since only taking two packs made no sense – you just kill the whole day to make chump change. There was no point in searching him, though, because he simply didn't have anywhere to hide any contraband. After he'd made a few dozen trips with his laughable two packs of cigarettes, the head of the customs office approached him and promised that he'd allow him to traffic anything and everything imaginable for three months if he'd just reveal his secret. Then the smuggler said he was taking bicycles into Hungary, not cigarettes, and that he'd walk back every time. He was running his whole operation right under everyone's noses, but those greedy numbskull uniforms had no clue!'

'So what are you three musketeers suggesting we do?' Tys asked, his eyes fixed amorously on the bottle.

'I think we have to dig right on the border. That'll be the easiest way to do it,' Ychi answered, looking like a wave of thought had just passed over him.

'Nah, that's pushing it. The People's Movement didn't march into the KGB building and hold their assembly there, did they?' The Genius of the Carpathians held an extended pause, downed his drink, and then, face contorted with disgust, rattled off his reply. 'We gotta dig in the town center. I mean, in Vedmediv, the town center is actually nowhere near the center of town, it's near the outskirts, closer to the border. It's the perfect spot. We just have to make up some excuse, like a construction project or something like that, so we can dig in peace. Well, not just dig, but drill and then take the dirt out by the truckload, right in front of everybody!'

'That's a bold idea, I'd say – a genius idea! Pour another round, Ychi. It's settled!' The host poured out the remnants of the bottle. Everyone clinked glasses and drank.

'Let's all go see the mayor tomorrow,' Icarus said. 'He's my friend. We'll persuade him, no problem. This is a genius idea, genius! In the town center, in plain view, sanctioned by the mayor! Oh yeah! It's just genius!'

Chapter 5:

In Which the Mayor Pours and Probes

Zoltan Bartok, the mayor of Vedmediv, had a large fish tank in his office. There were no fish in it – or water, for that matter – it was full of pickled tomatoes. Tys walked around it a few times, eyes shining with patriotic admiration.

'Mr. Bartok made that all by himself, by the way. He gathered the tomatoes himself and pickled them himself, so there'd always be snacks for revered guests of the city. The mayor has proposed changing the old imperial coat of arms – a bear – to a glass and a little pickled tomato to follow the shot, which would restore historical justice and raise the city's prestige, along with its appeal for tourists,' the secretary mumbled, her voice slow and measured. She was an esteemed member of the community, despite looking like an old broom.

The whole group turned toward the tank and scrutinized it; Tys sniffed the pleasantly piquant aroma that was to lure tourists to their city. Zoltan Bartok was in a meeting, so they had to wait a bit. Icarus and the Genius of the Carpathians settled into the comfortable chairs by the door. They looked the most respectable in their dark, nearly matching suits, dark dress shirts, and black shoes. Neatly combed hair, strong and silent. Ychi showed up wearing dirty, greasy jeans and an old, striped sweater; he leaned on the windowsill to the secretary's left and just stood there the whole time, staring blankly at a cabinet. Tys, on the other hand, just couldn't stop squirming; he'd sit down on a stool, cross his legs, jolt to his feet, walk around the fish tank, and step out of the room whenever he heard something in the hallway. He tried making small talk with the secretary a few times and asked her about the price of cabbage or if she was pining for her deceased husband, but the conversation kept flagging, so the teacher started doing laps around the office again, cracking his skinny fingers one by one. A discerning eye would immediately spot the tell-tale symptoms of a hangover in all this agitation. Yesterday, the originator of the project got drunk off his ass with his associates, and then after Icarus brought him home, Tys decided to swing by the bar near his house – to give everyone an update on Count Svyatoslav's comings and goings. So it's no wonder the guy looked like Dresden after the bombing. When Icarus, Mirca, and Ychi came by to pick Tys up, he was still sound asleep, while Marichka was listing all his relatives with pains- taking care so the whole neighborhood could hear, emphasising his family's genetic disorders and other shortcomings and masterfully linking them to the position of the stars when they tied the knot all those years ago. Her constant refrain was about how blind she had been to let the devil led her astray. These minute details – which would only be significant to future biographers telling the story of the mastermind behind this grand project – didn't interest Tys's associates, so they woke the teacher up without undue tenderness and gave him five minutes to get ready. A true gentleman remains a gentleman regardless of circumstances, even the morning after getting hammered, so within the time allotted to him, the teacher put on his snow-white suit, black button-up shirt, wingtips, and hat – and voila! To some, his look may've been reminiscent of an employee at a small-town circus who had to act as both ticket collector and security guard, but the unprejudiced eye would recognise that his outfit went quite well with his thick, bedraggled salt-and-pepper moustache.

There was some shouting coming out of the mayor's office, but it was hard to make out what was being said, though disparate words, such as 'plumbing,' 'Tanya,' and 'f-u-u-ck,' suggested that intense and assiduous work was being done to develop Vedmediv, that glorious city above the Tysa and below Black Mountain. Strictly speaking, the portly Zoltan Bartok truly was a patriotic son of his city; he was a real go-getter who put all of his force (all 300 pounds of it) into developing and cultivating the city entrusted to him by his constituents. He was already serving his second term as mayor, which spoke to his popularity and effectiveness.

Just 10 years ago, at the dawn of the 2000s, Zoltan Bartok was a scrawny young man taking his first steps into the business world. He was working as a porter at the market in town, but then he realised that he'd pile up ailments faster than cash doing that kind of work, so he decided to chart his own course. It all started, like everything else in newly-independent Ukraine, with common theft. Or with an open heart and a helping hand, depending on how you look at it. There was just one outhouse behind the city bazaar – both vendors and customers would scurry on back there when nature called. The employees took turns buying a new roll of toilet paper, and the security guard would put it on a shelf in the outhouse every morning. The young porter Zoltan Bartok would only go back there when he felt the urge, but that all changed one day as he squatted with his feet on the seat – so he wouldn't get all dirty – puffing on his bitter Priluki cigarettes. That's when that most Ukrainian of all business ideas dawned on him – stealing the toilet paper. He tucked the roll under his jacket and stepped outside, with his head held high, the head of a young porter, yet also a soon-to-be full-fledged businessman. No sooner had Zoltan left the outhouse than a marketgoer, eyes bulging from mounting tension, undoing his belt on the run, raced into the outhouse. A moment later, a sound similar to a volcanic eruption came from inside, followed by a squeaky, frightened voice.

'Oh, where's the toilet paper?' It was Zoltan Bartok's time to shine. He approached the heart-shaped aperture in the wooden door of the toilet and articulated his proposition judiciously.

'I can help. I got toilet paper… it costs a hryvnia, though.' The guy proffered a bill lightning-fast, and the fledgling entrepreneur thanked him with a sheet of the recently pilfered toilet paper.

From that moment on, the future mayor didn't unload a single box. Instead, he stood behind the outhouse and waited for just the right moment to offer his assistance. He'd earn ten hryvnias performing manual labor, but now, intellectual – and, to a certain extent, humanitarian – work put twenty to thirty singles in his pocket every day. His business wasn't exactly flourishing, but it was steady. Some people took issue with it, though, especially the employees at the market who would contribute money every month to cover various expenses, like the toilet paper that would vanish every morning – tucked under the young businessman's jacket. When Zoltan got caught red-handed, a furious crowd of vendors started hollering about a new form of lynching, which would involve stuffing the young thief's various orifices with whole rolls of toilet paper.

But at that very moment, Bartok's inner politician awakened. He started putting on a spirited performance for the crowd, captivating his persecutors, instantly turning them into appreciative listeners. Firstly, the woeful businessman emphasised that everything he'd done was for the good of his fellow Vedmedivites. Secondly, he didn't cause anyone any harm, although a demon had floated the idea of mixing some phenolphthalein into the city's water supply, which would've made his flow of patrons rise like dough in an oven. But no, he always followed God's will; he was always trying to do good for the people. Well, he needed to get his start-up capital from somewhere, so he took some toilet paper and began allocating it fairly. He did it with the greater good in mind, though; now nobody could tear off a piece twice as long as everyone else's and fold their extra portion in half. Yes, the young guy did charge a meager price for his modest services; however, he ensured justice for all.

The crowd quieted down and released the thief. Just a month later, fliers appeared in every single mailbox around the city. They stated that Zoltan Bartok, an entrepreneur and homegrown Transcarpathian patriot, was running for mayor to make every resident's life better today. It also said something about how 'Bartok and his team of like-minded individuals' were founding their own citizen-run organisation called the Helping Hand. For some unknown reason, Zoltan followed up with a long tangent about the Black Hand, a Bosnian organisation that operated a hundred years ago. Their most famous member, of course, was Gavrilo Princip, who murdered Archduke Franz Ferdinand in Sarajevo, thereby causing World War I. 'Unlike the murderer and radical Princip, the young Vedmedivite Zoltan Bartok uses his hand for good, helping his countrymen now that they're feeling the pinch of these trying times,' went the campaign flyer. At the very bottom, there was a picture of Bartok holding a roll of toilet paper in one hand and a set of keys (to the city, according to the caption) in the other; his bio was off to the side – special attention was given to the future mayor's business record. 'He was the son of a peasant and became the lord of a profitable business. He was a porter – he worked like a serf! – but his genius drove him to create a job for himself and become a giant of free enterprise.' Vedmedivites had always loved honest, industrious people, so, just one month later, they elected Zoltan Bartok as their mayor.

A lot of water had passed under the bridge and into the Tysa since then. The mayor got elected to a second term, and he'd gotten roughly twice as big, mostly around the middle. Once lean and mean, the mayor now looked like a bloated can of preserves propped on rickety legs. Nobody else in Vedmediv had a gut like his – well nobody else was mayor! Zoltan Bartok's belt couldn't fit around his waist – if you can call it that – so he just wrapped it around his body somewhere below his stomach, which made it look as though a rope had popped an enormous boil just above his skinny legs. Droplets of sweat glistened on his bald spot, which he periodically wiped with a grimy handkerchief. Glasses, which were meant to give Vedmediv's top official a more intellectual look, rested on his potato nose. Was he pulling it off? Eh... Moreover, like most Vedmedivites, he perpetually reeked of garlic. A dirty cotton ball stuck out of his right ear – according to local belief, that could prevent colds, a major concern with drafts blowing between East and West, as Ukraine kept emphasising its mission as a bridge between them.

His door sprang open, and some government officials filed out like a brood of ducklings. The mayor's round head poked out from behind them, and he sized up his visitors.

'Come on in, come on in, come on in.' He often repeated the same phrase a few times – perhaps political consultants had advised him to talk to his constituents like that so they'd remember and understand what he said better. There was some jostling by the door when Icarus and the Genius of the Carpathians both lunged forward to get inside first. They noticed the mayor's surprise, so they began politely waving each other through. Tys took advantage of the resulting chaos and entered the room (elegantly removing his hat and nodding at the mayor), followed by Mirca, Icarus, and then finally Ychi, who gruffly slammed the door. At that very instant, it swung open again; careening by – holding a swallow pose, like a ballerina – was Bartok, who turned to his secretary.

'Zoya, bring us five portions of delicacies, please, please, please. My most sincere gratitude!' The visitors sat down on both sides of an oval table. The mayor sank back into his leather chair. He had an entire iconostas behind him: up on his mantle was the president, the prime minster, the chairman of the Verkhovna Rada, the head of the penitentiary service, the head of the state security service, the head of the auditing service, the Patriarch of Moscow, Pamela Anderson in her younger years, and the head coach of FC Dynamo Kyiv. Shortly thereafter, the secretary came in and placed porcelain saucers with pickled tomatoes on them – along with small dessert forks and napkins – around the table. The mayor, in his turn, pulled a set of shot glasses out of his desk drawer, walked over to a bust of Taras Shevchenko by the window, unscrewed his head, and pulled out a bottle.

'Well then, my dears, let's get started, let's get started, let's get started. What brings you here?' The mayor of Vedmediv scanned the visitors, his expression hospitable. Then he smiled and made a sign with his eyebrows; everyone drank. The members of the team exchanged glances, then the next instant Tys, Mirca, and even Ychi instantly started staring at Icarus, who'd brought them all there.

'Mr. Bartok, we've come to see you, a patriotic son of our grand city, and as patriots ourselves, who would, first and foremost, like to thank you for all the work, the bulk of which you've had a hand in—'

'Let me stop you right there. Let's dispense with the pleasantries. Yes, I'll keep my hand on the tiller, don't you worry. As we say in Transcarpathia, you gotta throw back that second drink before your wife picks up the broom,' Bartok interrupted Icarus and began pouring another round. 'Keep going, keep going, keep going.'

'Well, to put it briefly… ' Icarus, who'd spent all night preparing his speech and now regretted that his seventeen-minute intro had gone down the tubes, was a bit out of sorts. 'We, as patriotic sons of our city, have come to you with an idea and a proposition.'

'Sounds interesting.' The mayor raised his eyebrows, and everyone automatically dumped the contents of their glasses into themselves. 'Keep going. Make sure you have a little snack, though, you've got to eat when you're drinking! I made the tomatoes myself, made them myself, made them myself.'

'The fact of the matter is that our magnificent city, which has delighted the eyes of travellers and remained in the hearts of its guests forever, is lacking a little something at this particular stage of its development,' Icarus continued grandly, as the mayor furrowed his brow and poured another. 'Among us sits a revered person, a person of great stature, a Vedmedivite of great stature, a true patriot, a distinguished son of our homeland, as well as a history teacher at a local school, Mykhailo Chvak, our friend Tys, as we know him. So, this man, a talented historian and true Vedmedivite, realized that the city's lacking a little something. Then he came to me with his idea. Once they heard the crux of the idea, Mirca and Ychi, two patriotic sprouts of Transcarpathia, a land fertile with talent, immediately backed us. Now we've come to you, the father of our city above the Tysa and below Black Mountain, with this idea. So, we want to give the city of Vedmediv, and, more specifically, our unmatched central square… a fountain!'

'A fountain?' The Genius of the Carpathians asked in reticent surprise.

'A fountain… ' Ychi mumbled dejectedly.

'We want to give, you know… ' Tys said, clearly befuddled.

'Hmm, a fountain! That's a wonderful idea! Let's drink to that!' The mayor could sense that something shady was going on.

Everyone drank, and then silence set in for a moment. After that, Zoltan Bartok continued. 'So you're telling me you want to give the city a fountain?'

'Yes, yes.' The visitors nodded in unison.

'As patriotic sons of our city?' The mayor persisted.

'Yes, as sons of our homeland!' Icarus declared spiritedly, summing things up and glancing around the room.

'Maybe you wanna suck a bear's prick?!' Bartok growled.

'No,' Ychi answered truthfully, after a short pause.

'Speak for yourself!' The Genius of the Carpathians pounced on him. 'Mr. Bartok, I'm afraid you misunderstood us. I mean, well, you haven't heard us out, you haven't heard everything we're trying to say.'

'Don't feed me that crap about some gift to the city. Either tell me what you're really here for or beat it! I might be willing to extend my patronage if I know the whole truth.' The father of the city's voice softened appreciably.

'Okay, okay, just don't get angry with us. We still haven't explained everything yet,' Icarus groveled. 'Now our revered history teacher, who came up with this whole plan, will tell you the whole truth. His idea is truly brilliant, just wait till you hear it.'

Everyone shifted their eyes towards Tys, who immediately got all flustered and turned bright red. The teacher swallowed hard, his Adam's apple quivering like a bobber. Tys got scared all of a sudden. His stomach gurgled, and his backside let out a little toot, so he apologized hastily, backpedaled out of the office, and made a run for the bathroom. The historian plopped down on the toilet seat as joyfully as Odysseus finally coming home. He stood up a minute later, now satisfied, and looked around but didn't see any toilet paper.

'Bartok's at it again!' Tys surveyed his environs, peered into the toilet, looked at the enormous dump he'd just taken (the kind you can only take after a night of heavy drinking), and wrinkled his nose, because it smelled like a thousand cats had died and rotted in the bathroom. He tried to flush, but there was no water in the toilet bowl. 'What should I do? What should I do?' The teacher repeated his question – just like the mayor – on the verge of a panic attack. That's when he saw the light! Eureka!

Being a history teacher has its advantages; you can call on the experience of past generations. More than seven decades ago, in the distant year of 1939, the English journalist Michael Winch spent some time in Transcarpathia. The purpose of his trip was to observe the division of Czechoslovakia, the creation of Carpatho-Ukraine, and the annexation of the young self-declared state by Hitler's ally, Hungary. The journalist wrote about those events in *Republic for a Day*. It was one of Tys's favorite books, as it described the history and customs of Transcarpathians in detail. There was one section where Winch complained about the Transcarpathians – he mentioned that a new, pristine hospital had been built for them, but they'd wipe their soiled hands on its snow-white walls after going to the bathroom, because they weren't accustomed to using toilet paper and considered it much too rough for them! Using his forefathers' experience, history teacher Mykhailo Chvak, better known as Tys, wiped himself with his hand and then dragged it along the wall. The brown streak looked like a comet's tail, which stirred his feelings. He stood in front of the mirror for another minute, checked himself out, stroked his mustache, made a sour face, buttoned his shirt and jacket all the way up, pulled a little comb out of his back pocket, ran it through his hair, winked at himself, exhaled, and then charged resolutely back towards the mayor's office.

This was the decisive moment – now Tys had to deliver the speech that would determine not only his own fate, but the fate of Vedmediv, Ukraine, and Europe.

Chapter 6:

In Which Tys Finally Announces His Idea

'If I may assume the floor,' the teacher began, and the mayor adopted a grave, official expression. He poured another round. Everyone downed their drinks, then Tys got down to the agenda. 'We're here because we're Vedmedivians... I mean, Vedmedivites. Fate has been generous to us. We live in the westernmost corner of our beloved homeland, in picturesque Transcarpathia – the Silver Land, the domain of magnificent people and miraculous natural beauty. The cultures of numerous peoples – Ukrainians, Hungarians, Romanians, Slovaks, Jews, Gypsies, Poles, and alcoholics – have come together in these parts. East meets West right here in these very parts, it's the center. No matter how you spin it, Transcarpathia has always been the center of Europe. People have tried selling it off a few times, but we all know the true center is right here and nowhere else. I drew upon the glorious history of Kyivan Rus' to arrive at my idea. Ages ago, the Rusyns lived here. There was nobody else around for miles and miles. Then our present neighbors, the Hungarians – who prefer to be called Magyars – elected to settle in a warm, fertile valley just over the Carpathians, where our city now stands. They crossed through Kyiv on their way from Asia, so naturally, a local count invited them to enjoy a feast and rest before continuing westward, thereby inaugurating a long history of friendly relations between our peoples. Later on, Anastasia, the daughter of Volodymyr the Great, another Kyivan count, became the wife of King Andrew I of Hungary, making her the Queen of Hungary. Our common history has been varied...well, it's been mostly bad, I suppose: the Hungarians mistreating the Slavs, forced assimilation, banning education, and so forth. For a thousand years, they tried to efface the mark Ukrainians left on Transcarpathia. They never built anything or invested in the region – that's why the cites of Galicia and Bukovina are richer and more beautiful. The Austro-Hungarian Empire may have been Austrian for some people, but we weren't so lucky – it was Hungarian for us. The Hungarians still aren't wild about us, to this very day. They're always mocking Ukrainians, but whenever my neighbor Choni – he's a Magyar through and through – tries talking down to me, saying I'm a savage Ukrainian because I use a rickety old outhouse, I yell right back at him. 'Oh yeah, you Magyar pig? I might have a rickety old outhouse, but Daniel of Galicia's army mopped the floor with you people back in 1227.' But that's not the point. My idea is actually designed to resolve ethnic disputes and soften lingering animosity. It symbolizes our hope for a united Europe!'

Tys's eyes began to water. The Genius of the Carpathians kicked Ychi under the table – the gravedigger was unabashedly dozing off. The mayor poured another round; everyone downed their drinks and had some of his pickled tomatoes for 'dessert.' The man behind the great idea gathered his strength, wiped a few tears from his cheeks, and continued his speech.

'Ukraine has been part of Europe since its inception. We're Europeans who've been separated from our natural homeland by a border. You know, my idea and my dream are simple – unifying Ukraine and Europe. Mr. Bartok, you ran for mayor on a platform that was all about that, so I think we're headed in the same direction. It is the syphilitic hand of Russian imperialism that has kept

Ukraine out of Europe, broken our legs, strangled us, and Asian-ized us, but Ukraine has never given up, because it simply couldn't. Claiming that Ukraine isn't part of Europe is like claiming that a man's heart isn't part of his body. If Ukraine is a European state, if the center of Europe is smack dab in the middle of Ukrainian Transcarpathia, then nobody will ever be able to tear us away from the bosom of Mother Europe. That's what Euromaidan stood for, after all. I'd say that calls for a toast!' Tys gave the mayor an entreating look, and he poured another round mechanically. Everyone threw their drinks back except Ychi, who was dozing again. The teacher looked at him with contempt, making a wry face, then another stroke of inspiration came.

'Ukrainians took to the central square of Kyiv and all of the country's other cities to prove that they're Europeans and they are striving for a European future. Our country made a geopolitical choice of civilizational importance, and we've been fighting an unbalanced war with Russia to defend it. But what did we get?' All the alcohol the teacher had consumed was firing him up, and he transformed into a gifted orator, masterfully wielding his intonation, holding pregnant pauses, and making the audience putty in his hands. 'We got jack fuckin' shit. Jack fuckin' shit, that's what we have to show for it, a fuck ton of shit!'

'Huh?' The Genius of the Carpathians had lost the thread of Tys's speech. 'Which is it? Did we get jack fuckin' shit or a fuck ton of shit?'

'We got both jack fuckin' shit and a fuck ton of shit at the same time – it was a one-two punch to our aspirations!' The teacher sighed dejectedly. 'That's why we have to fight for our right to join the European Union, finish what we started, and integrate ourselves into the common European space – euro-integrate ourselves! We, the sons of Vedmediv, must get to work without delay. The EU-Ukraine border runs right past our city. Everyone gathered here today has already... how should I put this...done some preliminary work to facilitate cross-border cooperation.' Tys winked at Icarus and the Genius of the Carpathians. 'These are people who have been building bridges between cultures, forging a path towards productive Ukrainian-European cooperation. We, as Vedmedivites, have to bring Ukraine and the European Union together! And we'll do that by building a fountain – the Fountain of Unity! Hurrah! Drinks all around!'

'What?' The mayor's face flushed with anger. 'You mean you came all the way down here to tell me that? To talk about some fountain of unity? You've decided to unite Ukraine and Europe?! Take your euro-integration and scram!'

'I'm afraid you've misunderstood us, Mr. Bartok,' Icarus said. He flashed an ingratiating smile, grabbed the bottle, and poured another round. 'The fountain will serve as a real, physical path, not a symbolic one – to unity with Europe!'

'Uh...huh?' The mayor lifted his glass with a certain degree of suspicion.

'Yeah huh! Don't you see? There'll be a tunnel in the fountain – well, under the fountain!' The Genius of the Carpathians blurted out. He'd been bursting to get to the point for a while now, and he considered Tys's preamble too long and too pompous. 'There's going to be a tunnel, underground, you see? With... like...a fountain on top. That tunnel will connect Vedmediv with Hungary.'

'Alright boys, we'd better have another drink, because I still have no clue what's going on here. What's the point of this tunnel?' Zoltan Bartok knocked one back, and everyone else followed suit.

'What's the point?' Tys clamored. 'It'll connect Ukraine with the European Union, and we'll checkmate all those bureaucrats over in Brussels who simply refuse to acknowledge the true European essence of the Ukrainian people!'

'Alright, let's say the tunnel does unify us. Then what?' The public servant, quite tipsy by now, still just wasn't getting it.

'Then there won't be any point having any borders...'cause they'll be above the ground. You can cross over without the European border guards seeing. You go down into the tunnel under the fountain in Vedmediv and then you pop out on the other side, in the EU. And then every single Ukrainian will cross the border, citizen by citizen, like the rats in *The Wonderful Adventures of Nils*, thereby slowly, gradually, and methodically euro-integrating themselves! Once all of Ukraine is inside the EU, those hapless bureaucrats will have no choice but to grant us membership! Nobody's ever done anything like this before – that's for sure – but we'll make it work. It'll be our own special path to a European future!'

'So, you're saying you want to build a tunnel that'll take every single Ukrainian to the EU?' Vedmediv's mayor asked in a businesslike tone.

'Yes!' His visitors chorused.

'But what do you need the fountain for?'

'We'll build the fountain downtown, because it's close to the border,' said Icarus. 'All the activity around the fountain won't attract any attention because there are always swarms of people bustling around there anyway. Keep in mind that the construction crew will be doing a lot of digging, which could attract a lot of unwanted attention if we built the tunnel somewhere else. But if we make it seem like we're removing excess dirt for the fountain, nobody will suspect a thing. I mean, you don't have to be a rocket scientist to know that fountains have underground pipes. There's no way the customs officers and border guards will get wise to what we're doing – after all, who would have the gall to do something like this right out in the open? We'll be totally in the clear. That's why we've come to *you*, since only you can sanction our construction project. Mirca and I have already worked out all the details. We have agreed to cover all the expenses associated with the construction of the Fountain of Unity. Think of it as two philanthropists' gift to their hometown. That'll be our contribution. Tys's contribution is the idea itself – he's the mastermind behind all this. Ychi will do the digging, that's his contribution. All we need you to do is sanction our project, Mr. Mayor.'

'Ah, I get it, I get it, I get it,' Zoltan Bartok said and emptied the contents of the bottle into everyone's glasses, clearly lost in thought. There was hardly any left, so each person received only a symbolic portion of vodka. Ychi, who'd been snoozing for some time now, got the least. The mayor glanced at the gravedigger.

'Somebody wake him up already,' he said with an affectedly harsh tone. 'A mayor's office is no place for sleeping, it's a place for serving the public good! People who come in should see a whirl-wind of activity!'

'I agree!' Ychi said dazedly – Icarus's foot had just brought him out of his slumber. Everyone downed their drinks.

'My esteemed Vedmedivite patriots, I see what you're saying, but I don't see why I have a compelling interest. I gotta have a compelling interest. So, what's my compelling interest, huh?' The mayor tucked the empty bottle away in a desk drawer and reclined majestically in his chair.

'First off,' Tys began heatedly, eager to rejoin the debate, 'as a candidate for mayor, you vowed to make every effort to promote good relations between our city and the neighboring region of Hungary, thereby integrating Ukraine into the common European space. So, this fountain is an opportunity to uphold your promise.'

'That's it?' The mayor flashed a sly, skeptical grin and then wiped a few beads of sweat off his glistening, bald head with his handkerchief.

'Secondly,' Tys said without hesitation, 'Mr. Bartok, you're an ethnic Hungarian, a Magyar, so your interest in bringing our region and the country as a whole closer to Hungary and Europe is genetic.'

'My interest is genetic? Is that right?' The mayor eyed him, clearly disappointed.

'Thirdly, and most importantly,' Tys said, raising his bony index finger, his long, filthy nail seemingly illustrating how much had gone into this moment of culmination. 'The fountain will be a gift to the city, and you'll be able to add it to your long list of accomplishments.'

All four of the visitors turned as a unit towards the mayor, who was noticeably flustered. Silence set in. There was nothing more to drink, and everyone had said their piece. All the group could do was wait for Zoltan Bartok's verdict as they strained to discern some sign of approval in his murky, drunken eyes.

'I'm not exactly over the moon about this little idea of yours,' the mayor stated disdainfully, yet wearily. 'Moreover, I'll be forced to inform the authorities—'

'Hold on there...it's a really good idea!' Icarus perked up.

'I didn't sign up to be the Moses of Ukraine on its quest for European integration, and there's nothing about tunnels in my platform. They'll crucify us for these antics of yours, and not without good reason! These kinds of things aren't done without running them by the higher-ups.' The mayor's eyes rolled towards the heavens.

'There's one very important nuance. I'm sure that you, as a true businessman, the best businessman in the city, must have already anticipated it... ' The Genius of the Carpathians tossed his hook into the water and waited for a bite.

'Yes, yes, yes, nuances, nuances, nuances, I like them very much!' Zoltan Bartok went for the bait.

'Icarus and I have been around the block, we've both been through a lot, although it hasn't always been together. I won't deny that I've been involved in promoting cross-border cooperation for some time. At first, it was just me gradually working my way up. Then I formed a team of real ghosts who could carry just about anything through the forest. Then I established a fruitful, long-term business relationship with our brothers, the Gypsies, and—'

'Speaking of Gypsies,' Tys interrupted the Genius of the Carpathians, but continuing his thought proved difficult as his tongue was getting all tangled up in his mouth like a fish caught in a net. 'Yes, the Gypsies, our brothers. Even *they* are more integrated into Europe than Ukrainians are – they're all over the world, and they're doing just great. They're lucky there's no Gypsy state because now nobody's barring them from entering the European Union. Cause there's no point, and if there was a point, it wouldn't be that—'

'Quit talking nonsense and quit interrupting!' The infuriated Genius of the Carpathians barked. 'I've collaborated with the Gypsies, now I'm euro-integrating the peoples of China and Pakistan, but that's getting harder with each passing day, what with crooked border guards hunting us down with their radar, ambushing us and demanding outlandish bribes, then they gyp us anyway.'

'Same here,' Icarus said. 'I've gone into Hungary every way there is. I built my own fleet. I took to the sky – designed and manufactured my own airplane – alright, fine, it was just a hang-glider...and it got confiscated right away. It took a record-setting bribe to get it back. So, what's next? Now I have no way to smuggle goods over the border. The airplane – the largest investment I've ever made – makes one flight a year, on Easter, when I take my wife down the streets of Vedmediv, scattering all the city's children and geese. The humiliation of failure makes me sick to my stomach. I want to get back in business, but there's just no way. The whole country rose up in protest, pushing for European integration, but the borders still haven't been opened!'

'That might be for the best. Personally, I'm strongly against lifting border controls and implementing visa-free travel,' the mayor objected abruptly, 'because as long as there are borders there will be different prices on each side, which means you can make money smuggling. You can sell counterfeit employment records and pay stubs and as long as there are visas you can transport illegal immigrants across the border for money. Visas are a status symbol, more than anything else. We – the government officials, smugglers, customs officers, and other esteemed individuals – have them. The common man, all that riff raff and poor trash, my constituency, can't even dream about getting them!'

'That's exactly what we want to fix!' Tys declared, like the true idealist he was.

'No, that's not it!' Icarus countered. 'I mean, yeah, that's pretty much it, but not quite. That's not the main thing. You see, our patriotic plan entails building a tunnel nobody will know about. First off, it'll be too narrow for all the citizens of Ukraine to fit through at once, so we'll send our cargo, packages, and so forth on the first few runs.'

'Well, then later on, in a few years' time, we'll expand the tunnel for the Ukrainian people.' The Genius of the Carpathians winked slyly and gestured at Tys.

'So, you're saying that during the initial stages of the project we'll be using the tunnel to satisfy our own modest needs?' Zoltan Bartok sat down at the table abruptly, his interest clearly piqued.

'No!' Tys objected.

'You betcha!' Icarus and the Genius of the Carpathians said in unison.

'How's it all going to play out?' the mayor asked.

'We – well, Ychi, will be digging the tunnel. We figure the job will take six months, tops. It should be ready to go by late fall. The tunnel won't be all that long, and we won't be digging too deep, so it'll be a piece of cake. Well, and it'll all look like prep work for a fountain downtown. We'll have the papers write about the Fountain of Unity, how Transcarpathia is super multi-cultural and all, European integration, and so forth. We'll dig the tunnel over into Hungary and send the first batch of our respective goods through. Meanwhile, there'll be a grand ceremony: the whole city celebrating, little munchkins peeing in the new fountain, and tourists taking pictures. Everyone'll be happy. Well, then we'll start integrating Ukraine into Europe, slowly but surely. That's the game plan.'

'But we have to transport *people* across the border!' Tys wasn't giving an inch.

'Mr. Chvak, digging a tunnel is a long, costly, and dangerous undertaking,' said the mayor – he had a good handle on the situation now, so he was trying to take control. 'So, our business associates are putting up the money to get it going. We'll send some goods to our brother country of Hungary first to make some money to expand and equip the tunnel. Once it's wide enough, Mircha will help a few batches of Pakistanis and Chinese cross the border – that's a nice thing to do, and it'll serve as a kind of experiment – since we wouldn't want to risk the lives of Ukrainians. We'll start European integration once everything is running smoothly. As a teacher, you must realize that we need to double-check everything first.'

'Yep!' Tys smacked his lips and raised his glass, only to discover that it was empty.

'Zoya!' The chipper mayor called. 'Bring us a complete set. It's not every day you meet such socially-conscious philanthropists!' Once another bottle and more pickled delicacies found their way to the table, Zoltan Bartok filled everyone's glasses, studied his visitors with a tender, fatherly gaze, and delivered a speech in the animated tone of a public servant. 'You are truly loyal and patriotic sons of our city and our homeland. Our national heroes, Taras Shevchenko and Valeriy Lobanovskyi, would be proud of you. I'm grateful you've come to me with this patriotic initiative. A fountain is a truly great gift that will make the city more beautiful, its people happier, and Ukraine,' the mayor snickered to himself, 'Europeanier! Therefore, I'm more than willing to extend my patronage. I order you to get to work immediately. Let's drink to the Fountain of Unity! To Ukraine and Europe!'

Chapter 7:

In Which Work Commences and Then Suddenly Ceases

The next morning, May 16th, 2015, Ychi rolled up to the central square of Vedmediv on his bicycle, with a shovel attached to the frame and a litre bottle of beer fastened to the rear basket. He started his workday with the latter, since he was feeling a little blue after yesterday's visit to the mayor's office.

His unfamiliarity with the terrain kept him from getting to work right away, though. More precisely, he didn't know where the city's – or rather Europe's – Fountain of Unity was to be erected. The gravedigger had to wait for the mayor, so he wound up cracking open a second bottle and lying down under a tree.

Ever since the days of the Bear Empire, it's been called Peace Square. It would've been damn near impossible to come up another name so ludicrous, yet so fitting – no matter what anyone may say, the Vedmedivites were good wine producers, industrious bakers, strong lumberjacks, and brilliant cooks, but they were never known as outstanding warriors, revolutionaries, or rebels. In other words, peace was part of the Vedmedivites' way of life, although, to be perfectly honest, it was usually imposed on them after they were defeated or occupied. No matter what country or empire Transcarpathia may have been joining at any given stage in history, this process always took place without the Transcarpathians' consent, or even their participation. So, the name Peace Square had a second, hidden meaning – Occupation Square. Way down south, people claim that Italians are the worst warriors because they're lazy, undisciplined hedonists. Folks in those parts obviously haven't heard about the Transcarpathians, who just won't fight at all. Perhaps that's where all that talk about Transcarpathia's centuries-old tradition of tolerance comes from.

Fortunately, Ychi didn't know about any of that. He was craving delicious treats as he shifted from sweet beer reverie to bouts of delirium. Salo, first and foremost, in all the varieties God had contrived. God had contrived quite a few varieties of that delicious cured pork fat: seasoned with spicy pepper, for pairing with single-distillation vodka; sweetened with red paprika, for white vodka; soft and boiled, for the fruit-infused kind; heavily salted, for your classic ice-cold poison; smoked and fragrant, for straight vodka, as pure as a tear.

'The Lord's miracle,' Ychi thought, or maybe dreamt. 'There are so many types of salo, and each of them goes with vodka. That's what the Almighty created them for, which means that God himself likes having a glass of the cold stuff. I may not go to church, but I'm a deeply religious man in my own way. A true Christian.' Then God – his most mundane, bearded manifestation – appeared to Ychi. He was sitting at a table and sharing a bottle – Him, his Son, and the Holy Spirit. They said 'Amen' and clinked their glasses, and then suddenly church bells tolled. Ychi shuddered from the loud noise, crossed himself, as if suddenly inspired, opened his eyes, and saw the large yellow bell swaying in the tower that overlooked the city's square.

In addition to the church, there was City Hall, built during the days of the Bear Empire, the House of Culture (which looked like a warehouse), a monument to the city's guardian angel (due to budget constraints, all the city did was replace the head on the old Lenin statue and add wings), an oak tree whose age gave rise to all sorts of outlandish legends, the city archives, the Bear's Share (a local restaurant), and the Hotel Vedmediv. A large, untidy flower bed sprawled out in the middle of the square, around the luxuriant oak tree. The gravedigger dozed there, and a ram, a white goat with a black spot on its left side, a white goat with no black spot, an all red goat, two sheep, two cows who had been looking at a new gate – the one on the archive building, specifically – since April, a brood of ducks, an uncatchable multitude of furiously active hens, a proud and elegant rooster, 17 geese, and a filthy pig were clustered around him and his bicycle, lying down, tied to something, or grazing. In the early 90s, some concerned citizens protested against this nature festival, calling it an open pasture and an utter disgrace. But the mayor managed to convince the city's residents that a pastoral landscape would have a calming effect on potential investors, who would see that Vedmediv was home to wealthy, hard-working, enterprising individuals and then decide to put their capital here. No investors had come yet, but the pasture remained. It did often come in handy for local drunkards, who could hide away somewhere in the grass and nap right there in the middle of town, soothed by soft mooing and a nice breeze.

Eventually, at around eleven a.m., the mayor and his entourage – the top city council members – who were much lauded by journalists at the *Vedmediv Star* and just so happened to be the mayor's wife, brother, and father-in-law – showed up in the square. Zoltan Bartok, as a man of dignity and integrity, didn't officially employ his beloved wife. Instead, she was listed on the books as a volunteer advisor at City Hall. His deeply patriotic wife would always voice the community's opinion whenever anything needed to be approved or ratified. After the mayor brought his underlings up to speed on Tys's idea and the unprecedented investment prospects that would open up for Vedmediv once the Fountain of Unity was built, he spoke dryly, addressing Ychi, who was still lying on the ground.

'Work has come to a standstill, I see.'

'It isn't at a standstill. It's lying down,' said the gravedigger in a proud, spirited tone. 'I brought my tools, everything's set. I don't know where exactly to dig, though. I need some sort of plan.'

'Don't you go telling the mayor what's necessary and when! You're familiar with the plan. We're not going to draw anything up. Start by digging down and then dig in the direction where the sun sets, use the steeple to get your bearings. I'll take care of the rest. Move, move, move!'

'But you've got a whole zoo here! They'll fall in!' Ychi wouldn't let up.

'We'll think of something, don't you worry. I've been meaning to bring my nephew on for a while now, he's an ace when it comes to this stuff. Get going already! Alright, my dears,' the official addressed his entourage. 'No use standing around here – go, go, go.'

Ychi got up lazily, had a lovely stretch, unfastened the shovel from his bike frame, stepped about 10 feet away from the oak, and started digging. Right around lunchtime, some snot-nosed kid sprinted over carrying a thin staff and ran the birds and beasts out of the square – Zoltan Bartok wasn't kidding about his nephew. Neither the gravedigger, nor anybody else around here ever saw the animals again throughout the entire duration of the project (envious tongues maintained that all of the livestock wound up in the mayor's backyard, but that's why they're called envious tongues).

The job wasn't easy. On the first day, Ychi dug a pit barely more than a foot deep and six feet wide. When Zoltan Bartok, Icarus, the Genius of the Carpathians, and Tys came by that evening to 'inspect the job site and track progress,' as they put it, they were extremely dissatisfied and ordered the gravedigger to try harder the next day and widen the pit, because it was supposed to be a world-class fountain, not a dinky little well in some village. Ychi tried his best, but didn't make much headway, because the ground underneath the square turned into a mix of clay and stone about two feet down, and the percentage of stone increased with every inch. So it's no wonder that he soon had to replace his shovel with a pickaxe. That nearly stopped the project. It'd take the gravedigger all day to hack three or four wheelbarrows' worth of that stony mixture out of the pit. Perhaps the Vedmedivites' ancestors had good reason to choose this spot for the city's main square. The ground was hard as glass, which made it safe for building and impervious to the many earthquakes that rock the Carpathians.

Ychi also had to make frequent appearances at his main place of employment, since the city's residents lacked the common courtesy to stop dying now that the Fountain of Unity was underway. He'd pick at the unyielding earth under Peace Square, head to the cemetery, where he'd hastily dig a grave for yet another corpse, and then stick around for the wake, where, as a devout Christian, he would imbibe the Lord's favorite beverage, for which He had contrived all kinds of salo. By that time, speaking, let alone digging, was out of the question, and the sun would already have dipped behind the church. Basically, the operation was moving slowly; he was hardly getting any deeper.

The same couldn't be said about the mayor and the Vedmediv Star. They'd launched a full-blown propaganda campaign. Just two days after the project got underway, the paper ran an expansive interview (covering three pages of the four-page publication) with Zoltan Bartok. On the remaining page, journalists portrayed Tys, Icarus, and the Genius of the Carpathians as homegrown patriots and downright wonderful people. At first, Marichka was very surprised when she read the write-up on her husband. Then she reread it and nearly fell in love with him again. After a third read, she ran over to kiss him, all proud and happy, but once she stepped into his rank, cluttered room, she changed her mind and opted for a string of choice curses instead. Other readers figured there had to be an election coming up, hence the candidates' mugs popping up all over the place again. At any rate, the idea of a fountain and the big PR push got the Vedmedivites all riled up.

On the very next day, a lot of onlookers gathered in the town square to stand in the shade and observe the languid, hung-over gravedigger at work, offering advice or derision. Two days later, the local TV station aired an interview with the mayor, which only added fuel to the fire. The journalists also illustrated Zoltan Bartok's inspired speech with a picture of the Trevi Fountain in Rome. This image roused the residents' imagination so much that some old guy even claimed to have recognised one of the statues lining the fountain as Emil Bartok, the mayor's bearded father, which he attributed to the fact that it was Ychi who had undertaken this project. Subsequently, a rumor crept around town to the effect that the vain, satanic mayor wanted to rebury his father in the very center of Vedmediv, in the central square, under a 700-year-old oak. Two days later, the mayor had to give another interview. He refuted that rumor and told the Vedmedivites – who were prone to exaggeration – about the idea of the Fountain of Unity. This time around, the broadcasters decided to forego showing the pictures; it was just the mayor's fat, sweaty, bald head on the screen, so all the insinuations abated over time. Just to reinforce things, the *Vedmediv Star* dedicated four pages to the fountain, once again. A billboard displaying a map of Europe – with Vedmediv as a big, fat dot in the middle – appeared in the city. A message sprawled across the bottom in bright cursive letters: 'Vedmediv will never be the same.

The Fountain of Unity is a new page in our European history. Mayor Zoltan Bartok and his team of activists.'

Although they were able to handle the first incident quickly, the 'activists' didn't like that half the city was bumming around the central square, keeping a close eye on Ychi's inch-by-inch progress. That's why a tall fence went up around the flowerbed, the oak, and the gravedigger. To keep the citizens from getting upset, they said the fence was designed to protect against construction hazards. The mayor had an old excavator from the utilities department brought over to the oak. Since the director of the aforementioned department had stolen all the fuel a long time ago, two horses – driven by the little Gypsy Mitya's whip – had to drag it the whole way, much to the residents' delight.

When the metal dinosaur got to the oak and the fence sprang up, the hype regarding the fountain died down; however, Ychi started growing indignant. Most notably, he insisted that the excavator actually be utilised for the project, presenting the reasonable argument that a metal scoop would make it faster and easier to dig a pit in the impenetrable ground, which was basically all rock. The mayor was all for it but not inclined to provide the fuel. He noted that Icarus and the Genius of the Carpathians had promised to handle all equipment procurement. They responded by saying that it was a myth that excavators could dig faster than people. Also, the machinery was too loud, and it would disturb the locals and disrupt city council sessions. Bartok and Ychi roared with laughter at that. Then the Genius of the Carpathians grasped for his final lifeline.

'Ychi,' he began in a tone meant to inspire trust, putting a friendly hand on the gravedigger's shoulder. 'Think about it. This is the central square of an old city that, as you know, is in the center of Europe. Wars started and ended here. Templars, knights, kings, and merchants passed through this area, and their valuables got lost and sank into the ground. Now you can find them – nobody else has ever dug around here! And you wanna start rooting around with an excavator?! You'll never spot a gold ring or a diamond in the scoop, or, worse yet, you could destroy some priceless treasure. You'd better keep at it with a shovel or pickaxe. It might be slow going, but you still have a chance to strike it rich!'

'Yeah, sure, I'll strike it rich diggin' up fuckin' kitsch,' Ychi said, growing surly. 'Don't try to put one over on me. I thought we were in this together, but you're up to your old tricks again. Just like my father when he wanted me to shuck beans. He'd say, 'son, I'd get shuckin', because there's one bean filled with candy in every bucket!' I'd shuck seven buckets' worth – my hands'd be bleedin' but I didn't get dick! No candy at all! So give me some fuel, and we'll start working for real. If I use a shovel, it'll be winter before I get the job done!'

Eventually, the team did have to fill up the excavator, and then the project started moving incomparably faster. Shortly thereafter, the pit in the central square of Vedmediv reached a depth of 10 feet. Now the second phase of the project was to begin – putting a canopy equipped with gutters over the pit so the rain couldn't wash out the future tunnel. Ychi, Icarus, and the Genius of the Carpathians undertook the task, while Tys was assigned the role of delivering lunch (Marichka would make all the meals for them). Meanwhile, the fifth 'activist' – Mayor Zoltan Bartok – was away on vacation.

A nice canopy shaped like a rectangular umbrella with tin gutters running around it sprouted up under the oak a few days later. Eventually, in the second half of June, almost a month after the project had begun, the key third phase – digging horizontally – got underway. The Vedmedivites weren't supposed to find out about it, though. Using the church steeple to get his bearings, Ychi slowly forged on in the right direction. The ground was still rather tough, and digging with a shovel would've been laughably slow. They had to set up a power line in the pit, so the gravedigger could hook his jackhammer up to it. Ychi forced the tool into the ground; all he had to do was toss the pulverized soil into a bucket, hoist it to the top of the ladder, and then dump it into a truck.

Carrying it up the ladder slowed the process down, though. The tunnel, despite all of Icarus and the Genius of the Carpathians' complaints and indignation, required a new apparatus that would enable Ychi to lift the pulverized soil to the surface more easily. They picked the cheapest device possible – a pulley attached to a branch of the oak. Ychi fastened the bucket to one end and pulled the other, thereby lifting the load. When it reached the surface, the gravedigger wrapped his end of the rope around a peg he'd driven into the ground, went up the ladder, and dumped the soil into the truck. Things could've gone faster if there'd been somebody else to catch the buckets and empty them, but after a short meeting it was decided that hiring yet another worker would've been way too risky – he might let the cat out of the bag and put an end to their monumental project.

The tunnel kept expanding, despite the extremely primitive nature of the work. Now the truck would deposit the soil at a different spot on the edge of town every day, to maintain secrecy. It was all because Ychi had finally embraced the idea of the project and begun to take pleasure in his work. And how! By the end of June, the tunnel had advanced by roughly thirty feet, expanding in scale and demanding fresh innovations. Every third day, Ychi would extend the power line to keep his jackhammer and overhead lamp alive. This was something he'd made with his own two hands, and that was exhilarating after all those years of digging mundane graves. The tunnel now resembled a mine, constantly growing in length with the gravedigger's every perfect and efficient movement.

With each stroke of the shovel, yank of the pulley, and heave of the bucket, Ychi's pride intensified. He thought of himself as a titan hammering at impervious glass, and it yielded, obeyed his hands, changed its shape under his pressure. More and more exalted aspirations bubbled up in the gravedigger's mind, but it was difficult for him to express them because he, unlike that other dreamer, Tys, wasn't all that educated and was a quiet, reserved type. His silhouette pushed deeper and deeper into the cool, damp space of the tunnel. This was his domain of solitude, the first truly creative job he'd done in his life, and perhaps the most important.

Ychi realized that the tunnel had crossed Peace Square and reached its outer boundary when his jackhammer hit something very hard and solid – a buttress of the church. 'It's a good thing we calculated everything, and that our tunnel'll pass under the church. We could've gone a little too high and rammed into its foundation.' The gravedigger chuckled smugly and pressed the clutch of the jackhammer. It started running, delving into the soil under the stone. O-n-n-n-ne, and the first bucket was filled up, two-o-o-o-o, and the second bucket was ready to go, thre-e-e-e-, and Ychi suddenly blacked out, dust and clay clogging his nostrils, a hellishly heavy load dropping onto his chest, as though the whole church had fallen and punished the gravedigger for this blatant sacrilege.

Chapter 8:

In Which There's Grief and Nothing But Grief

The sun had already crossed well beyond its midday threshold when Tys showed up at Peace Square in the center of Vedmediv, bearing the large cooler in which he brought the gravedigger his lunch every day. The teacher had his own key; he looked around conspiratorially, quickly opened the lock on the chain link gate to the site of the future fountain, and slipped inside. He put the cooler on a table under the canopy, walked over to the ladder, bent down, and yelled.

'Time to eat, come on up! It's borsch and garlic bread!' The only reply from down below was silence. Tys yelled once again, but to no avail. 'He-l-l-l-o-o! Ychi!' Tys called as loud as he could, but the gravedigger still wasn't responding. 'Heh-heh, maybe the tunnel's so long that he can't hear a thing.' The originator of the grand idea spat with pleasure and rubbed his hands together, then he clumsily swung his foot onto the ladder and went down to get his friend.

The tunnel sure was impressive – it was a ten-foot climb down the ladder, and then came the black, gaping void of Ukraine's path to Europe. Tys hadn't been down in the passageway for nearly two weeks; his role in the project had been reduced to the point that he was little more than a delivery boy, so he wasn't surprised it was dark in the tunnel now. He took his phone – the cheapest Nokia model available – switched on the flashlight and forged ahead.

The light from his phone reached no more than a foot and a half into the gloom, so the teacher was basically just groping his way along, feeling out the ground ahead of him with the pointy tip of his shoe before every step. Tys shouted again once he'd gotten another fifteen feet into the tunnel, but his voice crashed against its walls and sank into the packed earth without producing an echo. The teacher turned around – the bright spot at the tunnel entrance was a long way off, and there was nothing but solid gloom up ahead.

'Y-y-y-chi!' Tys yelled again, severely straining his vocal cords, but there was no reply. 'Whoa, things are really coming along,' he thought to himself. The tunnel's already so long you get tired walking through it. Soon we'll be seeing the light on the Hungarian side! We could really use a light bulb down here, though – it's as dark as the devil's asshole!' Tys walked another dozen feet or so, yelled, once again to no avail, then took one more tentative step, and felt his foot connect with something soft. He bent down and directed the flashlight at the area around his feet but only saw dirt, then stepped on the soft thing again, more resolutely this time, but instantly sprang back in fright. He could hear panting under the soil! 'The devil! Evil spirits!' went the thoughts whizzing by in his mind. Lurching back in fear, Tys started crossing himself and saying a prayer. When he'd backed up to a safe distance, he pointed his flashlight at the far corner. His eyes had mostly adjusted to the darkness, so he could finally see the end of the tunnel, the dark wall of earth, the heap of clay on the ground – a jackhammer jutted out of it – and then… a human arm with no body! Tys gulped like a fish in a net, hopped up, and blazed towards the exit, falling and getting up again; his legs were giving out, his heart was pounding, and his every sound was getting lodged in his dry throat like a tiny fish bone.

The teacher only regained his senses when he was back on the surface, under the oak. His legs just couldn't hold him up anymore, so he plopped down, his back resting against the trunk of the tree and his bulging eyes continuing to look into the tunnel opening, seemingly in a trance, yet wary – what if something was chasing him? The daylight and fresh air calmed Tys down a bit, but fear was making his stomach churn. An unbearable queasy feeling overcame him; he quickly scrambled around the tree, undid his belt with trembling fingers, and dropped his pants. A sound of such intensity erupted out of the teacher that he immediately remembered why his students maliciously called him Carbide. Tys finished up and exhaled with relief. His heart slowed its furious, adrenaline-fueled rhythm. After another fearful look at the tunnel entrance, he sat down and began feverishly contemplating his situation. What he'd seen was so preposterous that no explanation would suffice.

'Who could that've been?' Tys tried thinking as rationally as possible. 'Was it really an evil spirit? But why didn't it attack me when I stepped on it? Why is it hiding underground? How could Ychi just step over a guy lying on the ground and keep working? What could the devil need a jackhammer for?' Beads of cold sweat appeared on his temples, and he started getting that queasy feeling again. Gradually, the realisation came to him that it wasn't an otherworldly being, a devil, or a beast lying down there, buried under a thick layer of clay, but a person. A human being. 'But who was it? Nobody besides us knows about the tunnel. The mayor is on vacation, and it's highly unlikely Icarus or the Genius of the Carpathians would've gone down there to work – they've got enough on their plates as it is. So who was it? Why would Ychi let someone into the tunnel? If word got out, our idea could be ruined. Ychi! It could only be him! The gravedigger's lying down there, at the end of the tunnel. Maybe he buried himself? But what for? Nah, something happened, like a cave-in. Ychi needs help!'

Tys peered into the eye of the tunnel again, this time beyond frightened, and decided to take action. He may've been a coward, but he sure wasn't a bad person. The teacher couldn't leave his friend to die in the tunnel, or just lie there, dead under a heap of dirt. It was time to take action, and fast. Tys got up, crossed himself, and climbed down into the tunnel once again. At the bottom, he lifted his head, as if he wanted to get one last look at the blue sky, but all he could see were the slate tiles on the canopy over the entrance and the mighty trunk of the oak off to the side. Not finding anything sublime in that picture to help him bid farewell to the world, the teacher turned around, took his phone out of his pocket, and crept forward, shining the light more and more cautiously and scrupulously with every step. His lips whispered some sort of magic spell, but it didn't seem to be providing sufficient protection, so he picked up a rock by his feet. Armed, yet far from fearless, he continued his advance. On step 34 – or 59 feet into the tunnel – the light from his phone was stopped by the earthen wall once again. Just like before, the tip of a jackhammer and a human hand jutted out of the ground. There was no doubt – that enormous hand belonged to Ychi. The teacher locked up for a second, as though refusing to believe that his friend was lying there, buried under a layer of clay. He tried to discern whether or not the clay was actually rising ever so slightly, replicating the up-and-down movement of the ribcage, but in the dim light, the shadows made it feel like everything – the walls, the floor, the jackhammer – was moving. It wasn't just moving, but dancing, and then Tys realised that was because the hand holding his cell phone was trembling.

Tentatively, as if sneaking up on something, the teacher moved closer to the mound, shut his eyes in fear, and reached for Ychi's hand. It was warm. That warmth transferred to Tys, sliced right through him, injected itself into every nerve, and filled him with strength and confidence. Fear wasn't part of the equation anymore, because the hand was warm, and that meant Ychi was alive. Tys set his phone aside and began digging through the mound with his hands. Just a moment later, the outline of the torso came into view from underneath the clay; Tys picked up the pace and was soon tenderly wiping dirt off Ychi's face. Then he pressed his ear against the gravedigger's chest. At first, he couldn't hear anything, but then he held his breath and listened hard, straining his hearing to the utmost, and from some distant, unseen depth, as if from an old, abandoned well, he heard a tired, fading heartbeat. Then he pressed his cheek against the gravedigger's face, and a stream of air tickled him. Ychi was breathing!

Elated, Tys kissed his friend on both cheeks and started brushing the dirt off his legs. Once he was done, the teacher reached under Ychi's arms and tried to hoist him. The gravedigger barely budged. Tys got on his knees and pulled with all his might. Ychi's body rose slightly, and he emitted a dry cough. The gravedigger was coughing up the clay that had clogged his throat. Tys turned him over on his side and patted him on the back to get him coughing more.

'Try getting up now, Ychi. Everything's gonna be alright. You're alive, you're warm, you're breathing. Well, come on now, pal, everything's gonna be alright. You're alive. We'll get out of here soon, and you'll feel much better. C'mon, Ychi, everything's gonna be just fine. Keep breathing, keep coughing, just like that. Attaboy! Good job.'

This lasted a few minutes, until Ychi coughed up all the dirt, let his head sink onto his friend's shoulder, and began wheezing steadily. Tys rose to his feet, heaved the gravedigger up, and began dragging him, straining and grunting. This wasn't the easiest of tasks, since Ychi weighed at least twice as much as Tys. The teacher wasn't giving up, though. Thirty-four steps separated them from the tunnel entrance, and those were the longest and hardest steps of both their lives. Ychi was still unconscious, while Tys could barely manage two steps before he'd have to lean against the wall, catch his breath, and wipe the sweat from his forehead. Off went his jacket ten steps in; his whole shirt was soaked. Unaccustomed to exerting himself, the teacher was short of breath and running on empty. The end of the tunnel was infinitely far away. He had to take longer breaks and shake his arms, as if that would help fill them with more blood, more strength. How long did it take him to cover that route, which seemed like an eternity, an endless hell he was doomed to endure and could never escape? How long did it last? Was it really no more than 20 minutes? To the teacher, in his ecstasy of fatigue, it seemed like the sun had set and risen again by the time he had spent his last ounce of strength to pull his friend to the surface.

Tys lunged forward one more time, then collapsed on his back and looked up at the canopy. Made it! He'd lugged Ychi all that way; they could see the light of day! The teacher lay there for nearly half an hour, contemplating the sublime and flawless – at least it seemed that way at the moment – structure of the canopy's slate tiles, breathing and feeling the immense pleasure of his drained body at rest. Then he extricated himself from beneath the unmoving Ychi and rose into a crouch.

'What should I do next? How do I get this hapless gravedigger up the ladder?' Tys thought. 'I'm wiped out. Gotta call for help. But who should I call? Any outsider will figure out that the Fountain of Unity is no fountain at all the instant he walks onto the construction site! And what if somebody goes down into the tunnel and sees that it stretches 60 feet toward the nearby – and strictly regulated – border? How do I handle this situation?' On his knees again, Tys touched the gravedigger's face, trying to revive him.

'Come on, try getting up. Don't crap out on me now. Open your eyes, look at me. We're already in the clear. You're breathing, it's a beautiful day out there, c'mon now, get up. I can't pull you out of this damn hole, I just can't!' No response. The teacher wiped his lips on his sleeve and started giving Ychi mouth-to-mouth. Anybody who saw them would've recognised true love at once. Tys really was trying to resuscitate his buddy. He sprayed air into Ychi's mouth, rubbing his bristly stubble against him, huffing and puffing away, but none of it helped. Now irate, he slapped Ychi three times, dumping all his resentment, exhaustion, and anger on this over-grown dope, this hulking nitwit who could blow their cover and cause this entire project and Ukraine's whole future to fail miser-ably, to crash and burn! Ychi wasn't responding to anything at all; he simply lay there, eyes closed, still wheezing. A sudden rush of energy, possibly fueled by anger, came out of nowhere, and Tys began lugging Ychi towards the ladder. He strained every muscle in his body trying to lift the gravedigger onto one of the rungs, held his breath, and pulled hard, but at that moment, a squeaky, falsetto fart came out, and he plopped down on the earthen floor. Him pull Ychi up the ladder? Yeah right. You'd need 20 burly men to pull a carcass like this all the way up there!

There was still the bucket Ychi used for lifting the dirt out; the pulley, although primitive in design, did make it faster and easier. But how was Tys supposed to lift the gravedigger in the bucket? One limb at a time? He grabbed the bucket and stuck Ychi's limp hand into it – nothing else could fit inside. Eureka! The teacher smacked himself on the forehead, untied the rope attached to the bucket, and wrapped it around his friend's waist twice. That's how you lift a carcass this beefy! Quite pleased with himself, Tys rose to his feet, spat on his hands, rubbed them together with gusto, grabbed the other end of the rope, exhaled, and then pulled. It was tough going; Ychi's body – not even his whole body, just his stomach – rose a mere ten inches, so the gravedigger had just bent slightly into an arch. No matter how the teacher strained, even when he tried to use his own body as a counterweight, nothing worked. Ychi merely began wheezing even louder. Tys just wouldn't be able to pull him out all on his own. Eventually, the teacher thought of calling his partners to tell them about the tragedy and enlist their assistance. The thought of getting some help enlivened him, so he started dialing Icarus's number anxiously – the recorded voice stated that the number he'd called was unavailable. Then Tys called up the Genius of the Carpathians but there was no answer. He dialed another dozen or so times, but the sluggish Romanian just wouldn't pick up.

The teacher decided to run over to his house. Maybe the Genius of the Carpathians was just puttering around in the yard and couldn't hear the phone. Tys took stock of his supine pal one more time and then went up the ladder. He was surprised to see the city was carrying on according to its own calm, steady rhythm outside the construction site. Nobody had the slightest inkling of what was going on; nobody knew that Ychi the gravedigger lay unconscious just 10 feet below them. Tys hastily tucked his shirt into his pants, smoothed out his dusty moustache, slicked back his ragged hair with some spit, and nearly ran down Station Street, lined with cozy one-story, lower-middle-class houses, to the Genius of the Carpathians' property.

Dread burned in the history teacher's chest; something unknown and unfathomable was gnawing at him, blazing inside him, hurrying him along, bringing tears to his eyes. In all honesty, he was most concerned about Ychi dying on him. He couldn't handle another death; he wouldn't be able to forgive himself for being so helpless – yet again – in the face of that hideous woman with the scythe, the figure of death from every Ukrainian folk tale. Death had already taken one person from Tys, and he had no way of getting her back, saving her. Death was already in his life, so he feared it. Another one would do him in.

Things used to be different, though. Nah, not just different – everything was marvellous! That was 20-some years ago, when he'd just met Marichka. What a day that was! The day of days! Tys was 20, Marichka 21. They were both studying at Uzhhorod University, the boy history, the girl biology. On that magnificent, unforgettable day, Tys was walking along the waterfront, from the pedestrian bridge to City Hall – there was a bar cheap enough for a college student in the hungry nineties tucked away behind it. The soon-to-be historian passed Korzo Street and went into a building across from School No. 1. It was October – perhaps the most magnificent time of year in Uzhhorod – when the air's still gentle and velvety and the colors hot and vivid, when people get dressed up, stroll around downtown all evening, greet each other warmly and crack jokes whenever they meet. It was fall, when the light from lampposts tears the yellowish crowns of trees out of the night's embrace and tints the twilight river silver.

There were some young people sitting on the benches outside the school, music was flowing out of a nearby restaurant, Tys was walking along – inspired and somewhat inebriated – when he saw the lonely, tender silhouette of a young woman standing a little off to the side, book in hand. In those days, the soon-to-be teacher would feast his eyes upon every young maiden passing by, giving them long, deep looks, seemingly tempting them with his impudence. But this time the girl's gaze was stronger, more persistent, more fiery. It defeated Tys, and he lowered his eyes and saw that she was holding a book. Not just any book – Taras Shevchenko's *Kobzar*! This proved to be the decisive moment that tipped the scales – the young student fell irrevocably in love.

After all, he'd decided to major in history because he was a Ukrainian patriot; ever since he was a little boy, he'd get goosebumps just thinking about the country's glorious Cossack past, Hrushevsky's beard, or Chornovil's mustache. He was jumping for joy when the Soviet Union fell, when Ukraine finally gained its independence! This, coupled with economic collapse and devasta-tion, led to some truly tough times; his gray-haired, denture-wearing elders were the only patriots left and young people had no interest whatsoever in the idea of patriotism. Tys was a member of all the patriotic organizations operating in the city: Prosvita, the People's Movement of Ukraine (he secretly joined Sobor, the Ukrainian Republican Party, too), Plast, and the Romzha Greek Catholic Youth Group. He even signed up to join the Ukrainian Women's Union (although he didn't pay membership dues). His peers were nowhere to be found, though. Elderly patriots would bring their grandchildren to meetings – mostly little tykes or school-age kids – but there were hardly any students, let alone coeds. The young historian had always dreamt about a magnificent, alluring, lustful, and – most importantly! – patriotic girl with whom he could discuss counts Svyatoslav and Volodymyr, the works of Shevchenko and Malaniuk, the heroes of Carpatho-Ukraine, and the Battle of Kruty. But there was no such girl. Anywhere.

So when he saw that magnificent girl holding a copy of *Kobzar*, his heart fluttered, a man's meager tear dropped from his eye, and his pants bulged with the unyielding erection of a true Ukrainian. Their first conversation by the school didn't exactly go smoothly, though. Tys was all anxious and befuddled, and he smelled of cheap alcohol and garlic, so Marichka reacted frostily when he introduced himself. When this pesky, skinny-as-a-twig guy asked what she was majoring in, she only answered so he'd beat it. Tys had essentially wrapped himself around her like a liana vine, latched onto her like a burr. She couldn't get a word in edgewise because he kept blab-bing – about himself, about his hometown of Vedmediv, about the history department and the bar behind City Hall, about Ukraine, her will, honor, glory, and people. Luckily, Marichka's friend showed up in the nick of time; they had to get to a play. The girls did wind up ditching that ignoramus, but it came at a high price – they foolishly told him their real room number at the dorm – 204. Many years after that night, Marichka still griped about that stupid tongue of hers. Why did she have to blurt out the truth? Why couldn't she have made up some sick grandmother or aunt or said she lived in the countryside or something?

After the happy and boundlessly infatuated Tys got the information he needed, he marched down to the local bar and kicked off an exceptionally lengthy bender. There was no sign of him for three days, and Marichka had begun hoping that she was in the clear. Five days later, her suitor did indeed come calling, bearing a bouquet of flowers and a collection of Vasyl Symonenko poems. The book in particular surprised her, since she hadn't shown any interest in literature in all her born days and couldn't stand poetry. It was only on their seventh date or so, when she posed the sacred question that's mandatory for all couples—'what'd you see in me?' – that she got a laconic and crushing answer: '*Kobzar.*' Marichka tried to get it into the hapless lover boy's head numerous times, both then and later on, that she'd never even think about reading poems, especially ones by that excruciatingly boring old Shevchenko. She'd simply needed a hard cover for her final paper; she'd failed the class the semester before, so she was resubmitting it. She didn't have a binder or anything, so she grabbed the largest hardcover from the shelf of books in her family's china cabinet, tore out the pages, tossed them in the trash, and then replaced them with her term paper. It just so happened that the book was Shevchenko's *Kobzar*, but the first and last person to notice that was Tys – Marichka couldn't have cared less.

Tys was an intellectual giant, even back then, so he refused to believe such a mundane, anti-Ukrainian explanation. He thought that Marichka's innate modesty kept her from flaunting her patriotism and genuine love for the nightingale lyricism of

Kobzar. Later on, Tys got it into his head that this magnificent girl yearned for him to notice her beauty, not just her patriotism, love of Shevchenko, and modesty. This version of events seemed most plausible to him. That's often how it goes between people in love – they refuse to hear the truth or even the very words their loved one is saying. It's easier for them to make up their own version of events, believe fabrications that idealise the object of their love. So, they have a fabricated ideal, instead of a real person. Tys fabricated a plausible explanation for Marichka's behavior, which merely heightened his insurmountable love.

That's how their romance started. Miraculously enough, Marichka fell for Tys shortly thereafter. But why? What was it about him? He was a guileless oddball, and if he loved something, he put the whole of his simple heart into it. That was the case with history, alcohol, Ukraine, and Marichka. She knew, she was absolutely sure, that this romantic goofball would grant her every wish.

She says go steal me flowers from the public garden downtown – he goes running. Sit and wait outside my lecture hall for seven hours – there he sits. Listen to a flood of insults when I'm in a foul mood – he listens and admits it's all his fault. Copy lecture notes – he copies away. Tell me you love me 300 times with your eyes closed – he goes right ahead and does it. He's just like a little kid, but he sure is sweet.

Meanwhile, he had forgotten all about his studies and all his other business. All he did was hang around Marichka. One day when he knew she had four classes, he just happened to be strolling down the street leading back to her dorm when the last one was letting out.

'Oh,' he exclaimed, 'it's like you're stalking me or something. You're always there, no matter where I turn!' he said, laughing at his own joke. He was cracking up, which got her laughing, too.

'Oh, you're such a dope... What am I gonna do with you?' Marichka said, her voice tender. Those were the words he loved most of all. In the evenings, he'd come by her room and distract her while she was trying to prep for the next day's classes. 'I'm just going to sit real quiet in the corner and admire you. You're just so beautiful!'

Late one night, when they were walking back home with a big group of friends, Marichka felt the urge to test his love, or maybe just show off her unlimited power to her girlfriends, prove she was the sovereign of this boy's soul. The bridge over the Uzh River was up ahead, and she issued her instructions in a loud, clear voice so everyone could hear.

'Mykhailo, my dear, we're gonna take the bridge, but I'm gonna have you swim across the river, okay? If you love me, that is. You don't have to swim across if you don't love me.' Tys didn't ask any questions, and he showed no sign of surprise. He merely looked at her, his loving eyes seemingly thanking her for so magnanimously allowing him to show her his love. Everyone held their breath as the boy approached the river and stepped into it, without taking off any of his clothes. While they were walking across the bridge, he was under it, cocking his head up at them from time to time and shouting 'I love you!' The water went up to his chest at the deepest part of the river, so he had to start swimming. When the amorous and sopping wet boy got out of the Uzh, crawling ludicrously across some slimy rocks, everyone was already waiting for him. The feckless and elated Tys ran over to hug and kiss Marichka, the water squelching in his shoes and leaving wet tracks behind him, but she stuck her hand out.

'Eww, you're all wet. Don't touch me!' She knew all her girlfriends were so jealous of her at that moment. That's love for you – merciless, stupid, willing to go to any lengths. True love.

This one time, completely out of the blue, he asked her to lie down beside him on the ground. They were coming back from the movies; the city was empty, beautiful, sleepy, and they were still all stirred up from the picture they'd seen. Then Tys suddenly hugged Marichka, right in the middle of the street, and whispered in her ear.

'Let's just lie down right here, on the ground, and we'll lie here together – just us and the sky.' Much to her own surprise, she agreed, and they lay down on the cool cobblestones, side by side. He took her hand, and they looked at the sky girdled by the crowns of old trees. The sky was spinning. Nobody would've believed Marichka, but she clearly saw the sky spinning, the stars swirling, like snowflakes in a blizzard, the wind shaking the thick blanket of leaves on the branches, and the whole world racing along with her heart. If Tys had said just one word at that moment, if he had broken the silence or the spell cast by the theater of sky and trees, had he made one peep or said he'd been wishing on a star for a girl like her, Marichka would've fallen out of love with him and left him forever. He kept quiet, though, because he, too, was perfectly content. Their conversation ran through their hands, and each of them felt the warmth flowing between them.

Only lovebirds' silence can be so eloquent. This final test – understanding each other without words – reveals such a deep bond between people that real trust becomes possible. He felt so good; as he looked at the sky, wordlessly, it seemed as though the sky was inside him, that he was filled with it, filled to the brim with a translucent, yet dark expanse dotted with occasional flashes, warm as a comforting touch. Marichka was so grateful for this rambunctious, goofy, and so terribly sweet guy happening in her life, out of nowhere, who'd found her – yes, purely by accident, but true love is always a pure accident! – who'd held his ground until she gave in, who was lying beside her in the middle of this bleak city, sharing the sky, silence, and the warmth of his hand with her. Silence. The sky. Hand in hand. Their boundless gratitude for finding each other. Marichka couldn't help but bite her lower lip as deep pleasure consumed her whole being. But suddenly, she heard quiet, yet persistent snoring! That dope was snoring! He'd fallen asleep! Just when she thought he was lying there in silence, soaking it all up and thinking about her! There he was, snoring! She didn't talk to Tys for four and a half days after that, though he never did find out why.

The funniest thing about Tys was how genuinely earnest he was, which fiercely clashed with his actions, his words, and even his appearance. He believed everything he said, even if it left everyone around him laughing their heads off. He particularly enjoyed talking about his remarkable feats and skills. One time, he came to Marichka's dorm and announced that he was going to make her and her roommates a meal. He'd just picked up some meat for the occasion. He cleared the table, took a butcher knife wrapped in newspaper out of his jacket pocket, and began cooking.

Tys accompanied this process with a two-hour monologue in which he boasted that: a) his family had been butchering pigs since time immemorial, and that he'd been helping out ever since he was a kid – by the time he was five, he was doing it all by himself, at seven, he slaughtered a 220-pound sow with one blow, and when he turned nine, all the neighbors started coming to him whenever they needed someone to chop off a hen's head or slaughter a hog; b) he personally didn't consider slaughtering livestock murder, since life's cruel, and somebody's got to do it; c) if we didn't eat them, they'd eat us; d) only men should cook meat, since they're genetically wired to prepare it; e) men in pre-historic times would chase after mammoths to feed their tribes, so this habit sometimes surfaces suddenly from the depths of men's subconscious, even in our day, and the only thing he loved more than chopping and cooking meat was perhaps reading about the history of Ukraine; f) you have to salt meat right after you've chopped it, not while you're cooking it – tastes better that way; g) when he prepares meat in Vedmediv, everyone flocks to his home, his neighbors, and even his most distant relatives, for the tales of his culinary talents resound through the nearby villages like the old Cossack-sich songs at the tables of patriots; h) unfortunately, he doesn't always have time to cook, because he's a very busy man; i) if he couldn't feed his family by teaching history, he'd just go work as a chef ; j) his friends are always offering him chef jobs at foreign restaurants or asking him to teach their staff how to handle meat properly, but he always just apologises and turns them down, since he has to graduate from college first, and, most importantly, he doesn't want to emigrate, because he has to help build a better Ukraine; k) a man's knife has to be firm, just like his honor and dignity, and don't let anyone give you the shaft if you're looking to buy, your meat won't be any good if you don't have the right blade, but hardly anyone gives that fact any consideration (he knows a thing or two about that); l) a real man doesn't choose his meat based on its color or smell, or based on the butcher's word on its quality or freshness – nah, a real man strokes his meat, squeezes a piece of it; and if it's as soft as a woman's breast, then it's no good, because fine meat should be as supple as a woman's buttocks; m) you shouldn't wash meat before you chop it – the bloodier it is, the juicier it'll be; n) spices merely stifle the real flavor of meat, sure if you want spices, go ahead and stuff your face with them, just don't put them on your meat; and o) he's telling them all of this because he respects them and loves Marichka infinitely.

After this long but certainly edifying monologue, Tys grabbed a skillet and charged triumphantly into the kitchen. He came back 40 minutes later, and then everyone took their seats at the table. The meal was god-awful. Some pieces were too small and overcooked, while others were too big and raw. Tys hadn't removed the plastic wrap, so the meat was all rubbery. It wound up being so salty that you needed to drink a pitcher of water after every piece. Beaming with joy, Tys kept asking the girls if they were enjoying their meal.

'Listen girls, take notes while I'm still alive,' he intoned as a modest parting shot. He nearly wept in sorrow at the thought of such a great teacher leaving this world one day; there would be no one left to explain the secrets of the culinary arts to these benighted girls. That's just the kind of guy he was. How could you not fall in love with him?

Marichka did. They started living together the following academic year. Naturally, they'd already been spending most of their time together; they slept, ate, read, and studied together. They only got married in the summer, though. Marichka kept waiting for a genteel Tys, white dress shirt and all, to get down on one knee, proffer an engagement ring, and swear that he couldn't live without her. She imagined herself hesitating for a bit, then smiling playfully and eventually saying a merciful 'yes.' It was supposed to be the evening of her dreams: candlelight, string quartet joined by a saxophone at the climactic moment, lots of dancing and laughing, and then planning their honeymoon. That's roughly how it all played out, except for all those extraneous details. One muggy June evening, Tys, who already had like seven shots of vodka sloshing around in his stomach, stopped by Marichka's dorm room. He was wearing shorts – his rail-thin, hairy legs poking out the bottom – a dirty t-shirt, and socks with sandals. He sat down in a chair and tried to speak slowly to conceal his intoxication, which only gave him away even more.

'Hey, Marichka… I saw the student housing director today. I asked him to give us our own room for next year, but that jerk told me those rooms are only for families. So… um… you know, let's get hitched. We'll show that dickhead!'

That argument proved irrefutable, so they tied the knot, held a modest reception, and then started living together in September. Next came the two toughest, yet happiest years of their lives. There they are: the country's in shambles, no money, no nothing, and they're struggling to get by as a young married couple still in college, yet they're living in harmony. After the wedding, Tys forbade his wife from accepting any help whatsoever from her parents, saying that he should be the one providing for her. She upheld her end of the bargain, but he wasn't doing all that hot. After all, how was a hapless, idealistic history major supposed to get by in the hungry nineties? Marichka had to mend her old dresses, buy discount makeup, and scour the city for the cheapest groceries, yet she still loved her husband fervently. He'd go to class during the day, and then go unload some stuff at the market or roam around old Soviet factories with this pack of swindlers; they'd scrounge for scrap metal, rip copper wire out of the walls, or pull the sinks out of bathrooms – just to sell it for chump change. Despite how little he made, he'd still bring treasures home to Marichka. There were days when all they had in their fridge was sauerkraut, but he'd surprise her with an orange – an unheard-of luxury back then. Whenever she said that he needed some new pants or a dress shirt, he'd always say his things were 'almost brand-new' and refuse to buy anything for himself. If he somehow managed to pull some strings and get a free movie ticket, then he'd take Marichka to the theater and wait for her outside, just sitting on a bench for two hours until the movie was over. He carried her all the way to the hospital when she sprained her ankle. He loved her so dearly that, despite all the uncontrollable mayhem that was shaking their country, she was truly happy.

During their last year of college, their daughter Tremora was born out of this enormous happiness. Things got even more hectic after that, but their love got stronger too, transforming from a simple, yet deep infatuation into a real bond of intimacy and kinship. Now Tys had to shoulder the burden of caring for two women, so he tripled his efforts. Not everything worked out for him, naturally. Well, actually, hardly anything did, but he kept his nose to the grindstone. They both still had to finish their studies. He worked all day and studied at night; he'd copy notes he'd borrowed from Marichka's classmates when she had to start staying home. They were determined to push through one more year in Uzhhorod, graduate from college, and then move to Vedmediv, into the house Tys's parents had left him. With a college degree, he'd be able to get a respectable job and earn some more money; they'd have someplace to live, someplace to really start their life as a family.

And indeed, that's how it all played out – a year later, after they'd defended their theses, they moved to Vedmediv and began building their little family nest. They were just so happy! Tys began working as a schoolteacher, while Marichka tutored high school students aspiring to study biology or medicine in college. Tremora was a healthy, cheerful child. Their life together was slowly taking on new shades of color; they were becoming a full-fledged family. Despite the constant hardship, those were some extremely happy years. Yes, Tys was becoming ever nuttier and more absent-minded, and his antics ever more outlandish and foolhardy, but Marichka loved him just the way he was. About 10 years into their marriage, she even started finding his jokes funny. For instance, she'd come into his study and demand he impose some semblance of order on 'his nest of filth, disarray, and contamination,' as she put it. He'd reply with a slogan from one of the Ukrainian nationalist parties 'Bandera'll come and there'll be no more scum.' She'd laugh and let him off the hook.

It seemed as though Tys and Marichka had become one whole, and that's not just some figure of speech. They could communicate with half a glance, half a word. They truly enjoyed their time together; after school, the history teacher would blaze home, where his wife and daughter would be waiting for him. In their family, humor would solve everything; they never had any explosive arguments, because there was never any reason to. Besides, after a few years of living together, their bodies had achieved perfectly complimentary shapes, as if molded from play dough. Marichka would curl up on her side of the bed, and Tys would lie down behind her, fitting snuggly against her; there wouldn't be a single crack between them. Whenever his wife would roll over onto her stomach, he'd hug her shoulders and swing his leg over to cover up her buttocks, and once again, their shape was flawless. Lying on top of each other in any pose imaginable felt so nice and so natural; it was as if they'd actually been made for each other, Tys for Marichka and Marichka for Tys. That wasn't exactly true, though, because they made themselves and tailored every single part, curve, centimeter, bone, and soft spot on their bodies.

Tremora, their pride and joy, was growing up. She had cried a lot as an infant and she liked playing nasty tricks on her parents as a toddler, but these unfortunate traits became less pronounced as she moved through elementary school. She transformed from an impish little girl into an angelic young lady. She started getting even better grades, was always careful with her school clothes, and stopped fighting boys and climbing trees. By the time Tremora turned 10, she was already momma's little helper. All the neighbors admired her; she could clean up around the house, peel potatoes, do the dishes, wash the windows, and polish the silverware. She could help her mom whip up pierogis and cabbage rolls, too. She was an avid reader; some nights her parents had no choice but to take the bedside lamp out of her room so she wouldn't stay up too late. She'd take out her flashlight and read under the covers anyway.

So, it's no wonder that by the time high school came around, she was set on becoming a philologist. At first, she wanted to move to Lviv for college, but her folks couldn't stand the idea of her going halfway to Timbuktu, or to the 'Far East,' as they put it (geographically speaking, that description was actually spot on). They wound up convincing their daughter to enroll at Uzhhorod National University. Shortly thereafter, Tremora passed all her entrance exams with flying colours and then became one of the top students in the foreign philology department. Marichka and Tys were so proud and happy... until disaster struck – and wrecked their lives.

According to the subsequent police report, Tremora Mykhailivna Chvak, 18, a freshman at Uzhhorod National University, was celebrating her birthday at 12 University Street, Uzhhorod, Ukraine 88000, dormitory No. 4, room No. 138. More than 20 persons had been invited to the celebration, so the guests had to temporarily move all unneeded furniture from the room to the hallway. Only two tables and chairs remained in the aforementioned room to accommodate those in attendance. The students violated dormitory rules, as they celebrated during quiet hours and consumed alcoholic beverages. At around midnight, Ms. Chvak became indisposed; she then fell and died, most likely by suffocation. A forensic medical examination will determine the exact cause of death.

The deceased's grief-stricken parents subsequently heard from one of her girlfriends that it was a lovely evening with good friends. They had been drinking, but not all that much. Like the foreign philology department as a whole, the party was mostly girls, so this was no booze-up; they just said toasts, clinked glasses, and sipped their drinks. Yes, they did temporarily move the bureaus, bedside tables, and fridge out into the hallway so everyone could fit in the room. They struck a deal with the dorm security guard: a bottle and some savory snacks to go with it and he'd turn a blind eye to a quiet party that wouldn't bother anyone. As per the old Ukrainian college tradition, everyone said toasts – for three whole hours! – starting with the person to the right of Tremora and going around until they reached the birthday girl herself.

Then it was her turn to propose a toast to the guests, to thank them, like how it's always done at these get-togethers. Well, she'd had some alcohol, and it was her first adult party – all on her own, no parents – and she started to feel a bit overwhelmed. She wanted to show everyone just how much fun she was having, so she stood up on a chair, but then she really started shaking, like someone with a fear of public speaking. She raised her glass with immense effort, arm crooked, smiled, and then… dropped to the floor. She began convulsing; an unrestrained fit smacked her around, twisting and shattering. At first, the guests just lunged back; some of them even ran out into the hallway screaming, while others hightailed it out of there. But after the initial shock subsided, several people came over and tried to calm her down. They had no idea how, though.

It was impossible to hold Tremora still. Her body had suddenly acquired tremendous power, her eyes bulged, and she foamed at the mouth. None of the freshmen had ever seen the 'falling sickness' – an epileptic seizure – before, so nobody thought to pin her violently-convulsing body to the floor during the first few minutes and cram a spoon or some other hard object in her mouth – even if they had to break her teeth to do it – and hold her tongue down so it wouldn't get stuck in her throat and cut off her airway. Instead, the students tried speaking soothing words and dousing her with water. Eventually, someone thought to call an ambulance, but, most unfortunately, it took too long to get there, as it always does, even though they could see the hospital out their window. By the time the paramedics arrived, the birthday girl was lying on the floor of her room, showing no signs of life.

Everyone, both young and old, wept at the funeral. Her whole family came in for it. Her classmates and professors made the trip to Vedmediv. The entire city was there – they all bawled their eyes out. When Tremora was driven across town she was in her white wedding dress, as is the custom for unmarried girls – it seemed as though even the city's cats and dogs were howling, the trees were whimpering, and the air was hot with mourning. When Ychi tossed the first shovel of dirt into the grave, and it slammed against the lid of the coffin, Marichka fell to her knees and wailed horrifically, the way animals do right before an earthquake.

She just wasn't the same after that, and their marriage came undone. With the loss of their daughter, it was as if they'd lost their minds too; they shut themselves up in their own shells, in their phobias, eccentricities, and abnormalities. They didn't get along anymore. Marichka started nagging Tys every chance she got; Tys would growl back at her, but, soon enough, he wouldn't even respond to her anymore. They started sleeping in separate rooms. Tys reverted to his youthful penchant for vodka and began frequenting bars once again, where he'd blab about Kyivan counts all night – just so he wouldn't have to go home, to that hell; his pride and joy Tremora was gone forever, and so was his goddess, his beloved Marichka whom he once loved so dearly.

Tys's legs carried him down Station Street; he just kept going, oblivious to everything. Panic gripped him as his whole married life flashed before his eyes. Ever since he'd lost his daughter, the only thing he'd really feared was the death of someone close to him, being unable to prevent it or help. For the second time, death was breathing down his neck, dashing his hopes of achieving his most cherished dream – the tunnel and the salvation of Ukraine. He reached Mirca's property, so completely spent that for the first minute all he could do was lean against the fence and wave for attention, spasmodically gasping for air. The Genius of the Carpathians spotted him, ran over, and started bombarding him with questions, but Tys was still too spent to answer; he was in a state of shock, just repeating his friend's name.

'Ychi, Ychi's there, he's gonna die, Ychi.' The Genius of the Carpathians dragged the teacher into his car, and the next instant they were whizzing toward the city center.

Ychi was still unconscious. Mirca and Tys discussed their options, grumbled about the mayor and Icarus being out of town, and then decided to take their injured friend to the hospital. The Genius of the Carpathians, the more composed and level-headed of the two, slung the limp gravedigger over his shoulder, pulled him out of the tunnel, and then began speaking, still huffing and puffing.

'We can't just take him to any old doctor; because the hospital'll have to report his injuries to the police. Then they'll start investigating this whole tragic incident, and they'll eventually find our tunnel. We need someone who knows how to keep a secret – hell, someone who *likes* keeping secrets, someone who doesn't exactly have the cleanest conscience. We have to take him to Kruchka, we don't have a choice. I think we'll probably regret this, though. Yes, she may be a coroner, but she's still a doctor. It's a bummer Bartok or at the very least Icarus isn't around, they definitely would've come up with something. But Bartok is off sunning his belly on some beach and Icarus is over in Hungary and won't be back until the evening. Ugh! Thing is, I don't know any other doctors all that well, and we need someone we can trust. It's gotta be Kruchka, though we may very well be handing him over to the devil. Let's get a move on!'

Chapter 9:

In Which the Femme Fatale Finally Makes an Appearance

The parties involved had reason to be afraid, since Ulyana Dmytrivna Kruk, better known as Kruchka, the coroner at Vedmediv Hospital, had a horrible reputation. Rumor had it that she kept company with Satan himself. There's no place in the world where coroners are treated well, but that's especially true for villages and small provincial cities, where superstitions, archaic beliefs, and prejudice are still alive and well. The fact that she wasn't originally from Vedmediv – her college in Galicia sent her here after she'd graduated, and she stuck around after her mandatory rotation – only fueled the locals' mistrust and antipathy towards her.

Maybe it was her staying that surprised them most of all. What possible reason could a beautiful lady like her have to stick around this Podunk town nestled between mountains and closed borders? Nobody, not even the most jealous wives, had any doubt that she was gorgeous enough to be an international beauty pageant contestant. They'd say 'why doesn't she just go spread her legs for some millionaire instead of seducing our husbands?!' She was tall and slim, with a perfect figure, luxurious black hair, super-thin arched eyebrows, large eyes – possibly even too large – perky breasts, and long, skinny legs, like a high school girl. Besides, Kruchka was always dressed like she was strutting down the catwalk amid flashing cameras, not the filthy streets of Vedmediv: short skirts or dresses, black stockings, low-cut sweaters or blouses, shiny extra-high heels, lusty red makeup, red polish on her long, elegant nails. She moved with the smooth grace of a cat, every motion fluid and well-calculated, seemingly winding some invisible mechanism that automatically shifted every other part of her body to show off her curves perfectly. For instance, when she fixed her hair, she'd bend her neck slightly, which tightened the lines of her perfect waist, which, in turn, pushed out her buttocks. Then she'd move abruptly – her hair cascading back onto her shoulders and her bosom rising provocatively. Honest to God, Kruchka's every movement was hypnotic, and she knew it.

She was single, though. Twenty years she'd lived in Vedmediv, and still no husband. People in town were always going on about how Kruchka was a tramp, but nobody ever caught her in the act. Moreover, nobody had ever seen her so much as holding a man's hand. That was doubly irritating. Just what was she? An attractive, promiscuous lady or some kind of ice-cold nun? She spent her younger years alone, isolating herself from men, and never laid eyes on anyone. Now she was 40, give or take, yet her beauty had matured and grown even more noble – yes, this Ulyana Kruk had become even more attractive and more sophisticated, a true lady, the most alluring woman in Vedmediv, without a doubt. Just one look at her led men into temptation, leaving languid fantasies to germinate in their minds for weeks on end. Ultimately, she exerted a positive influence on the men of Vedmediv; one glimpse of her, and they could make love to their wives all night long, astounding them with their indefatigable tenacity. Their wives didn't have the slightest inkling – or masterfully feigned not having one – that when their darlings closed their eyes in those blissful moments, they were picturing her, Ulyana. She couldn't care less, though. For years, she'd been living in that big house on the edge of town, secluded as a convent.

That elicited consternation and suspicion. How could a single woman who worked as a coroner at the city's run-down hospital live so grandly? Where'd she get the money for a house like that, fancy clothes, and her own car? Yes, you could make a killing if you were a surgeon, a gynecologist, or the head of the committee that granted disability status and medical draft exemptions. But the coroner in a quiet – murder-free and nearly assault-free – town like Vedmediv, what kind of bribes could you even get? So, most people thought that Kruchka turned tricks, although nobody had ever caught her in the act. Others – an absolute minority – advanced some rather flimsy hypotheses about her having rich parents or an inheritance. Nobody dared to ask Ms. Kruk herself; that's just how cold and unapproachable she was. The whole business had a whiff of devilry about it, of something ominous and otherworldly; everyone could feel it, but nobody could really articulate it.

One more thing heightened suspicion. Kruchka didn't go to church – any church at all – although Vedmediv had its fair share of them: two Orthodox ones (Kyivan Patriarchate and Moscow Patriarchate), Greek Catholic, Roman Catholic, Reformed Church... Fine, it's not obligatory to attend services every day, but how could someone just stroll past places of worship on Easter or Christmas, when the aroma of home-smoked sausage and the atmosphere of a shared celebration complements the smell of incense? After all, where else, if not at church, was this young single woman supposed to find a wealthy, upstanding man? She wouldn't be meeting anyone at the morgue; the men were already dead when they got there. Maybe that was her type though? Why else would she have chosen that profession? So she led the life of a recluse, holed up in her house, behind a high fence that hid all her secrets, perversions, and witcheries. That's roughly how the Vedmedivites saw it, anyhow.

She was power-hungry, too, the kind of person who always had to be in control. She'd been elected to the city council twice, both times on the ruling party's slate. That party had changed three times during her tenure, but whatever party was in power, her sex appeal took her straight to the top of it. Everyone at the hospital was afraid of her; they thought she wanted to oust the supervisors and take over. But no, she didn't seem to have any designs on the top job. But then what did she need a seat on the city council for?

Kruchka's every word and action left people chewing the fat for days, but they couldn't discern any particular logic or strategy behind them. This confounded Vedmedivites. On nice days, she'd walk across town to work, making a good half of the population insane with jealousy and excitement; when the weather was nasty, she'd drive to work and go straight home at the end of the day. So, she spent most of her time among corpses; that was the company she kept. Everybody said she wasn't much of a doctor, because she never actually treated anyone.

Tys's knowledge, which happened to be common knowledge in Vedmediv, didn't go beyond that. So as they careened toward the hospital, Tys, who thought of himself as a sober-minded thinker, was less unnerved by Kruchka's aura of devilry than by Mirca's decision to take Ychi to a morgue. The Genius of the Carpathians was wholly focused on the road; his taciturn temperament kept him functioning smoothly, even in this moment of stress. He looked ahead, pursing his lips tightly...but he had his share of stories to tell about 'the Succubus,' that's for sure.

That's what the Genius of the Carpathians called her in the privacy of his own thoughts, but he never used that nickname in her presence. He regarded her as a colleague, since they did have complementary businesses – of the sort which zipped lips. After Ulyana moved to Vedmediv in the hungry nineties as a medical resident, she, like the rest of the locals, would head over to Hungary whenever she had some free time, taking vodka and cigarettes with her and then bringing back candy and fruits that were exotic as far as dismal post-Soviet Ukraine was concerned. She made enough to get by. Then her doctor friends advised her to break into the pharmaceutical industry by providing Hungarians with the medicine they needed and then bringing back medication that was scarce in Ukraine. Shortly thereafter, she, like everyone else endowed with a doctor's pad, began writing prescriptions for controlled substances – that yielded a large profit. Right around that time, she had a life-changing experience.

She wrote a prescription, received a box of powerful anesthetics – narcotic pain medication, in other words – and then headed for the border. Something went haywire that time around, though – either the wrong guys were on duty that day or they weren't in a good mood, so they searched her and found everything. After they'd established that she was just a medical intern, who didn't have influential parents – or any relatives in Vedmediv, for that matter – the customs officers told the alluring lady that they were in a position to condemn her to a lengthy prison sentence, led her to a little room at the back of their office, and… undressed her. At first, she resisted, but then she broke down crying and let them do whatever they could think of. Over the course of that evening, four of them had their way with her – several times, one by one and all together. Within narrow circles, a most piquant detail made the rounds – the young, fiery intern got so riled up during the gang rape that she actually started raping the customs officers.

Mirca knew the real reason the Succubus had no interest in the men of Vedmediv; no man could satisfy her. Well, no one man could satisfy her; she needed at least two, and if a third was available, she'd merely flash a pleased and lustful smile. That evening, the customs officers instructed her to come back again for their next shift, three days later, saying she could bring whatever she wanted across the border. As time went by, it wasn't exactly clear whether she was going to the border to smuggle or to see the voracious Ukrainian customs officers. That's when the tasty medical resident, whom nobody in Vedmediv had heard of, started looking like she'd just walked off the cover of a fashion magazine – her modest wardrobe had changed radically, and she started turning heads around town. Even the top customs officers took an interest in this young woman, whose beauty was so unusual for the Transcarpathian forest. After that, she hopped up to the next level, leaving the drooling, rank-and-file customs officers, driven bonkers by their own powerlessness, behind forever.

With her new level of connections, Kruchka reached a new level of smuggling, as even more expensive – and more illegal – medicine whizzed across the border; it was like a conveyor belt. Roughly around this time, the first advertisements calling for people to sell their hair appeared in Vedmediv. This was a real sensation – salvation for the destitute. After all, everyone has hair. Hundreds of Vedmediv women ran to the salon, where they chopped off their long hair and sold it by weight. Those were years of near starvation, when there was hardly any money around and people resorted to barter, but you could sell hair for actual cash. Many people thought of growing their hair as a profitable and stable business that could support them for their whole lives. Mothers would have their daughters' curls cut off; older girls would get bob cuts and sell their locks. Then they'd wash their hair with this weird shampoo they'd make from eggs and nettles, because a newspaper once wrote that this combination sped up hair growth. Kruchka joined this venture, too, not by chipping in her fabulous mane, which nobody could take their eyes off, but by contributing hair cut from the bodies in her morgue.

Soon enough, the enterprising Kruchka found out that people were buying up hair in Vedmediv for factories abroad, where it'd be made into wigs and extensions. She soon contacted one of those factories directly, then bought up all the hair in town and used her safe passage across the border to take it directly to her clients. That's how she started really racking up capital – meds and extensions – then she built herself a house on the edge of town in no time flat. Later on, it proved to be the perfect spot, since you could do secret, illegal – and therefore very profitable – things behind that high fence, far from prying eyes. Once Ulyana had ingratiated herself with the big manufacturers, they made her an offer, a much more demanding and dangerous one. Shortly thereafter, thanks to foreign medical experts, an entire laboratory was established in the basement of that house behind the high fence.

Nah, this was no drug lab. High-level politicians had occupied that niche long ago, and Ms. Kruk's area of expertise lay elsewhere. The Hungarians proposed that she become their blood supplier. Human blood. As the medical field continued its rapid development, the demand for blood was constantly growing. There was always so little of it, though. Besides that, in certain parts of the world, buying it from the public raised certain legal issues. For instance, in Hungary, you were only allowed to donate blood, without receiving any compensation. A black market emerged, since the volume of donor blood was insufficient. Therefore, the prospect of getting cheap Ukrainian blood immediately intrigued Central Europe's medical mafia. The poor were willing to give up a pint of their blood monthly for meager pay – by European standards, anyway. So Kruchka exploited her position to strike a deal with a blood bank; she'd take all of their 'product,' but not without rewarding them handsomely first. Soon enough, they couldn't provide nearly enough blood for her robust business, so Kruchka talked all the nurses into taking two or three hundred millilitres from more or less healthy patients so they could 'run some tests.' Her colleagues agreed readily enough, since they'd sometimes go months without seeing a paycheck from the hospital. She paid them cold, hard cash – precious foreign currency, no less!

Like everything in nineties Ukraine, this business grew at an astronomical rate. She went through that first batch of blood within a month. Then a city-wide blood drive was organised under the auspices of the local government. All the state employees – teachers, bureaucrats, municipal workers, etc. – were forced, under threat of being fired, to donate blood for the betterment of the country's medical system, voluntarily, of course. The resulting profit was ludicrously high, so the mayor instructed the principals to collect blood – a smaller dose, but still – from all the students in town. Mounds of gold, much higher than the ones yielded by the mundane cigarettes-and-vodka hustle, grew out of this business. Moreover, the human body replenishes lost blood, and if you eat right you can decant a new dose of red gold once every few weeks. So, once Kruchka had pulled off her first large-scale operation, she went way beyond the customs officers and added the city fathers to her circle of contacts; it didn't take her long to secure a spot on the city council.

All kinds of rumors started flying around. One version held that there was a blood farm outside of town, where they kept over a hundred people as slave donors. Nobody thought Ulyana was pulling the strings, though; everyone believed that the 'farmer' was the mayor or Vedmediv's chief prosecutor, because it's not like anyone would be coming after them. Nobody knows if a blood farm actually existed or still exists. Right around that time, a tabloid ran a piece about something like that going on in India, and the Vedmedivites could've just heard the story wrong and run with it. The truth was that the Succubus slept with the mayor and the chief prosecutor – often with both of them at the same time – to further her scheme. The Genius of the Carpathians was 100% sure of that.

Her blood business ran dry some time later, not due to talk of the mythical farm, but simply because Kruchka found a more profitable vein. Finding it didn't even require any prospecting; it'd been right under her nose the whole time. All Kruchka had to do was open her eyes, which she did when one of her foreign clients inquired if she could sell him a bone or two.

'A bone or two?'

'Yes, preferably in good condition. A complete set if you got it. Human bones, of course.' It didn't take long to get Ulyana up to speed. Tons of medical corporations and universities in Western Europe and the United States were willing to pay big bucks for human skeletons so they could use them for training. The law now bars them from plundering graves and exhuming corpses without the express written consent of the deceased, so most medical institutions around the world have plastic cadavers. They won't do if you want to get a good education, though. After all, no form of technology can compete with nature, especially when you're dealing with a masterpiece as ingenious as the human body. Consequently, doctors that specialise in transplants or plastic surgery, who are supposed to know every millimetre of every single bone, often aren't able to obtain the necessary skills and training. India, Pakistan, and various African countries provided a large number of skeletons but demand still outstripped supply.

Kruchka enjoyed this new endeavor more than her previous job, because she no longer had to worry about transporting her 'product' in mini fridges to keep it fresh. The bones were there for the taking! She handled all the homeless people that nobody came for and dead folks whose families lived far away. They always appreciated the morgue offering to take care of burying the body. All told, she could move three or four skeletons a week, for a profit of 20 or even

30,000 US dollars. Her business flourished and enabled Vedmediv's most disadvantaged citizens to go to the world's top universities. Granted, they weren't in a position to enjoy it, but still, they were moving up in the world. There were plenty of people who never made it to any university at all.

Well, where there's bones, there's meat. Once the supplier's clients saw her omnipotence at work, they started dropping subtle hints about how they'd be glad to get an extra kidney or a healthy heart. The Succubus had even more of those goodies than bones; you could only get bones if you had a whole body that wouldn't be missed. But when it came to missing organs, not even the deceased's relatives would notice their absence.

The entire human body doesn't die right away. Not only do nails and hair keep growing – thousands of post-mortem processes take place in a person's body. For instance, the dead continue digesting their food for some time. Their insides stay warm, gradually decreasing in temperature for the first 20 hours. After that tipping point, the bacteria come out to dance. They multiply and kick off the first active stage of decomposition. That's why you should cut a kidney, heart, joint, or piece of skin out of a recently deceased body as promptly as possible, then process them for storage. With the right handling and equipment, you can make sure these organs will still serve another body just fine.

So, in Kruchka's hands, human bodies turned into extremely lucrative products. Complete skeletons went to universities, while individual bones were sold to medical implant manufacturers. A cornea for living, breathing transplant patients at Western clinics was worth $2,000-3,000. They had no idea they were now looking at our sublime world through the eyes of the dead! Fresh human skin – primarily from the buttocks – went to Hungary for women who aspired to look more beautiful or burn victims who simply needed it. Whenever a fresh corpse was sent from the hospital to the morgue or the paramedics dropped off a car crash victim, it was a golden opportunity for the Succubus: she'd harvest both kidneys, a few joints, both corneas, the liver, and the heart. Hearts were more valuable than anything else; they were worth as much as the whole rest of the body. They'd go for $100,000 or more, but it was a messy business, and you had to transplant them within the first 24 hours.

Over time, her house turned into a laboratory and warehouse where dozens of human organs were stored and then shipped out. Kruchka didn't shy away from live product either – she'd never turn someone willing to sell a kidney away. More precisely, these donors were drawn from among Vedmediv's needier citizens – even more precisely, Gypsies. They were the easiest people to deal with, because they were typically healthy, and they didn't see any value whatsoever in their internal organs. On numerous occasions, mothers wanting to throw their daughters a kick-ass wedding would turn to the Succubus. Or Gypsies who'd run into trouble with the law and wanted to pay off the cops would hop on the operating table and wake up down a kidney but up $5,000. These people generally weren't too concerned about the future, and in most cases, they didn't experience any health problems – at first, that is. Down the road, when their bodies started glitching out on them, they never attributed it to the organs they'd sold four or five years earlier.

The saddest story involved a Gypsy who'd already sold one of his kidneys and then found out a few years later that his wife was dying of cancer. He decided to sell the other one to give her one last chance. Ulyana agreed, without the slightest pang of conscience, removed the kidney, and made a bundle on the rest of his organs in the process – she didn't pay the widow a dime, obviously, or even bother telling her she'd removed them. Instead, she issued a death certificate. Cause of death – kidney failure. Well, she wasn't lying.

Her house gradually turned into a real death factory, while the unassuming former medical resident became a multi-millionaire and one of the most pivotal players on Europe's black market for human organs. Hardly anyone in Vedmediv had any clue what was going on, which was fine by the Succubus, as was the fact that she wasn't the least bit successful in the eyes of Vedmedivites. Actually, she was considered a rapidly-aging failure. She hadn't even managed to find a husband! She had so many men in and around her, but she was a woman who knew what she wanted. No respectable Vedmedivite lady would believe her eyes if she saw one of the cocaine-fueled orgies at Ulyana's place.

So, the Succubus was irrefutably the most dangerous person in Vedmediv, and the Genius of the Carpathians was well aware of that. Nevertheless, she could keep her mouth shut, which was crucial in their business. Mirca was already mulling over his seductive proposition, even before his blue Toyota pulled up to the morgue.

As soon as the car stopped, Tys lunged out of his seat, ready to pull Ychi out of the back, but Mirca stopped him with one commanding gesture. He and Tys stepped into a white room where a stunningly beautiful woman sat at a large table. When she got up to greet them, they both noticed that she wasn't wearing anything under her white uniform except black stockings. Once she saw the Genius of the Carpathians, she clicked on over, swaying alluringly on her extremely high heels.

'Well, hello, my dear,' the Genius of the Carpathians said, affecting a careless drawl.

'Hmm, look who it is.' The Succubus came over and hugged him – her supple breasts pressing up against him and her breath caressing his neck – then gave his earlobe a playful nip. 'What brings you here? You're not planning on dying, are you?'

Tys, who was standing on the other side of them and couldn't see their little game, proffered his hand at the most inopportune moment, thereby separating the close – by all appearances – couple.

'Mykhailo Chvak, history teacher. But you may call me Tys.' He extended his muddy hand, his gold tooth glinting beneath his mustache.

The Succubus looked at him, completely uninterested, didn't shake his hand, turned around, and went back to the table, favoring them a flicker of slender legs in lacy stockings. Then she jerked back around, sending her hair flying around her neck and shoulders like myriad black spider webs.

'Okay, so what brings you boys here?' she asked, adopting a drier tone.

'We've come to you with some serious business, don't you worry,' the Genius of the Carpathians began, nodding at Tys as if apologizing for having brought him along. 'Our buddy's injured. We brought him here—'

'For disassembly?' Ulyana arched an eyebrow, clearly intrigued.

'Nah, this is a fix up job. Could you take a look?'

'So I guess I was the only doctor you could find?'

'Well, the thing is, what we're doing isn't exactly legal. Gotta keep it under wraps.'

'So, where is he?'

'In the car.'

'What are you standing around for then? Bring him in. There's a stretcher over there in the corner if you need it,' she said, nodding at the door.

The guys carried the gravedigger inside.

'Oh, I know him. You could say he's one of my associates.' The Succubus was even more intrigued now.

'He's a wonderful guy, a real patriot,' Tys interjected.

'He's our associate, too,' Mirca interrupted him hurriedly.

'What happened to him?' Ulyana asked, examining Ychi's body.

'There was a cave in. Down in the tunnel.'

'Like a railroad tunnel?'

'Nah, we have our own tunnel. I mean, not yet, but we will. He's the one digging it,' the Genius of the Carpathians said, looking at the floor.

'What do you need a tunnel for?'

'The tunnel'll run under the border, into Hungary. This is all hush hush, though. The project is already underway, but then the damn thing caved in… '

'Oh, so you're building a Europe without borders?' Ulyana asked with a giggle.

'Yes, Ukraine should be part of Europe – and we're going to make it happen!' Tys declared resolutely.

'Listen Ulyana, once the tunnel's ready… ' Mirca tensed up and started speaking with a drawl again. '…you'll get to use it, too, just so you know. I know it'll come in handy. That's why we came here. You help us – and keep all of this strictly confidential, of course – and then the tunnel is at your disposal.'

'Alright. Who's this guy?' the Succubus asked in a contemptuous, yet businesslike tone, pointing at Tys.

'Mykhailo Chvak, history teacher, but you, respected member of the medical community that you are, may call me Tys.' He smiled, showing all 19 of his teeth.

'The project was his idea, he came up with the whole thing. He's our partner. You can trust him,' Mirca said, trying to salvage the situation.

'Is he in our business, too? I've never heard of him,' the Succubus said, surprised.

'Nah, he's all about euro-integration for Ukraine. That's what the tunnel is about. He's one of those guys, those...um... patriotic types,' the Genius of the Carpathians said with a sly smile.

'Ah, gotcha. Still, your proposition sounds interesting. When's the launch date for this tunnel of yours?'

'This fall, if everything goes alright with Ychi...if he snaps out of it and finishes digging!'

'Whoa, this fall? Sure about that? July's just around the corner.'

'I'm sure. We calculated everything out.' Mirca sounded confident.

'Where are you digging?'

'In Peace Square.'

'What do you mean in Peace Square? I thought you said it was a secret!'

'Yeah, we camouflaged it as a fountain, the Fountain of Unity. You might have heard something about it already. We went with the square because it's close to the border. Also, nobody'll think to look for a tunnel there.'

'Wow, I'm impressed. Great thinking! Well, now I'm definitely in,' the Succubus said, licking her red lips with relish.

She examined Ychi for about half an hour, listening to his heartbeat, checking his blood pressure, holding smelling salts up to his nose, and even giving him a shot of adrenaline, but none of it elicited any reaction. Then she went over to the table, gathered her things, tossed them into her purse, turned toward the guys, and addressed them in a commanding voice.

'Things are looking pretty shitty, boys. I'm not exactly sure what's up but I can tell he's in a coma, and who knows when he'll claw his way out of it. I'll do everything I can to help, though. It's in my best interest, too. But we can't keep him here. Let's take him back to my place.'

Chapter 10:

Scrambling for a Solution

Zoltan Bartok, Icarus, the Genius of the Carpathians, the Succubus, and Tys had gathered around a table in the mayor's office for an emergency meeting.

'So you're telling me that lazy bum could just lie there like that for a year? And there's no way to wake him up?' the mayor of Vedmediv asked the Succubus incredulously.

'No, there isn't. It's out of our hands now. People often come out of comas spontaneously,' she replied.

'And I cut my vacation short just so I could hear that in person? Couldn't you have told me over the phone?!' the mayor asked reproachfully, his glare boring a hole in Icarus.

'Well, we didn't know what was going on. He's been conked out for over two days now. I had to come back from Hungary, too. I dropped everything and raced home as soon as I got the call – no hot springs or any of that jazz for me!' Icarus said defensively.

The office doors suddenly opened. First, a tray came into view – pickled tomatoes flashed red on little saucers – then Zoya slid in behind it.

'We don't need anything. This is a business meeting. Leave this instant, close the doors, and don't let anyone in!' the mayor barked in a fit of anger.

'I just—'

'Close the doors, now!' Bartok growled through his teeth, eyes bulging.

His secretary left, and silence set in for the next minute or so, because nobody wanted to be the enraged mayor's next victim. Then he took a deep breath and continued in a remarkably agreeable voice, as though nothing had happened.

'Guess it's good I came back. You guys are dumb enough to get us all thrown in jail! Why are we hiding the digger? Why isn't a regular doctor taking care of him instead of a coroner? Ulyana, sweetie, you know how much I love you, but we need a specialist for something like this. It could make or break the project. What, was the vet busy?' Zoltan Bartok asked in a mocking, yet jovial tone.

'We had to make a decision, and fast. I think I did the right thing, given the situation. You guys were all out of town. What could Tys and I have done? Ms. Kruk is an excellent specialist, plus she has a vested interest in the success of our project,' the Genius of the Carpathians countered.

'I don't doubt that Ulyana is excellent from every angle. But what are we supposed to do now? Wait for the gravedigger to rise from the dead?'

'That's what this meeting is about, we have to discuss everything and make a decision together,' Icarus said, trying to get the conversation moving in a more constructive direction.

'Let me reiterate – Ychi could get better today or seven years from now. He's on life support back at my house. That's all I could do for him. At this stage, modern medicine is powerless.' The Succubus wanted to have a serious discussion, without all the yelling and carrying on.

'Okay, so does anyone have any ideas? What do we do now? Freeze the project?' Zoltan Bartok sized everyone up, waiting for an answer.

'No way!' Tys cried. 'We just can't. This isn't just our project. It'll decide the fate of Ukraine! And Europe, too!'

'This guy keeps blabbing about the same thing, on and on,' the mayor sighed. 'I'm asking you what we should do!'

'Well, I don't know. We can't just give up, though. I think we'll have to do it ourselves. Everyone'll just have to put in one day a week. For instance, Icarus could dig tomorrow. Then Mirca the day after that. Then you, Mr. Bartok. Just like that, taking turns. I'll bring you your meals, and Ms. Kruk will give everyone vitamins. It's not as if we expect a lady to dig,' Tys answered.

'How come you'll just be bringing us meals, instead of digging? You're the one who came up with all this, but you'll pass on the digging part?' Mirca asked.

'I won't do you any good. I couldn't even carry Ychi out of the tunnel. This project'll drag on forever if I try to dig,' the teacher said with a shrug.

'What kind of idea is that? That's dog shit. D-o-g s-h-i-t! The mayor digging in Peace Square, who ever heard of a thing like that? You must be kidding, right?! This kind of work has to be done by professionals, professionals, professionals.' Zoltan Bartok suddenly remembered his advisors' tip about repetition.

'I agree that this kind of work has to be done by professionals. If you really want to have a tunnel by the fall, then gravediggers just won't do. You need specialists, otherwise the whole thing will be a pain in the ass,' the Succubus said, crossing her legs.

'Where are we supposed to find these professionals? Why don't I run an ad in the paper? Or stick a bunch of fliers on telephone poles around town?' The mayor was running out of patience.

'I think I could help. A new batch of Pakistanis should be coming in any day now. I could get them to dig the tunnel, so they wouldn't have to go through the mountains or the woods. That way everyone'll be happy: we won't have to pay them, they'll be too afraid to tell anyone anything, and they'll be motivated to work fast because the tunnel'll be their ticket to Europe,' the Genius of the Carpathians said, folding his arms across his chest. Just then, the phone rang, and the mayor picked up.

'Hello! What? What fuckin' fruit festival?! Call my deputy about that bullshit! I got enough on my plate as is! What?! Go fuck yourself, fu-ck your-self. Got that?' Zoltan Bartok yelled, then slammed down the receiver as hard as he could, apparently satisfied with his assessment of the state of agriculture. 'Festival... Fucktival! Where did we leave off?'

'Pakistanis... ' Mirca reminded him timidly.

'Fuckistanis! You're shitting me about the Pakistanis, right?! You really do want to get me shipped off to prison, don't you?! So, there'll be a horde of Pakistanis running around downtown with shovels! That's what you're suggesting? Sure, just finish me off and bury me and leave Vedmediv with no mayor. That's what you want, right? A wise woman just spelled everything out for you. We need specialists. Specialists, you got that? Not dipshitists, spe-cia-lists!'

'Then I'd like to make a suggestion,' Tys interjected, and everyone looked at him in surprise. 'If we need specialists, then we have to go where the specialists are. We have a trade school in Vedmediv, and they have lots of people studying civil engineering. We should do some scouting around—'

'Who brought this dope here? Do some scouting around, he says! Do some scouting around in July? What're ya gonna do, dig another tunnel under the lecture hall so you can scope them out in secret? Working with morons isn't easy!' said the dejected mayor, wiping the sweat from his bald spot with his already-wet handkerchief.

'First off, I'm not a moron. The whole project is my idea,' Tys said, raising his index finger.

'Second off, I'm gonna kick you out of my office right now! What does it matter whose idea it is? I'm asking you what we should do now. N-o-w. Do you hear what I'm saying?! None of this reaching out to the public, no damn billboards. What should we do now? And nobody, I mean nobody, can find out about this!'

'Well, everybody's going to find out about it eventually,' Tys persisted. 'Once we finish digging the tunnel, all forty million Ukrainians will go over into Europe, so it'll be pretty hard to keep that a secret.'

'What forty million Ukrainians?' The Succubus was dumbfounded.

'Uh, he wants to euro-integrate Ukraine through the tunnel. Like the European Union has officially closed its borders to us Ukrainians, but we can get there another way, without any official documentation,' Icarus sighed mockingly.

'How about he euro-integrates Ukraine through his asshole?' said the Succubus, exasperated.

'I'll ask you to refrain from using such pejoratives in relation to the future of Ukraine!' Tys instantly adopted a solemn expression, and his voice became more uplifting. 'Ukraine has experienced Euromaidan and faced Russian aggression, and now we need a new direction. We've already seen Peter the Great's 'window to Europe.' There've been doors, gates, and borders, too. Now it's time to build a tunnel, since nothing else has worked thus far. Ukrainians, and Transcarpathians in particular, have always nurtured a dream of joining Mother Europe. We're merely a tool in the hands of the genius of the people! The Transcarpathians, boxed in by mountains and checkpoints, need the borders to open up like no one else! We just can't breathe in here, we're suffocating! Our gift to Ukraine will be blazing a path to Europe. Transcarpathia, the land of patriots, will become a place of unity!'

'Working with morons really isn't easy,' the mayor repeated, his voice tired and dejected. 'I don't know what you've been teaching our kids, but you've got diddly-squat when it comes to brains. What makes you think that Transcarpathians want open borders? Yes, we live in a region that borders four different countries. Yes, for centuries, we have lived between East and West, at the intersection of various cultures. I make that point, speech after speech. Yes, we are the westernmost region of Ukraine. Yes, Ukrainians took to the streets to be part of Europe, for the right to be Europeans, and for the freedom to travel. I'd like to remind you, just in case you've forgotten, although I was part of the previous government and belonged to the ruling party, I backed Euromaidan almost immediately – by the middle of February, a mere three months later! Then I came out with an official statement of support at the beginning of March. So I was in the revolutionary vanguard, at the forefront of the movement – I don't think anyone can deny that. But… there's one thing you have to realize – while Ukraine as a whole may benefit from euro-integration, it would kill us Transcarpathians. We'd have nothing without those borders. Sure, people may consider us second-class citizens, but who gives a damn? Just so long as there are borders! The more borders, the better! Because where there's a border, there's smuggling. And smuggling is the Bible, Torah, and Koran for Transcarpathians. Tys, why do you think it is that Transcarpathians, the people who live in the westernmost region of Ukraine, have always voted for the pro-Russian Party of Regions and Yanukovych? Because that party is for closer ties with Russia, which automatically causes problems with Europe. In other words, it means borders. Trust me, our priests are petitioning God not to do away with our borders. Because if He does, there'll be no more smuggling, and we'll all go hungry. What else can you do here? Can you picture a Transcarpathian working in a factory? No way. We need borders, and if I have to, I'll build a half-mile of border with my own money and stand guard on it!' The speech made every-one freeze. Tys turned beet red, then suddenly went completely pale.

'You didn't understand anything I was trying to say,' Tys finally began. 'I knew it'd be hard to assemble a team of like-minded indi-viduals. But I had to try, because I had an idea I'd give my life for. You're out to make a quick buck and you're willing to sell Ukraine out for thirty pieces of silver. Well, when I decided to call myself Tys, I knew things wouldn't be easy, that they'd be tough, very tough. And that I might be misunderstood by my contemporaries, but that our descendants would certainly thank me one day. And that the name Tys would go down in history, exalted as the name Tiberius. I didn't have high hopes for you. I'll be perfectly honest, I realised that everyone would pursue their own goals when I got you involved. Mine's the salvation of Ukraine and Europe. Yours is a tunnel for smuggling. But at this stage of the project, we can still collaborate, although it pains me very much that you don't have a drop of patriotism left in your hearts—'

'Now we're getting somewhere,' Zoltan Bartok said, livening up. 'I like this new attitude of yours, all business. I guess you're not completely hopeless, Tys. So everyone has their own separate inter-ests, but now we're all facing the same issue. What should we do?'

'I think I have an idea,' Icarus said, inspecting his nails. 'We need to bring someone else on board. Someone who can take over for Ychi.'

'Brilliant!' The mayor clapped his hands. 'We never would've thought of that without you! We just have to iron out one minor detail, though. Who the fuck are we gonna hire instead of Ychi? Huh?'

'That's what I'm saying,' Icarus continued, slightly offended. 'I have someone in mind. I think you all know him. Ihor Lendian.'

'Yeah, I know him. Why him?' the mayor inquired.

'Because he won't go blabbing around town. He has his own smuggling interests, so he'd be a perfect partner. And his brother Yosif is a building contractor. They're close and all, so we'll bring both of them on. You'll get the professionals you wanted so badly. Well, and Ihor has some real organisational talent, too.'

'Hmm,' went the Genius of the Carpathians, clearly interested. 'I know him. He's a good guy. His brother is too.'

'I know them both...very well,' the Succubus said, giggling alluringly. 'Those boys are real slick!'

'That's what I've been saying – professionals, people in construction, that's who we need! I'm not sure about bringing them on, but I'm with you if you think we should,' Tys said with an air of importance, although nobody was waiting for his stamp of approval.

'I know them, too. They can get the job done. When exactly did he demonstrate his 'organisational talent?' Please, enlighten me,' the mayor said.

'At Eurovision,' Icarus answered quietly, almost conspiratorially.

'Eurovision?' The mayor sounded disappointed.

'You mean that singing contest on TV?' Kruchka asked incredulously.

'Yeah, that contest on TV. Ihor organized the whole thing.'

'Well, if that's the case, then maybe we should get him a job at the cultural center downtown. He can teach our kids to sing and prance around in their underwear. How's he gonna help us? Are we going to hold an underground Eurovision so Ukraine can win?' the mayor asked, bursting into laughter.

'Nah, that's not what I'm getting at. It's actually a good thing you haven't heard much about Eurovision. That proves just how professional Ihor really is. He'll never let us down. He'll take our secret to the grave. I've done business with him in the past. I let him use my buses once, for modest compensation, of course. You don't actually believe that the person who sings the best and is most liked by European viewers is the one who wins Eurovision, do you?' Icarus asked, trying to pique their interest.

'I don't give a damn,' Zoltan Bartok answered, shrugging.

'I don't either, but there are people out there who do care. Like the performers themselves. Winning a competition like that opens the doors to superstardom, and that means big money. That's why they're willing to invest hefty sums to ensure they win. A few years back, the Russian participant… Dima Clan, or something like that, decided to buy himself a Eurovision victory. Vedmediv's very own Ihor Lendian helped him do it, but the BBC never told his story,' Icarus continued.

'But how?' the Succubus asked.

'Well, as you know, we live on the border, right next to four different countries, right?' Icarus was building up some real rhetorical fervor.

'That's the truth, the solemn truth,' Tys replied, crossing himself.

'What did you watch back when they showed the Communist Party plenary sessions on TV? Foreign channels, right?' Icarus continued.

'Sure, I won't deny it.' The mayor still wasn't following Icarus's logic, though.

'But why?' Icarus asked him straight up.

'Well, because they had more color. There were Western cartoons, you know, Tom and Jerry and stuff, cool music—' The mayor still didn't really know what was going on.

'That's not why, my dears,' Icarus said triumphantly. 'It was because the antennas on your roofs could pick up those channels. Nobody in Poltava was watching Slovak television, but we were. Every household can still pick up foreign channels. And foreign cellular networks, too. Ihor took advantage of that.'

'But how?'

'He didn't come up with this plan, but he made it happen. Somebody approached him and offered him a job working for Dima Clan. He was told that half the Eurovision votes came from the jury and half from viewers sending texts. Since we can get coverage for Romanian, Hungarian, Slovakian, and Polish cell phone providers here in town, we can vote on behalf of those countries. So, it was just a matter of buying an enormous number of SIM cards over there – twenty to thirty thousand – and then hiring 'fans' who would start sending texts from two phones at a time. Once the moment came – voting lasted for forty minutes – one person, alternating SIM cards and sending 15-20 messages from each phone, could vote 400 times. And that's exactly what they did. Ihor picked up nearly 500 students in Uzhhorod, parked his buses near the border, handed out cell phones and SIM cards, gave everyone the signal when it was time, and voila! Thousands and thousands of texts for their beloved Dima Clan flew to Belgrade for Eurovision. The Hungarians were just floored that their country had given a Russian singer nobody had ever heard of the top score. That's how it went with the other countries, too. So, Dima Clan rode a wave of made-to-order international acclaim to victory.' Icarus flashed a patronising smile, quite satisfied with the effect his story had produced.

'Wow!' the Genius of the Carpathians said, raising his eyebrows.

'Those dirty Russkies… they're a bunch of cheats. That's why we need euro-integration. 'Away from Moscow!' as Khvylovy wrote!' Tys offered.

'Even still,' Zoltan Bartok said, giving Tys an indulgent look, 'that's quite impressive, I have to say. Scams on that scale are only possible in Transcarpathia.'

'Well, obviously, it had to be Transcarpathia, given its location and all the borders nearby,' Icarus concurred. 'But Ihor told me they were operating in other European countries, too. Like there was an airplane full of students from Lviv who flew to Spain just so they could vote from their hotel rooms. Some others went over to Latvia or even France. It was a major operation, and Ihor did a magnificent job!'

'Impressive, impressive,' Kruchka said pensively. 'I think we need to bring him on right away. He'll definitely come through for us, too!'

'We just have to have him, we need him, he was made for this – there's no questioning that! Icarus, run on over to his place and work out the details. This is the perfect solution!' The mayor was beaming. 'I assume there are no objections?'

'I'm with you,' said the Genius of the Carpathians.

'Me too. I think this calls for a drink,' Tys said, blushing.

'It positively cries out for one! Positively cries out! Zoya, my dear, bring everything on over, lickety-split! Don't want to keep these good people waiting!' the mayor ordered.

Chapter 11:

In Which the Tunnel is Revived!

Zoltan Bartok, the Succubus, Icarus, Mirca, and Tys were sitting at the table under the oak in the central square. An incredible heat wave had hit Vedmediv. Flies were practically falling asleep mid-flight because they just didn't feel like moving anymore. There wasn't even the slightest breeze; it was unbearably hot, even in the shade. The group was drinking chilled kvass out of large plastic cups, but it didn't really help. Suddenly, a head of curly hair popped out of the tunnel. It belonged to a young man roughly twenty-five years of age. He swiftly climbed up the ladder and then came over to the table. It was Ihor Lendian. His brother Yosif, a bit stockier than him and wearing blue work overalls, followed him, and they sat down.

'What an ungodly smell, it's like someone just took a shit!' Yosif made a wry face and started sniffing around.

'Ah, that's just the flies,' Icarus said, swatting at them.

'Nah, I'm telling you, somebody just took a huge dump!' Yosif said, his nostrils narrowing as he kept sniffing. Tys blushed and looked down at his kvass.

'Would ya drop it already?' the mayor commanded. 'Alright, what do you say, boys?'

'The short answer is we'll do it,' Ihor answered, taking a sip of frothy kvass and wiping his lips on his sleeve. 'But we gotta redo everything.'

'I've never seen such shoddy work! You're lucky Ychi wasn't killed a few feet in. That tunnel could have been his grave. I think the roots of this big ole oak saved him from a major cave-in and kept the whole square from collapsing on top of him,' Yosif remarked contemptuously.

'Well, yeah, Yosif's right,' Ihor continued once his brother finished. 'Icarus and I checked on Google Maps yesterday – we only need to dig 750 yards to reach a safe spot in Hungary. It's 525 yards to the actual border, but it's too dangerous to come up right there. There's no way Ychi would've finished a tunnel that long all by himself before the fall. Most importantly, we can't keep digging like this – we're not building a treehouse here. The first major storm would flood that tunnel in no time. We have to reinforce the walls and ceiling – and with concrete, not beams and two-by-fours. Pouring that much concrete would take a year – that's not going to work for us. There's another way of doing things. I'll tell you about it later. This is how I see it – we have to fill in what we have now, make another pit – about fifteen feet deep – and *then* we can start digging.'

'How long's that going to take? When can we expect the project to be complete?' Icarus inquired.

'Well, it's pretty much up to you. I'll give it to you straight – and my brother can back me up on this one – you don't do things like this with your hands. I mean you can, if you're Robinson Crusoe or the Count of Monte Cristo, like if you're put in extreme circumstances and you don't have any other options. That could go on for years, though. Today, you use heavy machinery to take care of things like this. You get the job done in a fraction of the time, and the final product is of much higher quality, much more reliable.'

'Well, we have a jackhammer and a pulley for the buckets of dirt. And we hooked up electricity down there, too,' boasted Icarus, who'd purchased most of that with his own money.

'I had a truck and an excavator brought in – everything's up and running,' Zoltan Bartok added in a businesslike tone.

'How about beach pails? Got any of those?' Yosif asked without even a hint of a smile.

'Cool it, alright? Please excuse my brother. He's a little rough around the edges. He's a builder, not a negotiator, you know,' Ihor said hurriedly. 'The thing is, none of that is heavy machinery. It's enough to make a cat laugh. You need real machinery to dig a real tunnel, like in the metro. We can rent it, but it won't be cheap. We'll get a half-mile long tunnel done in three weeks, though – by the middle of August.'

'By Independence Day!' Tys said, beaming.

'That's allowing for any delays or unforeseen setbacks. We might even finish before that,' Yosif said.

'What kind of price tag are we looking at?' Ulyana asked.

'Roughly two to three hundred thousand dollars,' Ihor answered nonchalantly, like they were talking about purchasing those beach pails.

'Screw that!' the Genius of the Carpathians spat.

'That's not gonna happen...' Icarus said, clearly dismayed.

'Now we'll never build a better Ukraine!' the teacher yelled in a fit of anger.

'Hey, hey, hold your horses now, boys,' the mayor said, brow furrowed. 'We're in this together. Everyone'll just chip in what they can – but that sounds like an awful lot to me. We're talking about a tunnel to Hungary here, not the damn space program!'

'We're not marking anything up, that's just the cost of the materials and machinery rentals. Icarus and I hammered the whole thing out. He said that my brother and I will have full access to the tunnel, and we'll be able to transport whatever we want. I agreed to those terms. As a shareholder, our contribution will be creating a design and then building it. Everything'll be ready to go in just three weeks. The price tag isn't actually all that high. That's how much building a nice house costs nowadays. A house doesn't provide any real benefits, though – just maintenance costs. But this tunnel can pay for itself in a month or two and then start bringing in a profit.'

'Three weeks… interesting.' Kruchka's fiery gaze was fixed on Ihor. 'What kind of technology are you gonna be using? What do you mean by 'like in the metro?' What's the tunnel gonna look like?'

'The technology'll be pretty basic, but we'll need a special machine that'll cost the lion's share of the budget. So, first we'll fill in this tunnel before the church collapses,' Ihor said sarcastically. 'Then we'll go right ahead and make a nice deep pit. While we're doing that, we'll order the machine we need from Belarus. It just looks like a big boiler, but it's practically a whole factory. It has this drill, like a gigantic screw, in the front, that'll mash up the dirt. There are some hoses filled with water behind that, so it can soak the mashed-up dirt and turn it into mush. That water has to go somewhere. It'll gush like a geyser, so your fountain idea was actually great. Some murky water'll be gushing out of the pit for a while, and everyone in town'll just think that we're doing some final prep work before the big unveiling.'

'That's perfect!' Zoltan Bartok exclaimed.

'So there's this thing, like an enormous vacuum, behind those hoses. It'll suck up all the water and dirt and blast it out of the tunnel. The dirt'll run through a sieve into a dump truck, and the water'll run into the sewer system. With this technology, the tunnel'll move along at roughly three to five feet an hour, and it'll be about four feet wide.'

'Whoa!' Icarus could hardly contain himself.

'Yeah, good luck getting that out of Ychi,' the mayor added.

'But that's not all.' Ihor was keeping them in suspense as long as he could. 'There's this press behind that vacuum thingy, with a large concrete pipe inside it. Once the drill mashes up some dirt and the water vacuum pumps it out, the press shoves a concrete pipe in its place. And it keeps going like that, foot by foot. So we get a concrete tunnel that'll never collapse or leak, not some crude underground pit. This is tried-and-tested technology. This is how they lay new utility and sewage tunnels in old Western European cities. You don't have to dig the whole length of the tunnel. All you need is a pit, and then you put this machine down there. It digs its way to where you need to go and installs pipe along the way. That's what makes it so fast.'

'That's incredible!' Ulyana said. This may have been the first time any of them had seen her express genuine surprise; she was generally so cold and unapproachable.

'Would ya just give them the whole spiel already?' interjected Yosif, who didn't particularly care for his brother's theatrics.

'Is there a problem or something? I just knew there had to be a catch. I know a thing or two… I mean, after running the city all these years… ' Zoltan Bartok boasted smugly.

'Nah, it's the other way around!' Ihor said, smacking his lips. 'So, this machine digs, sucks up the soil, and lays pipe. More importantly, though, the pipe has railroad tracks at the bottom and cables running at the top. But this isn't just a pipe with lamps and electrical wiring in it, no sir! A small train can run on the tracks! All right, fine, it's more like little carts, not full-sized cars, but still! The pipe isn't all that wide, but you can fit a cart system about the size of what you'd find in a mine inside it. You can haul up to 650 pounds of freight in one of those carts, and the run to Hungary's no more than ten minutes!'

'So, you're telling me we won't need people crawling through the tunnel with cartons of cigarettes?' Icarus asked, fully entranced by this point.

'Nope! Just one person on this side loading the carts – you can send up to ten of them through at once – and another person unloading them on the other side. And one person up front, driving – like an engineer. He'll have this remote control, just five buttons. That's about it,' Ihor replied.

'Hold on just one second… are you telling me people can ride in these carts, too?' The Genius of the Carpathians recognised what was in it for him.

'Did you say 'people?'' Tys could also sense that his dream might be about to come true.

'Yeah, not very many, though. One person can fit in each cart pretty comfortably. It's not like a nice sleeper car or anything, but the ride's real fast. You just lie down, curl up, and then hop out ten minutes later. The tunnel's well-lit, so it isn't scary. The carts go slow, so they don't make too much of a racket. It's dry down there, and you can even install a basic ventilation system to keep a good airflow going.'

'Alright, say we drove the train over into Hungary. How does it get back? Where does it turn around?' Icarus wanted to hear every last detail.

'Why does it have to turn around?' Yosif asked in surprise. 'Our tunnel's gonna be dead straight. The engine in the first cart'll propel the whole train along the tracks to Hungary. Then it'll switch into reverse and push the train back toward Ukraine.'

'That's unbelievable!' The Genius of the Carpathians was genuinely impressed.

'So, we'll get a tunnel, and this train of yours, in just three weeks' time?' Zoltan Bartok asked.

'I think the whole project will take about three weeks. Worst case scenario, it'll be ready by August 24th, by Independence Day, like Carbide – uh, I mean Mr. Chvak – said.' Ihor gave Tys, his former teacher, a respectful nod. 'We'll definitely get the job done by then. We'll spend two or three days filling up the old tunnel and digging a new, wider pit. The machinery'll be comin' in from Belarus around then. By the time we set it up, the pipes'll be coming in. And then once we start digging, the carts and the engine for our mini-train'll be ready. There's nothing to it. This is tried-and-tested technology. Pretty standard stuff.'

'Alright, what'd you say this engineering marvel was gonna cost us?' Kruchka loved the idea of an international metro system, and she was ready to bite.

'Somewhere around two to three hundred thousand dollars. Let's do the math: first off, ya need high-voltage cables for this kind of job. That means we have to replace the transformer substation downtown. That's forty thousand dollars right there. Second, you have to rent the actual machinery – that ain't cheap – fifty thousand dollars a week. That'll motivate us to work as quickly as possible. If we're shooting for three weeks, that'll be one hundred and fifty thousand dollars. So, our running total comes to one hundred and ninety. A half-mile's worth of pipe and track will cost seventy thousand – that makes two hundred and sixty. The engine and the ten carts'll cost roughly twenty thousand. So, we have a grand total of two hundred and eighty thousand American dollars. There'll be some additional expenses, obviously. You should always allow for them – that'll be ten percent of the budget, so add another thirty thousand. Yosif and I are willing to put up that amount, though. That'll be our contribution – in addition to our labor. Right, Yosif?'

'Right,' his brother answered frostily.

'I'll put up forty thousand dollars – for the substation.' The mayor's unheard-of generosity shocked everyone. 'Vedmediv isn't some one-horse town,' he continued. 'It's a major city in the center of Europe! People are always complaining about power outages.

It's about time we put a modern transformer vault downtown. I'll have the city pay for it, the councilmen'll back me up.'

'I came up with the idea and brought everyone lunch—' Tys started, but he was immediately cut off.

'We don't need anything from you. Your gold tooth could buy you a bottle of vodka and two beers. What else do you got? Good job coming up with the idea,' Icarus said. 'I can chip in twenty thousand, but that's it. Ever since the airplane crash, I haven't been able to reach the same entrepreneurial heights as before. I've been reduced to small-time jobs. I'll give you the money I've saved for a rainy day. Twenty thousand.'

'Well, that's sixty thousand so far. Not even close to enough,' Ihor continued.

'And lunches,' Tys added resolutely.

'God, something just reeks!' Yosif said, sniffing around again.

'Knock it off! We're trying to focus here!' his brother barked peevishly.

'I'm willing to put up two hundred thousand,' Ulyana announced unexpectedly, with a devilish glint in her eyes. 'On one condition.'

'Well, well, for two hundred thousand, we'll indulge your every whim! Isn't that right, guys?' Ihor asked everyone in attendance.

'Of course,' Tys agreed, now overwhelmed with self-importance.

'What's your condition?' Icarus inquired tentatively.

'It's very simple,' Kruchka answered. 'I'm willing to put up two hundred thousand dollars, which, I'll remind you boys, is two-thirds of the project's budget, if I get one of the carts all to myself. There'll be a lock on it, and I'll be the only one with the key, and nobody, I mean nobody, will be allowed to look inside, ever. Not ever!'

'No problem. We'll even put your name on it and paint it pink for you,' Icarus agreed gladly.

'I'll paint your balls pink,' the Succubus said, flashing her seductive smile. 'And then I'll chop 'em off. And sell 'em.'

'Alright, alright, cool it, you two. I, personally, don't have anything against our sweet and magnificent Ms. Kruk having a cart she'll use for her own purposes,' the mayor said in a conciliatory tone. 'Any objections?'

'I'm in favor,' the Genius of the Carpathians answered in his typical reserved fashion. 'And I'm willing to cover the rest – forty thousand – if people can actually ride in those carts and if everything's actually ready by the end of August.'

'Fantastic! That's the full amount, and we won't be needing anything else!' Ihor exclaimed. 'We'll be able to send people to Hungary and ride over ourselves. With this kind of money, we'll definitely get the job done by the end of August, at the latest. Now that's how you do business! And you were afraid we couldn't do it!'

'Well, that figure of three hundred thousand just knocked the wind out of us. Three hundred thousand! There's no way we would've pulled this off, if not for the wonderful Succ—' Icarus faltered. '—Ms. Kruk.'

'You guys are too funny: you develop a project like this and start trumpeting it all over town, but you won't put your money where your mouth is. Thank God the tunnel caved in so soon. Another two feet and the church would've been gone. Also, it's flat out impossible to dig a tunnel like this with just a shovel. You read one too many adventure stories as a kid!' Ihor said, clearly loosening up. 'Actually, Ychi got real lucky. He got a slap on the wrist for his foolishness. He could've gotten buried down there.'

'Speaking of which, what are we going to do with him?' the Succubus asked.

'Nothing. Keep him in that fortress of yours for now,' Zoltan Bartok said. 'Good thing he doesn't have any relatives. Maybe,

God willing, he'll come to sometime soon. And then we'll take it from there.'

'When should we expect the money?' Impatience had overcome Ihor.

'I'll have my share ready by tomorrow morning, in cash,' Ulyana said, as though she'd only be handing over a few hryvnias.

'I'll need a week – no more, I guarantee it – to gather up the full amount,' the Genius of the Carpathians answered, businesslike as always.

'I'll be ready by tomorrow, too, no problem,' was Icarus's reply.

'I came up with the idea and brought everyone their lunches. In our country, teachers aren't—' Tys began once again.

'Shut it! We got it already!' Zoltan Bartok interrupted him. 'Now boys, start filling in the tunnel and prepping everything else. I'll allocate the necessary funds in a week. Can't go any faster – that's the law. Don't think I haven't been meaning to replace that substation for a while now. The city needs a new one. You just came along at the right time.'

'Excellent! Alright, then we'll get to work tomorrow. I'll order the machinery tonight. By the way, you can watch some videos of how it works online – just google 'Lovat' or 'Lovat MTS.' It's some pretty interesting stuff. One of those machines'll be parked in downtown Vedmediv in a few days! I'll make the rounds tomorrow morning and pick up the cash that's ready. I'll be looking forward to getting the rest soon. Everything'll be up and running by Independence Day!' Ihor said, standing up and downing the rest of his kvass, which was almost hot by this point.

'What a spectacular birthday gift for Ukraine!' the teacher said, his eyes rolling back with pleasure. 'Finally, our ancient land will be reunited with Europe! And we won't need any European parliaments, summits, or agreements. Vedmedivites are our own European Parliament!'

'It's time to get a move on. We've been out here so long my shirt's soaked with sweat. Gotta buckle down tomorrow!' Zoltan Bartok said in parting.

'It really does smell like shit. Human shit. I'm telling ya, somebody took a huge dump here,' Yosif declared. He surveyed the area one last time and then walked away. The Genius of the Carpathians locked the gate to the construction site, then the sweltering square went quiet, and black clouds – the harbinger of a fierce storm that would put an end to this unbearable heat wave – poked out from behind the crown of the age-old oak.

Chapter 12:

In Which all the Extras Exit the Stage

Construction was in full swing near the oak in the main square of Vedmediv. They had to make room for the Lovat, so they'd expanded the construction site and replaced the fence. It was now adorned with large pictures of old Vedmediv – more precisely, Mediv – taken by unknown photographers in the sumptuous heyday of the Austro-Hungarian Empire. This may have been an effort to emphasise the value and significance of this fountain that was supposed to return the city to those times of wealth and prosperity. A rather skilled designer had the Fountain of Unity integrated into its surroundings, so now one side of the fence displayed the future layout of Vedmediv's Peace Square. The majestic oak – an imperturbable witness to many initiatives and endeavors, the rise and fall of governments, the creation and disappearance of new countries, the raising of monuments and their subsequent destruction, marches and parades that participants preferred to keep quiet about a few decades later – towered over all of this. Under its regal crown, a machine was gnawing away at the soil, slowly, just like a worm, forging Ukraine's path towards the European Union. Or, at the very least, tearing a path towards riches coveted by a few individuals. Hardly anyone had any clue about that, though. Instead, Vedmedivites were delighted to see the sign by the construction site stating that the Fountain of Unity would be unveiled on Independence Day, August 24th, 2015, at 11:00 a.m. There were two weeks left until the celebration.

A small announcement in the *Vedmediv Star* made the rounds, stirring up the town's August apathy. It stated that the Road to Paradise, a municipal association that managed the cemetery on Partisan Street, among other things, was asking Vedmedivites to come forward with any information they had regarding the whereabouts of their employee, Ychi the gravedigger. It also stated that local law enforcement agencies had launched an intensive search.

Vedmedivites are always thirsty for sensational news and rumours, so the municipal association's phones were soon ringing off the hook. Somebody insisted that they'd seen Ychi on the train to Odessa, drunk as a skunk and apparently on his way down to the beach. One local slut hurried to inform everyone that she'd seen Ychi on St. Elijah's Day – July 20th. He was walking around on the outskirts of town, holding a torch, absolutely oblivious, not even responding when someone said hello to him. A local alcoholic nicknamed 'the Hose' didn't have a phone, so he showed up at the office of the Road to Paradise in person to provide them with some truly valuable information. According to him, a week ago, while he was walking home after the liquor store had closed, he saw Ychi, who was carrying a coffin on his back. The Hose shouted that he could help him – for a sip of vodka, that is. But Ychi didn't turn around and didn't even pay any attention to his old friend. Then he snuck up on the gravedigger as a joke, and tapped on the coffin

'It's me, your death, open up,' he said, and Ychi spun around abruptly. He held the coffin in one hand and clocked the Hose with the other. 'His eyes were all red, like a vampire's, and blood was dribbling out of the corner of his mouth,' the drunkard said, asking for nothing but a bottle of vodka and some green onion to go with it as a reward for coming forward.

Ychi's mysterious disappearance caused many people in town to speculate that he might have emigrated. For some reason, nobody could even conceive of misfortune striking him. After all, who would dare attack the burly gravedigger? Him being mugged seemed pretty improbable, too – what were they gonna take? His shovel? Therefore, he must have moved, abandoning Vedmediv and his job at the cemetery.

'We really are done for it if even Ychi decided to leave,' the old-timers in town said. Everyone could understand young people moving abroad, students staying where they went to college, or girls rushing into marriages with the first guys they met in the big city. Nobody was surprised when migrant workers decided to stay in Prague or Moscow, leaving their families behind. Women who moved to Italy or Portugal to look after feeble old people hardly ever came back home – maybe once every five or ten years, and that was just to show everyone they'd made it. That all made perfect sense, but they were really done for if even Ychi had decided to leave. After all, what did he have to offer? Perpetually unwashed, dirty and unpolished, honest, yet unskilled, kind, yet frightful-looking – how could he make it in the big, wide world? Who would hire him? What would he do? Scare kids?

'Oof,' went the old-timers, their sighs devastating. 'Someday, there'll be nobody left around here.' Obviously, Vedmedivites continued to die, despite the gravedigger's disappearance, so the government had to replace him quickly. Miklos Svyscho, better known as the Fisherman in Vedmediv and the adjacent villages, became the city's new gravedigger. The Fisherman was a decent guy and a hard worker. He didn't much care for that nickname, but he got it when he was young, and it just stuck.

This is how it went. Miklos and his buddy were drafted into the newly-formed Ukrainian army. Back then, you could buy your way out of anything, so his parents offered a pig as a bribe to make sure their son would serve as a guard on the nearby border, instead of on the other side of the country. The army wasn't all that bad – he had his fair share of food, booze, and girls, but he still had to report for duty once every four days. Every evening, a two-man patrol armed with assault rifles would be sent from one outpost to the next. The patrolmen were expected to cover 5-10 miles by the next morning, keeping vigilant watch over the western gates of the young Ukrainian state. Nobody really felt like trudging along the banks of the Tysa or through the Carpathian forest, though, so generally, the border guards would report for duty, start walking, and then peel off towards the nearest bar, where they'd pound drinks until morning, then take a taxi to the next outpost right before sunrise.

One March evening at the dawn of Ukraine's independence, Miklos decided he didn't want to freeze his butt off in the swamps along the border. Instead, he opted to throw a few back at this hospitable old guy's house near the village of Vylky. He was a local celebrity because his pear-flavored moonshine was so stupendous that not even the Queen of England would turned her nose up at it. Moreover, in those days, when everyone was strapped for cash, he'd willingly swap his booze for army boots or pea coats. So, once their shift started, Miklos and his partner headed straight for his place, where they exchanged their leather shoulder harnesses and officer's messenger bags for a litre of 125-proof moonshine. The kindly moonshiner even let the guys spend the night in his barn. A remarkable idea struck Miklos when there was just a little of the wonder-working liquid still sloshing around at the bottom of the bottle.

There were some large fishing nets hanging on the walls of the barn, and some rods and reels neatly propped against the wall off to the side. The old guy clearly liked fishing, just like Miklos – that was all he really did as a kid.

'Hey, you know what I was thinking?!' His buddy had already started nodding off, but Miklos suddenly sounded inspired. 'While the old guy's sleepin', we should borrow his rods, head down to the river, catch some fish, and then put everything back where it was by morning. Well, everything but the fish. It's the end of March, they're just waking up after a long winter, they're hungry as a bunch of dragons!' His partner was delighted by this plan, because he, too, really enjoyed fishing, although he just hadn't been able to find the time for his wonderful hobby for the past five years or so. The Tysa is an exceptional river where you can do impossible things. For instance, in Ukraine it's illegal to catch the Danube salmon that lay eggs upstream; however, it's perfectly legal in Hungary. The border between Ukraine and Hungary runs down the middle of the river, so clever Transcarpathian fishermen simply cast their lines over to the other side and catch the – legal – Hungarian salmon. To a certain extent, everyone in these parts is a fisherman, if only in their hearts. That includes the border guards.

So they headed out. The night was dark and cloudy; not a single star lit the young anglers' path. Miklos remembered that the closest lake was about a twenty-minute walk from the old guy's house. They took one rod each and hid their rifles, which they wouldn't be needing for a fishing expedition, in the attic of the barn. Relative to the warm, stale air inside, the night felt fresh and crisp, chilling them to the core and making them quicken their pace. It's a good thing they'd swiped another bottle of moonshine; it would keep them warm and alert, in case a fish – a huge one, obviously – tugged on one of their lines. Time and distance always seem to stretch out at night, and the boys' drunken impatience only made it worse. They were just five minutes into the walk, but it felt like half the night was already gone.

'You sure we're going the right way?' Miklos's partner asked him.

'You betcha! Hell, I know every dog in these parts...and I'm no stranger to the fish either!' he answered.

In another five minutes, Miklos's boot landed on something squishy. 'Woah there. Stop, we're here,' he commanded. That night, the sky, in its utter blackness, blended with the earth; visibility was no greater than a foot. They'd been more or less groping their way forward the whole time, unable to see anything around them and relying on Miklos's instincts, as he was certain they were on the right track. Then they took a step back and started getting their reels ready. They fastened large cannonball sinkers – actually, just rolled-up hunks of bread, because they didn't have anything else – to their hooks.

'Don't you worry, we'll snag a huge carp before long! You know what kind of carp they have over here? Ah, you wouldn't know! Lemme tell ya. When I was a kid I'd catch fish bigger than me! I remember this one time, I used a chicken thigh as bait, and an enormous catfish went for it. I couldn't reel it in, no matter how hard I tried, because it was heavier and stronger than me. So I tied my rod to a tree and ran over to the nearest village for back-up. A few adults came over, but they couldn't pull that monster out of the water either. Then they came over in their truck, attached the pole to the back, and stepped on the gas. Then that catfish finally saw the light of day! Everyone called it the Whale because it was just so big. The water level in the lake dropped six feet when we finally pulled it out. Everyone wanted their picture taken with it. That's the kind of fish I catch! We're gonna reel in a nice big carp, you'll see! Oh yeah! I don't even know how we're gonna carry it back to base,' Miklos said, exultant.

Once they'd settled in, the fishermen took a few sips out of the bottle – their little libation for a successful catch. First Miklos swung back his arm and cast his line, then his partner's hook flew in a different direction.

'Hey, I didn't hear a splash. How come?' he inquired.

'Probably because we cast our lines too far out. That's a good thing, though. An experienced angler knows not to disturb the fish,' Miklos replied.

With their lines cast, they sat down on the ground, had a smoke, and then got back to their bottle. About an hour later, fatigue, moonshine, and the warmth of their pea coats got the better of them, and they were soon sleeping like babies. They both had the same dream: a gigantic, mustached catfish was riding around Vylky on an old bicycle, a peaked military cap perched atop his head. For some reason, the catfish had legs, which he was using to pedal. He would pull up to the villagers' houses, lift his leg, and drop a portion of caviar in the buckets they'd placed next to their front gates. They'd smile, thank him, and make the sign of the cross over him as he pulled away. He'd ride by all the pretty girls in the village, cigarette smoke curling out of his mouth and a devilish glint burning in his eyes. None of them had legs, though – just tails and fins, so the local boys never really chased them. What was the point? The two border guards were sitting at a bus stop and savoring their moonshine and all kinds of delectable treats that the grateful villagers kept bringing them. After all, Miklos and his partner had caught the catfish that so generously doled out delicious caviar by the bucketful. They sat there until a bus pulled up and the driver started honking the horn, as if to say, 'hey, champs, hop on!'

A bus really was honking its horn, the anxious, intermittent sounds tearing the boys out of their slumber. Miklos reluctantly forced one eye open and saw the thing parked right in front of them, its god-awful headlights blinding them. Still in the no man's land between sleep and waking, he looked around and saw the dark, dismal desolation of March fields slowly brightening as the sun rose. His partner lay next to him.

'You fuckin' dead or something? Get outta the damn way, ya pissants!' yelled the exasperated driver, reinforcing his angry words with another beep. Miklos looked around again, finally coming to and realizing that he and his friend were lying in the middle of the road. A six-foot-long puddle sparkled in front of them, clenched in a thin crust of morning ice – temperatures had indeed dipped below freezing that night.

Waking up, his partner started shaking his head. Meanwhile, the driver hopped off the bus, cursing the boys loudly and wishing all sorts of misfortune upon them. The fishing rods rested next to them in their metal holders with little bells on them. Once the driver saw them, he burst into roaring laughter; he couldn't even talk for the next few minutes. At that point, the bitter truth hit Miklos – in the pitch-black night, he had mistaken the puddle for the edge of the lake. There was no splash because they'd just cast their bait right in front of them – Miklos on the road and his partner into the field. Then they fell asleep, and at five a.m., their little fishing encampment obstructed the driver's first run. Miklos tried to explain himself and laugh the whole thing off, but the driver wasn't buying any of his stories. Well, in the early 90s, it was pretty hard to believe that a green border guard sleeping in the middle of the road, his moonshine-laden breath carrying all the way over to Hungary, was actually on a covert assignment the nature of which he, unfortunately, couldn't reveal due to legal concerns. After that night, nobody in the Vedmediv area would call Miklos by his name anymore. His new nickname, 'the Fisherman,' said it all, and it was pretty menacing, too.

Now he'd replaced Ychi as the city's gravedigger. Nevertheless, the furor around his predecessor showed no sign of dying down.

Where had Ychi disappeared to and why? It wasn't just gossiping old ladies on park benches pondering this question; some people had a professional obligation to get to the bottom of things. Anyway, even though nobody had filed a missing person's report – the former gravedigger didn't have any relatives – the announcement in the newspaper was grounds enough to initiate an investigation. The police searched Ychi's home. As expected, there was no sign of a struggle. Granted, there was one fact that could've easily stirred everyone up again. Police Staff Sergeant Lysenko, a true patriot and proud son of his city, weighed all the pros and cons, and remembered that it was his duty to maintain peace and tranquility, so he decided to conceal the fact in question. For the good of the community, of course. When rooting through the missing person's effects, the vigilant law enforcement officer found two thousand American dollars stashed under the mattress, which was clearly Ychi's life savings. If the Vedmedivites had found out about Lysenko's discovery, then they would've spent the next few months talking about where Ychi had gotten all that money. 'You see, he's been ripping us off when we're down and out, living it up and putting away thousands of dollars!' they'd gripe. Therefore, Lysenko decided to spare the Vedmedivites' nerves and patriotically tucked the money away in his pocket.

Although, if you give it some thought, finding the cash under the mattress could've led the officer to draw a few conclusions; after all, that money was a testament to the fact that Ychi hadn't gone anywhere, not to mention the sheer greed of a gravedigger who wasn't ashamed of exploiting other people's grief. If a person that had been saving up for years suddenly decided to pick up and leave town, they probably would've taken the money with them before setting off into the unknown. So Ychi must have disappeared suddenly, due to something not even he had expected--he hadn't packed his things, planned his departure, or made any prior arrangements. Still, it was impossible to imagine that someone had kidnapped or killed Ychi – the gravedigger was so strong and so scary that death itself feared him. Whether the officer had considered that or not, he still had to run around town and take statements from people who knew Ychi. He gathered testimony from the employees at the Road to Paradise and the missing person's neighbors, and then it was time to head to the fountain.

One hot August afternoon, Staff Sergeant Lysenko came to the construction site in Vedmediv's central square so he could talk to the workers. When he started yanking on the door handle, Yosif Lendian stepped outside and told him that Ychi hadn't been around for a while.

'He left work one evening and then just didn't come back the next morning. That's it… Nah, nothing was stolen from the construction site, nothing went missing, and nothing strange happened either… Nothing seemed to be bothering Ychi. He just disappeared one day, just vanished into thin air.'

Much to the young sergeant's surprise, about five minutes into their conversation, Ihor Lendian came running over – then Zoltan Bartok, who looked bewildered and even frightened, showed up a few minutes after that. Once the mayor ascertained that the officer was merely gathering testimony about Ychi's disappearance, he loosened up and advised him to go look someplace else, where he wouldn't be impeding the construction of the Fountain of Unity, which would soon grace their fair city. Staff Sergeant Lysenko, surprised and confounded by the mayor appearing so quickly at the construction site, apologised for disturbing them and then headed to the station. Also, they couldn't do much talking there anyway; the powerful machine, which had been running non-stop all week, was buzzing so loudly that even the pigeons had abandoned the central square. The ground kept vibrating, as if Peace Square had turned into one gigantic anti-cellulite massager. So the officer, his conscience clean and his appetite for dollars satisfied, closed the case due to lack of evidence – nobody was looking for Ychi, nobody had reported any tragic news about him, and, after all, he was a big boy who could roam the globe at will without telling his colleagues, neighbors, or the police first. Soon enough, Ychi was no longer the talk of the town. Yeah, some guy disappeared, just up and left. So what? Someday, there'll be nobody left around here.

Tys wasn't too concerned about all this Ychi business. He knew that the gravedigger was in Kruchka's house. It sure was a shame that had happened to a hard-working, upstanding guy like him, though. The teacher still held out hope that, God willing, he would come out of his coma. Man, he'd be surprised to see how much progress they'd made on the tunnel! The Lendian brothers were right when they compared Ychi's efforts to a kid building a tree-house. What they had wasn't a real tunnel, more like a primitive ditch, like something dug by a medieval laborer. Not anymore!

Ihor and Yosif got to work right away. As promised, they filled up the old tunnel, which they'd dubbed 'a tapeworm-infested small intestine,' within a few days, and then began digging a new pit. Meanwhile, the Vedmediv City Council convened for a session where Zoltan Bartok delivered a spirited speech. He candidly admitted that the city was in dire straits, that a city in this condition should be ashamed to be in the centre of Europe, and that nobody flying overhead could see Vedmediv, which explained why no tourists had any idea their ancient settlement even existed. The mayor argued that this was due to the fact that their ancient European city was drowning in darkness. The flow of electricity downtown was so weak that switching on something as small as an electric teapot would blow fuses. They simply couldn't go on living like that – either the City Council members would back the mayor's resolution to allocate funds to purchase a new substation for downtown Vedmediv or he'd get really mad and not talk to anyone for a whole week.

Go big or go home. The City Council members exchanged glances, allocated the necessary funds from the budget, and then spent the next few weeks talking about the image that impressed them the most: a 747 flying at an altitude of 30,000 feet, the passengers' faces plastered against the windows; they're staring down at the ground because they know one of Europe's most ancient cities, smack dab in the center of the continent, is right below them, but all they see is black emptiness. Six days later, the fitters had started installing the new substation on one of the streets adjacent to Peace Square.

The heavy machinery came as soon as they'd hooked up the power. One morning in late July, the Vedmedivites, mouths agape, watched the gigantic machines roll into town. The workers transformed Peace Square, like a bunch of stagehands doing a scene change – first they tore down the fence around the construction site, then they removed the canopy, table, benches, and mounds of dirt and garbage. Finally, a crane picked up this crazy box thing off the back of a truck and lowered it right into the pit, the soon-to-be fountain. Then they unloaded an enormous drill, which looked like a self-tapping screw enlarged a thousand times. A few more trucks dumped hundreds of concrete pipe sections in the square; the workers arranged them in four separate stacks around the oak.

All this commotion attracted crowds of onlookers, both young and old. Grandmothers brought their grandchildren, drunkards and deadbeats retreated to the shade, beers in hand, mothers did laps around the square with their strollers, politicians, businessmen, and bureaucrats observed this miracle out the windows of City Hall, and Zoltan Bartok paraded around the construction site. Vedmedivites kept asking him questions about what all the pipe and machinery would be used for, but the haughty mayor just kept throwing out catchphrases about the fountain, building a new Europe, harmony in the home, and Vedmediv's prospects for the future. Then some old fogey, deciding to take a break from doing nothing, asked Bartok if the fountain was really going to be so powerful that the jets of water would reach the sky. I mean, what else would you need such massive pipes for? It wouldn't have been right to tell an elderly man off, so the mayor patiently explained that they'd be drawing water from the Tysa – for the municipal water supply, not just the fountain.

There was a decent proportion of insolent grumblers – there always are! – who are never pleased and bash every new idea. They moved from group to group, smiling sardonically and bemoaning the fact that the city was squandering the taxpayers' money and that the mayor had lost his marbles, building a fountain instead of adding a new wing to the hospital, remodelling the school, or patching up the roads.

'Just take one look at all that machinery – this ain't gonna be cheap. There's no way a crummy town like Vedmediv can afford this,' they'd say. The fountain had these venomous detractors all worked up. 'Our public bathroom downtown is just an outhouse, and it reeks so bad that people are afraid to go inside, so they just do their business *near* the facilities. It's like a mine field down there! People are going to come from all over Europe for the unveiling, but where are they supposed to relieve themselves – in the fountain?!' Much to Zoltan Bartok's credit, he didn't let any of those slanderous remarks get to him. As per usual, he called all of his opponents 'bought-and-paid-for foreign agents.' They let him have it, too, excoriating him as totally shameless – 'you spit in his eye and he will reply it's just dew from the sky.'

Everything was unloaded by evening. The trucks left, and then you could hear rhythmic hammer blows as a few workers started putting up a new fence. The construction site had expanded tremendously and now took up nearly the whole square. The mighty crown of the oak towered over everything, imperturbably observing the furious activity. By the next morning, the square had been fenced in with painstaking care, and the large photographs of old Vedmediv returned. Much to the Vedmedivites' surprise, yesterday's workers were now gone. They'd complained that City Hall should've hired Vedmedivites for such an extensive construction project, instead of bringing in bumbling outsiders all the way from Uzhhorod, but now they had to bite their tongues because there'd actually only be two guys on the job, Ihor and Yosif Lendian, and they were both locals. The machinery was state-of-the-art; hardly any manual labor was needed.

'Sounds about right,' the Vedmedivites thought. 'They're just building a fountain. This isn't rocket science.' They would've been even more surprised to hear that only one person, not two, was needed to operate the machine. Considering the expensive rental fees, it was decided that the Lendian brothers would work around the clock in two shifts to speed up the project. This is how it played out – in the morning, Yosif would feed sections of pipe into the machine, then it lowered them onto the ground and pushed them down the tunnel. One person would sit in a small booth and monitor the operation and direction of the drill using a system of cameras and lasers. You had to empty the truck full of wet soil twice during the day and once at night and feed new sections of pipe into the machine once a day – that's all there was to it. The machine did the rest, methodically gnawing into the soil and assembling the tunnel as it went.

The Lovat drilled the tunnel, foot by foot, without a hitch. Within just a few days, the mayor and his associates were confident they'd finish on schedule and send the first cart down the tunnel by Ukraine's Independence Day. Everything was going smoothly. They just had to switch off the machine once a week to re-equip it. Ihor would watch the monitor, while Yosif crawled into the tunnel. He'd hook up electric cables to the fittings in the tube, twist in light bulbs, and clamp the rails together to get them ready for the mini-train. Also, once a week – generally after sundown, so as not to attract too much attention – Zoltan Bartok, Icarus, the Succubus, the Genius of the Carpathians, and Tys would come to the construction site. They'd inspect the brothers' work and examine the map that displayed the newest stretch of tunnel, their eyes wide with wonder. Before they knew it, Ihor was inviting them over for a glass of champagne to celebrate crossing the Ukrainian border. Now their apparatus, which was parked under the oak in the central square of Vedmediv, was steering a drill gnawing away at Hungarian soil. They were jumping for joy!

Tys was full of childlike happiness; his idea had only appeared that spring, but it was rapidly coming to fruition. That fueled his delusions of grandeur, so now he could spend days at a time slumped over in the armchair in his study, imagining his future fame and his place in European history. He'd close his eyes and see a chapter entitled 'Tys' in 8th-grade textbooks all across the country. It would tell the story of the Silver Land's renowned son who gifted Ukraine to Europe. His house would turn into a museum offering audio tours in 20 languages. Nobody would be allowed to tidy up his room ever again so they could preserve the pristine chaos that inspired Mykhailo Chvak, better known as Tys, whose renowned name was derived from that mighty, yet elegant, eternal river.

For some reason, the history teacher relished thinking about his own funeral. He saw a 100,000-strong procession carrying his coffin through the streets of Vedmediv and then burying him near the entrance to the tunnel – his greatest and most important brain-child. Everyone would be crying during the prayer for the departed – Marichka would be crying and admonishing herself for the unkind words she'd said to her brilliant and loving husband; the mayor and the president of Ukraine would be crying since they'd realise there was no chance future generations would remember them; Silvika, the cashier at the liquor store who refused to sell him alcohol on numerous occasions and mocked his stories about the Kyivan counts would be crying; the head of the customs office would be crying because Tys was the only person who could outsmart him so devastatingly; the kids who once so rudely gave him the nick-name 'Carbide' would be crying; and Tys's breathless body would be crying, too, tears flowing, because he would be sorry to leave this world so young, when he still had so many plans, so many things he wanted to do for Ukraine!

Tys's days passed in sweet contemplation. Now he had absolutely nothing to do – the Lendian brothers had refused his offer to bring them lunch, and it was still summer break. Miraculously enough, even Marichka had stopped nagging him with her constant reproaches and discontent. It wouldn't be fair to say that harmony and tranquility had returned to their family, but she had been much more well-disposed towards her husband lately. She had no clue what was going on, though – Tys, bound by a vow of silence, hadn't confided in her. Just the fact that the teacher now rubbed elbows with respected businessmen and philanthropists (sure, they were smugglers, too, but whatever!), instead of drunkards, made less frequent visits to the town's bars and liquor stores, and had established friendly relations with the mayor himself, was enough to soothe her aching heart. Tys had clearly found some pursuit that had completely absorbed him, a project to which he'd wholly devoted himself, so Marichka didn't rebuff Tys when he asked her to make hearty lunches that he took to the construction site every day. Marichka didn't care to know how her husband had gotten involved in a project so utterly unrelated to his profession. After all, this was the first time Tys had acted more or less normal since Tremora's tragic death, so she kept off his back.

Now that the drilling machine had been installed, the tunnel had no use for Tys whatsoever. The teacher would just lie around and daydream, but he got sick of that pretty quickly, although he had tried to do some research. For instance, he calculated how many years it would take to get all of Ukraine's citizens into the European Union. His forecast wasn't too encouraging – if the Succubus took one cart exclusively for her own purposes and Mirca was going to be trafficking Pakistanis, then euro-integration would drag on for another year and a half. A tremendously ambitious project was coming to fruition right below the surface, and that made the partners a little antsy. So, when they got together for a glass of champagne to celebrate crossing the border into Hungary and Kruchka invited them over to her house for a little party that coming Sunday, everyone eagerly accepted.

The Genius of the Carpathians picked up Tys on Sunday evening, and then they headed towards the Succubus's house. The history teacher had put on his best suit – the white one – and he was holding some summer mums he'd picked from his garden. They wound up being perfect for the occasion, since it was Kruchka's birthday. She hadn't told anyone that, though. They exchanged some brief greetings and pleasantries – like the Succubus saying 'Don't bother taking off your shoes. It'll be easier to just vacuum the floors than spend two days airing the place out' – the guests sat down at the dinner table.

The luxurious décor was truly impressive. Tys didn't get where a doctor in Ukraine could find the money for the most expensive furniture and the most state-of-the-art appliances or how she could've paid for the artwork that filled each room. Or why she had decided to put a gold toilet in the guest bathroom. Was she just swimming in money? The best part of all that wealth was her endless variety of alcoholic beverages that the teacher had only seen in foreign movies. Surrendering to the celebratory mood, he poured himself grappa, Becherovka, Jägermeister, white rum, dark rum, bourbon, scotch, rye, red Italian wine, French rosé, prosecco, Serbian rakija, Bulgarian pelinkovac, Romanian tuica, Calvados, Armenian brandy, French Armagnac, absinth, Finnish vodka, Polish zubrowka, and Belgian beer in turn. Once he'd sampled them all, he settled on the plum-flavored Serbian beverage, since it was the closest thing to Vedmediv's traditional moonshines.

Lounging in their deep chairs, they were discussing their future prospects. A bit tipsy by that point, the Succubus said that she'd be able to buy a small island in Indonesia if she kept her cart running all year. Zoltan Bartok announced that once the tunnel was built, he'd step down as mayor and devote himself to beekeeping. He'd erect his own 100-hive apiary with its own therapy room. The bees would swarm below the bed; after all, their bio-fields heal people and slow the aging process. Icarus shared his plan to use the profits from the tunnel to pay off all the European politicians and get them to lift the public smoking ban, which would boost tobacco sales. And who would provide all of Europe's smokers with cheap ciga-rettes? Why, Icarus, of course! Now relaxed as could be and nearly supine in his chair, Tys dreamt about euro-integrating Ukraine by gradually taking all 40,000,000 Ukrainians through the tunnel, because they deserved it, because of Count Svyatoslav, because of all that stuff. The Genius of the Carpathians added amicably that it wouldn't hurt to euro-integrate Pakistan a little, too, which he planned to do in his own way.

Tys'd had a fair amount to drink, so he had to go the bathroom. He excused himself, and then stood there, his forehead resting against the wall, until a powerful jet smashed against the innards of the gold toilet. Once he'd finished and let out a grunt of satisfaction and relief, he decided to go downstairs, into the basement, where he and the Genius of the Carpathians had dropped off their poor friend Ychi two weeks earlier. Without saying anything to anyone, Tys plodded and zigzagged down the steps. Once he got to the bottom, he stepped inside the room where his injured companion should have been lying. Much to his surprise, the teacher didn't find anyone in there, although the life support machine was right where it had been before. Thinking he'd made some sort of mistake, Tys started opening all the doors, but every single room in the basement was completely empty. Actually, some of the doors led to gigantic fridges jam-packed with various kinds of meats. He was genuinely surprised that a delicate single lady like her could need such colossal food reserves. Tys headed back upstairs, poking his head into all the rooms he passed along the way, but the gravedigger was nowhere to be found. In the living room, the banquet was still going on; he interrupted it with a question.

'Where'd the patient... well, the gravedigger... um... you know, Ychi, go? I can't find him anywhere. I wanted to sit next to him and tell him how much progress we've made. I've heard that people can still hear everything when they're in a coma, and if he knew about how far we've come, that would give him extra strength to bounce back. So, I went down to where Mirca and I left him, but he wasn't there. The life support machine was there but Ychi wasn't!' Tys exclaimed, shrugging in drunken dismay.

'Don't worry, my dear. Our colleague's doing just fine. You could say I've already euro-integrated him,' the Succubus answered playfully.

'What do you mean?' the teacher asked, dumbfounded.

'A little here, a little there, bit by bit. First an arm, then a leg, and then the rest. So, he's already in Europe – he pulled ahead of the pack!' Kruchka cracked up, and then everyone else, except Tys, exploded with furious, roaring laughter.

Chapter 13:

In Which Reality Intertwines With Illusion

It was as though the ground had disappeared beneath his feet. Tys reached his chair on autopilot and collapsed into it like bird droppings landing on a coat painstakingly selected for a big date. He couldn't believe that Ychi was no longer with them. This all seemed like some terrible joke, some elaborate drunken prank or bad dream. He sat in his chair as if he were in a different reality, underneath a film of dark water that muffled all the light and sound around him. Loud, distant laughter eventually reached him, as if from another planet. He saw dark, blurry smudges in front of him – people's silhouettes – but his consciousness refused to accept that he was sitting next to them. His legs went weak, his pulse nearly disappeared, and cool, sticky sweat appeared on his forehead. Somewhere deep inside of him, he felt that an invisible centrifuge was starting to pick up speed, which elicited this queasy feeling that inched up towards his throat. Then suddenly someone insistently passed him a cigarette.

Tys latched onto it like a lifeline. Although he hardly ever smoked, he stuck it in his mouth, struggling to repel a volcano of murky puke, push it back inside. The thick smoke gripped his throat like a vice, constricted his esophagus, and made his ribcage lock up. This smoke was a little weird, much thicker than from his cheap Priluki or Prima cigarettes. It was acerbic, too. One drag paralysed his throat and dried up all his saliva, turning his mouth into a rancid desert. He grabbed his glass of rakija off the arm of his chair and dumped its contents into himself so he could come back to the real world and start breathing again.

Pleasant heat flowed through his body and scorched his taste buds, overpowering that dry, acerbic feeling in his mouth. The teacher started to feel so good that he took another drag – deeper and longer this time. Once again, his throat dried up and went numb, but this time it was thoroughly enjoyable, because every part of his body the smoke soothed had practically disappeared and ceased sending signals to the brain. Tys sat there, seemingly with no mouth, throat, or chest. He felt a faint burning sensation in the pit of his stomach, like it was crawling with ants. Actually, it was just the potent rakija continuing to caress his insides. He liked that feeling. He puckered his lips, readying himself for another drag, but somebody ripped the cigarette out of his hand. Tys slowly turned his head, like a robot, and saw that the Genius of the Carpathians was smoking it now. He pushed out his lips, closed his eyes, and held the cigarette – it was a hand-rolled one, dark gray paper – prudently, with the tips of two fingers.

Meanwhile, somebody poured Tys more rakija, and he immediately emptied it into himself and then kicked back in his chair. He started to feel positively celestial. He closed his eyes, soaking it all up. Time sprawled out, and every thought lasted an eternity. It seemed like he'd been sitting there for vast swathes of time, listening intently to his inner universe. That queasy feeling had receded, giving way to cosmic weightlessness. Voices were coming from somewhere far away. The teacher listened hard, intrigued, and then felt that he was suddenly all ears, just a big seashell sucking in all the sounds like a black hole, and the sounds were accompanied by the awesome din engendered by the universe. This is what Tys heard:

'Marijuana's dope, real cool stuff, that's for sure. But there's something else that hit me so much harder,' the Succubus said in a confiding tone. 'I went to Amsterdam two years ago. I've got a couple clients over there who like buying corneas wholesale. But that's not what I'm getting at. So, I headed to Amsterdam. I decided to do a few days of exploring once I took care of my business. This was in April, early April, so it was pretty warm, but hanging around outside all day wasn't exactly tons of fun. Well, I walked around the city and went up and down the canals on a yacht. It's really beautiful there. All the houses are well-kept and everything's real clean. Also, it's really nice how everybody minds their own business. My associates were so courteous, they even agreed to keep me company and show me around. They suggested we go to some museums. You know, Rembrandt and Vermeer or whatever his name is, but I didn't feel like doing that. Then they suggested we go to the Red Light District. That sounded fun. I'd heard a lot about it. Honestly, it was a pretty big letdown. It was just a few narrow streets with half-naked women sitting in windows – and they're generally kinda old and ugly. They spin around so provocatively, twisting and turning, and beckon to you, but I only saw one person actually go inside in the twenty minutes I was walking around. It seems like people generally just go there to goof around and gawk at the girls. Basically, just wankers and tourists hang around there, but they don't have the guts to actually get a hooker.'

'I was disappointed. My associates invited me to a coffee shop to perk me up – in Holland, they sell soft drugs there. I hope you know that Holland and the Netherlands are the same country, nobody else seems to, ha-ha. So, we went into the coffee shop. They sell single joints there or just marijuana and hash by the gram. We each got a joint and a cup of coffee and lit up, which calmed me down a bit. I went up to the counter and started looking at their selection – there were dozens of different kinds of joints, as well as some strange boxes and Ziploc bags. I asked what was inside. Turns out, it was mushrooms. Nah, not champignons or Carpathian boletuses – hallucinogenic mushrooms. There were these colored slips of paper on the boxes. The colors showed how strong they were. For instance, they recommend beginners start with the green ones. Everything was so nicely sorted – they had packs of 2, 3, or 5 grams.'

'I was just dying to try them, and my associates were all for it. We bought a 5-gram bag for next to nothing – something like fifteen or twenty Euros. It isn't a great idea to take shrooms in public, so we headed over to the condo I was renting. We split the shrooms four ways – for me and the three guys I was with – and started chewing. They didn't taste great, but it's not like they were gross. Didn't taste like anything really, just a tad sour. We chewed them like they were gum for about ten minutes. It was strange, but nothing was happening, nothing changed. I was starting to think we'd been ripped off, but my associates told me everything was fine, we just had to wait a half hour or so.'

'Well, so I waited. I was sitting at a wooden table, checking out my nails, when I suddenly saw it was no regular old table. Bright flames – really colorful – started glowing in the grain of the wood. I looked at them intently, absolutely dumbfounded, until the image totally engrossed me. I saw this highway, somewhere out by San Francisco. The night was black, the sky was dark blue, and the stars were bright – fireworks were exploding and gushing like fountains in between them. Incredible sports cars were flying by, faster than the speed of light, leaving their own red and white glow in their wake. There were palm trees all around me, with myriad flashes of signs for casinos and night clubs beyond them. Everything was so real and so sublime that I nearly lost my mind from the sheer luxury of it all. I lifted my head and saw that my guests were seeing things too. Each of them was looking in a different direction, their eyes entranced, yet focused. I shifted my gaze to the light bulb up by the ceiling.'

'Light was flowing out of it in pulses, in colored waves, like a rainbow. It reminded me of the circles on French Renaissance dresses – the light was looping around the bulb. It was so wonderful. All the colors in the room grew more intense, more beautiful. The thing is, I was still completely with it. Nothing scary was going on or anything. I was moving around the room just fine and talking to people like normal. I just saw everything differently – it was all sharper, more distinct. I wouldn't call those mushrooms hallucinogenic; they just heighten your senses by about a million times. It's like you have butterfly vision. I bet artists could use them—'

'Oh, I can tell you a thing or two about hallucinations,' Mirca said slowly, his tone relaxed.

'Wait a sec, I wasn't finished. When you're on shrooms you see everything like you're a butterfly or a dolphin. Your perception of sound changes, too. So, about an hour later, I decided to put on some music. Nobody was saying anything because we were all tripping balls. Everyone was in their own dimension. I couldn't find the TV remote, so I just played some music on my phone. It was one of Zemfira's old albums. Oh Lord, it was just sublime! I lay down on the bed and closed my eyes. The music was celestial. I felt like I could completely tune out reality, drown myself in her voice, just let it swallow me up. The strangest thing was that when I closed my eyes I didn't go tumbling back into darkness – it was still there, the sky above San Francisco and the colored explosions of light, and I could distinctly see a control panel, like the one on Winamp. There were some dials, like on a radio, labelled "voice", "guitar", "drums", and "piano".'

'So, I was lying there and I could turn them with my eyes and adjust the music in my head. For instance, I could turn the voice dial and just hear Zemfira singing or turn the piano dial and make the keys produce a more intense sound. I've never heard anything better, and Zemfira's been my favorite singer ever since. I've never felt music like that before. They say that you should go to the opera when you're on shrooms – the symphony orchestra and the high, powerful voices give you unforgettable joy. I didn't go to the opera, though. Instead, my guests saw I was in bed, so they came on over and started undressing me, and I kept listening to Zemfira, and she filled me up just like those Dutch guys. That was some sublime sex, like true art or something. I thought about taking shrooms again, but I never wound up doing it. I know we have them in Transcarpathia – they grow out in the polonynas by Perechyn. People gather them and eat them, and they have the same effect as the Amsterdam ones, but I never had the guts to try them. After all, I'm in the medical field, so I realize how important it is to have the right concentration and dosage. There I was, these Hutsuls gave me forty or fifty little shrooms and told me to start chowin' down. I was too afraid. Now Amsterdam, that's a whole 'nother thing – colored labels, government labs doing quality control, 2–3 gram doses. Boy, I'd love to try them again!'

'Sounds awesome,' Mirca said the instant Kruchka had finished her story. 'I tried some hallucinogens one time, much heavier ones, though. Don't ever want to again. That was a long time ago, I was still a real young guy. That's when you want to try everything. My buddies and I mostly drank moonshine back then… because we didn't have the money for real vodka. We'd drink ourselves silly, even senseless sometimes. There was a rumor going around town that a guy we knew had gotten hooked on drugs. That sounded cool. I asked him, and he told me that he didn't do drugs – he didn't have the money for them, and back then none of us knew where to get them anyway. His product was all natural, Ukrainian-grown. Its name says it all – 'devil's weed.' It grows right along the road. The thing is, you gotta pick it before it blooms. What you want is the seeds, and they're inside the flower. You can get about one or two hundred out of each one. First you dry them out a bit, then you just chew 'em. That's what my buddy told me. Then he hooked me up with some seeds – a whole bagful. He said you're supposed to have about thirty seeds at a time, no more.'

'Then the world changes, and the trip takes over. I was so into it. I had thirty of them as soon as I left his place. I was walking home, but nothing was happening. Then I figured that given my body mass, I probably needed more for them to have any effect on me. So I ate another dozen or so. Nothing. That got me so worked up that I popped another twenty in my mouth. It all started a few minutes later. That was the worst night of my life – the scariest, that is. I lost all control over myself. It was like I was a character in a computer game and I was just watching myself. It was so terrifying. I was just walking along and then suddenly I saw snakes! They were coiling up by my feet! And tons of different ones were slithering up my legs. But the scariest thing was the way they were staring right at me, their eyes empty, extinguished.'

'My heart was pounding. I ran down the street towards my house, hopping over the snakes, blind to everything else. I'm telling you; it was like a computer game – the road, the snakes, my legs, and everything around me was like props on a stage. The buildings on both sides of the street looked like dark plywood smudges. The trees were flat. Nothing in that image was moving, though – nothing besides me and the snakes. I ran home – front door locked. Oddly enough, the key wasn't underneath the vase on the windowsill. That scared me, so I punched out the window and climbed inside. I ran into my room, hopped in bed, and pulled the covers over my head. But there was this lingering fear, and these noises, some ultra-high frequency sounds grating on my ears. It felt like ants and spiders were crawling on my skin. I abruptly threw the sheets off me and got out of bed. There were all kinds of devilish creatures all around me – ants, rodents, snakes, and rows of bats hanging from the light fixture and the curtain rod.'

'Thing is, it wasn't actually my house. I raced back and forth between the rooms, but I didn't recognise anything. None of the furniture looked familiar. It seemed like I'd lost my mind or gone on to the other side. I punched out another window – this time in another room, because I couldn't find the way I'd come in – and climbed outside. I saw that this wasn't my street. This house was at the end of the row, like mine, but it was the wrong street. Partisan Street – where I lived – ran parallel to this one. I darted home, and the nightmare kept raging all around me. Once I got to my room, I closed all the doors and windows, grabbed a knife – just in case – put it under my pillow, and then lay down on the bed. It felt like it was gradually starting to wear off. At the very least, I wasn't as scared anymore and I had a better handle on reality. An odd fatigue came over my eyes, I was really sleepy all of a sudden. As I was falling asleep, I looked at the Weeping Madonna of Mariapocs icon hanging on the wall across from me. She looked at me, her eyes turned sorrowful, and then blood started trickling out of them. I watched it happen, like I was in a trance. The last thing I remember about that night was a little black beetle crawling out of her ear. It kept shaking its head, making its antennae tremble – ugh, they were like hairs in some vile mustache. That was the scariest and darkest day of my life. I was absolutely fine when I woke up the next morning, but I never touched that stuff again. And I wouldn't try it if I were you. It's horrible, terrible, frightening… it's like the hell that's inside all of us. You take it and all your fears come spilling out.'

'You're an odd bunch, poisoning your bodies with all that junk,' Zoltan Bartok said, shrugging. 'Trying something I know is bad for me has never even crossed my mind, although I have the money and my position would allow me to get banned substances easily. But no, I just don't like that stuff. It's gross! I like things that taste good. A glass of the cold stuff – now that's what I call getting high. I just look at it, covet it. And then bam! – I dump it in me. It goes so well with pickles, a piece of Borodinsky bread, smoked salo, and spicy ajika. M-m-m, delicious! You could say I'm a man who appreciates the finer points of drinking. Yeah, I've been known to get a little rowdy and do some shameful, regrettable things. Especially in my younger days. But I've been around the block, and now I know my limits – I call it quits once I fall down! There's nothing better than coming home after a hectic day at work and enjoying a bottle with some greasy, spicy food. I've been known to throw a few back at work, too – you've witnessed it yourselves, no point in hiding that – but I keep it classy and I never overdo it. I like when things look and taste good. That's why I serve pickled tomatoes on porcelain saucers with dessert forks. That's the top-grade stuff! This marijuana of yours didn't even faze me! Better have some more vodka!'

'Seems like it's already hit me. Smoking was a good call. My body's nice and relaxed, I feel so calm. I'm listening to you guys and soaking it all up. Let's have another hit,' Icarus suggested. The Succubus grabbed the joint, took the first drag, and then passed it. Icarus took a hit and continued. 'You're talking about all kinds of drugs, but I'm just sitting here, listening – and the whole time I can't get our tunnel out of my head. I close my eyes and see it like it's a movie – a big tunnel with trains, carts, trucks, people, planes, and rockets whizzing back and forth. In our very own Vedmediv, under the big oak tree. There's a train station underground, just like the one in Vienna. And I'm overseeing all of it and collecting tribute. I send off my product and then carts of cash come back. And all of it is mine. Just like that guy we read about in school who could ride his horse for days on end and everything he could see belonged to him.'

'Everything belongs to all of us,' the Genius of the Carpathians corrected him graciously. 'I find myself picturing an endless procession walking into the tunnel under the oak and disappearing underground. And the cash keeps flowing. Soon our tunnel will be the main way out of Vedmediv, believe me. There'll be more people going out of the city that way than on the Uzhhorod highway, you'll see!'

'I believe you!' Tys interjected. The grass and rakija had erased the image of Ychi's hideous demise from his mind. 'I can see it, too. This won't be the first time in human history people have taken a tunnel out of a city, though. Not too long ago, just down the road – in the former Yugoslavia – people built a tunnel to escape from besieged Sarajevo. That was the longest and most horrifying siege since World War II. The Serbs had that city in a vice for over three years. People were left without electricity, water, and basic necessities. There were only two ways out of Sarajevo. Taking to the skies – to heaven, to God, by dying – or going underground – into the tunnel the people had dug to flee, to save themselves. Just like our tunnel will help Ukraine flee from Russia to Europe.'

'Well, that's how Ukraine'll get into Europe, doing it all ass-backwards,' the mayor said, trying to make a joke out of the whole thing. 'We'll do euro-integration like everything else – illegally. We'll smuggle it through.'

'Incidentally, smuggling is as old as the hills,' Tys said, growing increasingly animated. 'In *Candide: Optimism*, perhaps Voltaire's most popular work, he even described people's various orifices being inspected at certain borders in Europe. In other words, border guards would stick their fingers up people's cornholes to check if they were carrying valuables across the border illegally.'

'Huh, guess nothing's changed. Our border guards'll turn your soul inside out!' Icarus added, and everyone nodded approvingly.

'This may surprise you even more, but Voltaire actually alluded to our neck of the woods, to Transcarpathia,' the teacher said, aiming to pique his listeners' interest. 'The heroine's name in *Candide* is Cunegonde. The infatuated protagonist is searching for her high and low and then finally finds her down in Istanbul, where she's working for a certain Frances Rakoczi, a Transylvanian prince in exile, as he's described by Voltaire. He's actually referring to Ferenc Rakoczi, at least that's what we call him here in Transcarpathia. The Transcarpathian Hungarian Institute in Berehove bears his name. He's a local. He was born not too far from Uzhhorod, although his hometown is now part of Slovakia. And Voltaire himself wrote about him! He has Cunegonde washing Ferenc Rakoczi's dishes – in other words, Candide's beloved is a Transcarpathian gentleman's servant!'

'Oh, wow!' Zoltan Bartok exclaimed. 'I know about Rakoczi. He's a national hero. Well, for us Magyars. But I hadn't heard that Voltaire wrote about him.'

'Yes, he's Hungary's national hero because he led a war of independence against the Habsburgs.' Tys continued in his customary history teacher mode. 'He spent his childhood in Transcarpathia. He grew up in Mukachevo Castle. In 1703, he boldly led a people's rebellion to throw off the Viennese yoke. At first, roughly half of his army was recruited from the Rusyn/Ukrainian population of Transcarpathian. Then later on, after he liberated more territory, a greater number of Hungarians joined his forces. They had remarkable success – his army managed to liberate Transylvania, and Ferenc Rakoczi was immediately elected ruling prince. The French backed him in his struggle against Vienna. They even officially provided him with arms. So it's no wonder that Voltaire knew about him. Rakoczi was poised to become the head of the Confederated Estates of the Kingdom of Hungary, a state independent of Habsburg rule. This rebellion and his quasi-state had a long history – eight whole years, all the way up to 1711. Then Rakoczi fled and drifted from country to country, eventually settling in Turkey, near Istanbul. And Voltaire writes about his exile there and makes Cunegonde his servant.'

'What a goofy name. It sounds like the French for cunnilingus,' the Succubus said, bursting out laughing, but nobody responded to her joke.

'There's one more Transcarpathian reference in Voltaire's story,' Tys continued. 'There's a lake in Solotvyno called Cunegonde. That's where the old salt mines used to be. Those mines are really old, and they've always been essential to this part of Europe, so it's possible people had heard about them in France. Lakes eventually formed where the deepest mines were. The water's just like the Dead Sea. The place is a resort now. Lots of those lakes are fed by hot springs, so the water's toasty, even in the wintertime.'

'We know. Just about every Transcarpathian has been there. It's sweet!' Icarus concurred.

'But Cunegonde is famous for other reasons, too,' Tys said, his voice suddenly grim. 'During World War II, the Germans would take Gypsies to those white salt mines and shoot them. A good number of Gypsies still live around here, but there used to be several times more. Everyone knows that the Hitlerites wanted to wipe Jews off the face of the earth, but hardly anyone knows that if the Nazis had carried their program through to completion, there wouldn't be a trace of the European Gypsies left today. For Jews, it's called the Holocaust, while for the Gypsies it's the Porajmos. So, the Germans, assisted by Miklos Horthy's troops, caught the local Gypsies and brought them to Cunegonde. It was a harsh winter that year. They lined the Gypsies up on the edge of the old mine shafts and shot them. Their bodies fell in. Eventually, there were tons of them piled up. But later on, the occupiers were ordered to get rid of the bodies, to bury them away from prying eyes. They went to the mines during a record-breaking cold snap. It was fifteen below, so the Gypsies' corpses were rock hard, and they were covered with white hoarfrost and a light dusting of salt. They looked like ice sculptures or something out of a fairytale. The extreme cold had kept their bodies from decomposing, so it seemed like they were alive, but frozen stiff. It was an eerie spectacle. The Fascists made the local villagers gather the bodies, one of them wrote about it in his memoirs years later. He mentioned that the bodies were so hard it felt like they were tossing lumber into the back of the truck. When the truck was nearly all filled up, they placed some bodies against the sides, forming a fence of sorts. Then they threw more bodies in. Can you picture that? There's this truck driving along and these white, frost-covered bodies, like in *Snow White*, propped up or just lying there in the back like logs. Gives you the chills!'

'Well, I heard that they have some pretty exotic ways of dying these days, too,' said Zoltan Bartok. 'A ton of Gypsies live in these parts, by Tiachiv, and a lot of them are very wealthy. They're millionaires, actually – they made their fortune smuggling. There are these enormous, 100-room palaces in a few villages along the way to Yaremche. They belong to the local Gypsy barons. Now *they* look like something out of a fairytale: towers, triumphal arches instead of gates, balconies the size of a gym. When one of those Gypsy barons dies, they dig an underground house for him, instead of a grave. It has everything down there: bed, TVs, table, fully stocked fridge, paintings, and pictures of his family. And they place the deceased's cell phone – charged and turned on – by his bed. That way, he can call his family if he wants. Then they put down stones and toss dirt on top of everything.'

'Yeah, that's true. The thing is, Gypsies' souls, which they call 'mulo,' don't die right away. They keep living for some time, so their relatives try to provide them with whatever they may need. Death is definitely not the end for Gypsies,' Tys added with a grave, pensive air. The marijuana was gradually wearing off, but the alcohol was pressing on his prostate, so the teacher was squirming in his chair and repeatedly cracking his long fingers. He had to go to the bathroom, but he was afraid to go off on his own; after all, the lonely soul of Ychi, an innocent man so recently murdered, was roaming around somewhere nearby.

Chapter 14:

In Which the Action Unfolds a Week Before
the Unveiling of the Fountain of Unity

On Monday, August 17th, 2015, Vedmedivites were just carrying on with their lives as usual. Those with jobs had gotten going bright and early. Those without jobs were just drifting around town. The men were sitting on coffee shop patios, brazenly monopolizing their tables as they sipped one cup for hours. A southern atmosphere – the kind suited for leisure, laziness, and motionless contemplation – reigned over everything. It wasn't the least bit unusual to see someone just standing in the middle of the street and staring off into space. In the summertime, Vedmedivites often spent more time in cafes than at work. The heat was so oppressive that even the flies wouldn't take flight, and the pesky mosquitoes only dared to come out during the cooler evening hours.

Transcarpathia doesn't just owe its juicy Southern feel to its fair climate; there's a certain geographical element to it, too. After all, there are the Carpathian Mountains that keep cold winds out of the valley, so spring comes to the region much more quickly – by the second half of February – and autumn recedes much more slowly. There really isn't much of a winter to speak of – snow and chilly weather never last longer than a few days at a time, so generally Vedmediv rings in the New Year amid light drizzle and dirty slush, giving the impression of a thaw. Summer temperatures rival those in Greece or Italy, so it's odd that people don't grow lemons, oranges, or olives in these parts.

Moreover, the natural geographical barrier of the Carpathian Mountains to the north has created an exotic cultural phenomenon in Transcarpathia. It feels like the most Balkan part of Ukraine. Like Bukovina, this really is the South, and the people have the mindset to match. One should note that they're significantly closer to the Balkan Peninsula than the Crimean Peninsula. Even prior to the arrival of the Slavs, nomadic shepherds roamed the local mountain ranges, transmitting knowledge, news, languages, culture, and diseases. Now hardly anyone acknowledges that 'vatra,' a word used by Hutsuls and residents of Verkhovyna that means 'hearth,' actually came from Proto-Albanian. It's easier to recognise musical or culinary similarities, though. If a Serb were ever to find himself at a Transcarpathian wedding, he'd feel right at home; greasy, spicy food, various types of paprika, alcohol made from whatever fruit is at hand – it's about the same from Uzhhorod all the way down to the southernmost Greek islands. Also, years of Hungarian rule brought Transcarpathians closer to the Balkan peoples. Transcarpathian Ukrainians and Slovaks lived on one side of the kingdom, while on the other side, the pecking order looked roughly like this: Balkans, Yugoslavs, Serbs, and then Croats. The two Slavic islands on opposite sides of the empire simply had to come together, combining their efforts to strengthen their position at the royal court in Budapest.

The Balkans… where there's no such thing as a wedding without a murder, where they fire guns straight into the air when a son is born, where they don't drink all that often, but when they do, they go to the brink of death, where men's skin is black from working under the baking sun and their hands are big, yet nimble, where it's hard to tell a streak of gray hair from road dust that's settled on someone's head, where a vagrant breeze is always blowing, so people walk around with cotton stuffed in their ears so they don't fall ill from the draft whipping through the door between

East and West, between warm and cold – and between North and South, too – the South where they serve up an enormous hunk of onion and a slice of bread with your two-egg breakfast, where everyone eats garlic, so its smell is tenacious and omnipresent – they eat it because it tastes good, because it protects them from various ailments, and because it fends off demons and vampires.

The Balkans is a land of extremes and emotional rifts. On the one hand, there's that lazy, drowsy disposition of theirs. Sometimes people just sit there and stare at the mountains all day. Or they watch the travelers whizzing down the road, who, in turn, write in their journals that 'the locals are all so strange and apathetic. The men can just stand outside for hours and look at the horizon, their arms crossed on their chests. And the only thing they'll do that whole time is spit, though they do it rather skeptically, which probably symbolises their contempt for this world.' Then, on the other hand, there's their incredible cruelty – or maybe it's happiness. If they decide to fight, there won't be a single living soul left, including the unborn children in women's wombs. If they decide to party, they go until they pass out, sobbing and laughing at the same time.

It's a common belief there that happiness is actually two-fold, dualistic. Combining joy with sorrow, pleasure with pain, is the greatest source of happiness. One should probably search for the roots of this idea in Iranian Manichaeism, which rolled through the Balkans back in the day, along with foreign conquerors, and then migrated farther north – in altered form – all the way up to Transcarpathia. Whatever the case may be, Good and Evil, Light and Darkness, are perceived as being inseparable in their dialectical unity, their endless battle of opposites. So at a man's happiest moment – for instance, at a feast celebrating the birth of his son – he seeks to combine euphoria with pain to feel the highest degree of pleasure. He drinks, and when the alcohol begins to numb his feelings, he grabs two glasses, grips them in his palms, and then slams them on the table, so the shards cut into his hands. That way, he achieves one of the most sophisticated forms of ecstasy – he's so happy he could sing, but he's bleeding and crying from the burning pain. This is the culmination, the moment of truth, the quintessence of the Balkans. Extremes, frenzied outbursts – either lazy apathy or frantic joy, mixed with cruelty and pain.

Moreover, this marvellous geographical and philosophical unit is the land of oblivion. There are various explanations for this, one being that their many centuries as occupied peoples under an imperial yoke left them without schools, universities, or an educated class, so there was nobody to attend to history. Memory was destroyed, burned out, scraped bare with knives and swords, giving way to assimilation and propaganda. A simpler interpretation may suffice, too. Perhaps there's just no such thing as memory here. Life is so hard, so bleak that you immediately want to forget each passing day, just get hammered at night so you won't remember anything the next morning. You may come across some dream diaries written by residents of Warsaw, Stockholm, or Hamburg, but it's highly unlikely you'll find one by someone from Bucharest, Ljubljana, or Uzhhorod. In these parts, dreams fade into oblivion the moment before waking; they fly off people's eyelids, never to return.

If anyone could understand that, it was Tys – after all, he was both a historian and a Vedmedivite. Oblivion consumed everything here, reduced it to an incoherent mash that looked like dirty winter slush. People around here didn't know how to take pride in themselves and remember important events or heroic figures. This may have been because it was too hard to figure out who was who. The peoples that inhabited these mountains and valleys had intermingled so much that they'd lost their primal visage. Two world wars and modern nationalism forced everyone to make choices. Which side are you on, buddy? Who are you? Paradoxically enough, Jews and Gypsies had it the easiest – at first, anyway – which then made their situation the toughest during the Holocaust and the Porajmos, because they definitely knew who they were. And everyone else did, too. But what was a guy like Mykhailo, who had Czechs, Serbs, Hungarians, Germans, Slovaks, and Romanians in his family tree, yet considered himself Ukrainian, supposed to do? When the sword of war hovered over the Transcarpathians, they had to choose an identity, which meant choosing an ethnicity, a set of heroes, and a version of history.

Consequently, many people got the short end of the stick. Take the world-renowned composer Bela Bartok, for instance. He hailed from Vedmediv. He had a Hungarian name, but he wrote music that crossed ethnic lines. After all, is it even possible to write home-grown music that belongs solely to one people? He gathered up folk songs and remade them for symphony orchestras, and then the melodies that played at weddings in Vedmediv were performed at the best philharmonic societies in the world. Once the young Bartok figured out he couldn't advance professionally here, he set out on a journey towards international recognition – going through Bratislava, Vienna, Paris, and eventually winding up in the USA, where he composed for the Boston Symphony Orchestra for many years. None of that meant anybody in Vedmediv would remember he existed, let alone try to commemorate him. There was simply nobody to do it. The Hungarian Vedmedivites couldn't consider him a purely Hungarian composer because his music had a rich Slavic, Ukrainian sound to it. The Ukrainians, in turn, were in no rush to call somebody with the name Bartok a national hero. He brought Ukrainian melodies to the world stage. But did that matter? A Magyar's still a Magyar.

So, nobody actually wanted to take the composer's memory under their protection, because as soon as the Hungarians started showering him with praise the Ukrainians would remind them reproachfully that his music was Ukrainian at its core. If the Ukrainians started taking ownership of Bartok, the Magyars would shove his ethnicity in their faces. But can a genius really belong to just one people? Those who rise above borders and break the mold face a tough fate in this part of the world, in Central Europe, where every discussion ends in conflict. So it's best not to start any conversations at all, just forget it. That's roughly what happened to Bartok – people steered clear of him, because they didn't want to take any flak. Consequently, Vedmediv didn't have a Bartok Street or a monument to him, and his pieces were no longer played at local holiday events. In Boston, however, there was a monument to him, as well as a Bela Bartok Music Festival and even a philharmonic orchestra named in his honor. This makes perfect sense, because there weren't any Magyars or Ukrainians fighting over his legacy. They could've enriched themselves by recognizing they shared something sublime, precious, and brilliant.

Tys had considered writing an article for the *Vedmediv Star* about Bartok to advocate for naming a street in his honor and putting a bust of him downtown. Initially, he was hesitant to do so because this would only fuel the Magyars' conceit. They still considered Vedmediv 'their' city, like true imperialists, although they'd never been the majority population here. Tys didn't want to earn himself a reputation as a traitor to his fellow Ukrainians who sold out for a 30-hryvnia honorarium. Instead, he continued going to the bar to shower praise on Counts Svetoslav and Ihor – who'd never set foot in Transcarpathia.

There was no way the teacher would take a stand for the composer now. Vedmediv isn't all that big, so there was only enough room for one person to go down in history, and that person had to be Mykhailo Oleksiyovych Chvak, better known as Tys. In the future, all of Vedmediv's streets and public institutions were to be linked somehow to his name or biography. Nevertheless, deep down, Tys had always felt a certain kinship with the composer, primarily because any person with a strong personality has to swim against the current, do things differently than everyone else. While everyone else was cashing in on their smuggling schemes and thinking only about money, Tys was leading the life of a poor teacher who put Ukraine's needs before his own. He justified being such a loser by claiming he was remarkable in some way. He presented Bartok, who immersed himself in music, instead of going into business or public service, which eventually made him immortal, as a justification. Who today remembers the names of the customs officers, notaries, and mayors who governed this area a hundred years ago? Nobody. But in Boston… And it was all because Bartok swam against the current.

Incidentally, this metaphor dredged up some less than pleasant memories for Tys. Way back when, his father Oleksa, named after Ukraine's national hero and avenger Oleksa Dovbush, demonstrated the formula for a happy and tranquil existence to his son. It was late May, the time of year when the heat isn't so unbearable and people can still enjoy being outside. Their whole family had decided to make a day of swimming in the Tysa, at a picturesque spot much loved by Vedmedivites. The water in the Tysa – a crucial artery that connects Transcarpathia and the Balkans, since it empties into the Danube down in Serbia – was warm and clean. The boy's father called him over, saying he wanted to show him something.

'Let's see who can swim against the current the longest, alright?' Oleksa Chvak proposed. The man and his teenage son, who were roughly the same height, waded into the water up to their chests. They turned to face the current and then started swimming at Oleksa's signal. Tys seemed to be doing fine at first, but then the current started to take over, sapping his strength. No matter how hard the young man tried, no matter how much he exerted himself, the best he could do was keep himself from drifting down the river. His arms turned to stiff wood, then to heavy zinc; he just couldn't lift them anymore. He just couldn't get enough air into his lungs, and his mouth and nose kept drawing in the water that swirled around him as if he were a rock by the shore. Once Tys had exhausted his last ounce of strength, he let his feet land on the bottom of the river and looked at his father, who burst out laughing and said that he wasn't tired at all because he'd tricked Tys. He'd actually been standing the whole time, just bending his knees a little and paddling to make it look like he was swimming. He gave Tys, who'd fought the current, quickly run out of steam, and then given up, a smug look.

'Never swim against the current, ever!' Oleksa said. 'Remember, son, if somebody challenges you, turn them down right away, because even if you win, you'll still be a fool and you won't achieve anything. Swimming against the current is pointless. Go with the flow, that's how you get moving, that's how you get faster and stronger. There's some real-life wisdom for you.'

Tys remembered his father's guidance, although he thought it was for philistines and conformists, a guiding principle for wimps and cowards. Admittedly, that's the kind of guy his father was. He willingly served whoever was in power and never expressed his opinion. Well, he never actually had one to begin with. Average people don't have their own opinions; they're merely tools in the hands of a few individuals with the drive to change the world. Individuals like Tys.

That's what the teacher was thinking about as he rolled his bike out of the barn on that nice summer morning, Monday, August 17th, a week before Ukraine's Independence Day and the unveiling of the Fountain of Unity. He pinned up his pant leg, put on a jacket and hat (even during a heat wave Vedmedivites value sophistication above all), and headed towards Peace Square to see how things were coming along. Tys's role had been curtailed once the Lendian brothers came on board. Now he was just the man who'd come up with the idea. Nobody wanted or expected anything from him anymore. Even Marichka's lunches – and she sure was a fabulous cook! – were of no interest to Ihor or Yosif. All Tys could do was sink into swampy idleness and devote all his time to daydreaming about his forthcoming glory and grandeur.

After all, he didn't even really have anyone to talk to. All of his associates were busy attending to their own business, so they hardly got together anymore. The mayor would stop by the Lendian brothers' booth every day, since they were nearing the end of the project. Being unable to talk, brag, or share his thoughts and dreams with anyone else was burning Tys up. He couldn't even confide in his darling Marichka because she had a remarkably big mouth. Her cousin, who worked in the advertising department at a regional newspaper, once joked that she'd recommend Marichka's services to her clients.

'Even if you put up 10 enormous billboards all around town, not everyone will get the message. But if you tell Marichka and make sure to add 'don't tell anybody, though,' a few times, everyone in the whole city, even newborn children at the hospital, will know within two hours! My cousin is more effective than any billboard. Just whisper something in her ear and ask her not to say anything,' she laughed.

Someday, Tys would certainly tell his wife about his grand tunnel project, but only when the timing was just right. Not quite yet. Not right now. For the time being, he had to keep everything under wraps, although he was itching to tell someone! Luckily, Marichka had never been all that interested in the project. She asked Tys several times why he'd been hanging around the fountain so much, but he merely scoffed at her and replied that he whole-heartedly supported the building of the Fountain of Unity, a most monumental undertaking for the city, that he came up with the idea, and that the city government was backing him. Marichka didn't buy Tys's boastful account, but she was still glad he had something to do and, at the very least, wasn't drunk every day.

The teacher was pedalling vigorously, yet making little headway, which only reaffirmed the old Vedmediv saying about biking, 'your butt's ridin' and your legs are walkin'.' The central square was empty. It was time for the city's afternoon siesta, and most Vedmedivites had opted to retire to their cool abodes. There was a monotone buzzing coming from behind the fence, where the machine was indefatigably drilling a tunnel the length of Tys's dream. After he'd looked around to make sure the coast was clear, he opened the gate with his own key, darted inside, and then quickly shut the door behind him. Everything looked much tidier and more professional than it had under the late Ychi. A control room of sorts had been set up under the oak, with Ihor and Yosif Lendian working at the computer. Next to it, three-foot pipe sections had been stacked and arranged in three rows. There were a lot fewer of them than at the start of the project, since most of the tunnel had already been completed. Two trucks and the machine that cleaned the soil – the naïve Vedmedivites took the stream of water gushing out of it to be the future fountain – were parked off to the left. The actual basin of the Fountain of Unity, which was admittedly rather crude, lay on the ground next to a statue of a beautiful woman, who was supposed to symbolise Europe – water would pour out of her mouth, ears, and bosom. In the corner, in the most inconspicuous spot, cars for the future train hid from the big, wide world in two gigantic crates.

Yosif was in the control room. Tys's arrival didn't elicit much of a response. Sure, they nodded at each other and said 'hello,' but it was clear that the taciturn builder wasn't exactly dying to strike up a conversation. The teacher felt like the builders, as well as the rest of the team, were always mocking him, snubbing him, looking down on him – they didn't respect him at all. 'That's just because they're all anxious and paranoid,' he consoled himself. The tension was mounting – just a few days and inevitably sleepless nights remained until the unveiling. Tys wandered around a bit, checking things out, and then sat down in the shade of the oak. Everything was just great, and they were on schedule – the Hungarian end of the tunnel would be open before Independence Day, then they'd put the basin and the Mother Europe statue together lickety-split, hook all of that up to the municipal water supply, and unveil the Fountain of Unity. It'd all be ready to go in a week.

The summer heat was starting to make him listless. He rested his back against the century-old oak, and every fibre of his being felt the tunnel's vibration. That trembling was a soothing massage for Tys's soul; it meant he was actualising his dream and following through on his idea. Every millimetre of progress truly was a step towards immortality. A sweet slumber embraced the teacher. He languidly covered his face with his hat and started snoring, head resting on his chest. In his dream, the tunnel appeared as a road to a world that was alien, yet better than this one, and he was Charon, transporting human souls. After all, Ukrainians making their way to Europe through a smugglers' tunnel was supposed to be a kind of initiation. They'd enter on this side and then surface in a different reality, coveted, and therefore happy. What they were achieving here was just like the Underground Railroad. After all, aren't Ukrainians just like black slaves, separated from prosperous Europe by a barbed-wire border? The only way they could get there was by overcoming this final challenge – building the tunnel. Tys would be in a big boat down there. In his dream, the tunnel was black, boundless, and filled with water.

Suddenly, Iowaska, who frequented the same bar as Tys and happened to be one of his worst enemies, came over to the boat. He'd always mock the teacher, laughing at his patriotism and calling Ukraine a cursed country and Count Svyatoslav a worthless nobody who'd screwed everything up. When he was proposing toasts, he'd invariably poke fun at Tys by rephrasing Ukrainian nationalist slogans. His drunken lips would turn 'you'll build the Ukrainian state or die fighting for it' into 'I'll build the Ukrainian state… or just leave and never come back.' The whole bar would erupt with mean-spirited laughter. Feeling a sense of power over Iowaska for the first time, Tys brought him onto the boat. But then in the middle of the tunnel, he pushed him into the water with his oar. His rival bobbed up and down, begging for mercy, but the teacher proved implacable – Iowaska eventually sank to the bottom of the tunnel. Tys peered into the dark depths for a while, relishing his victory until the gold fin of death glimmered at the bottom. Tys took a closer look and suddenly got the chills; he saw himself down there. That was his gold tooth, not a gold coin glimmering in his mouth. Tys woke up in a cold sweat, his heart racing wildly.

The Fountain of Unity would be unveiled in a week. Just one week, seven days.

Chapter 15:

In Which the Protagonist Hears Something He Shouldn't Have, and the Protagonist is Transformed Into a Coward

Marichka was inspecting herself in the mirror. Curly, chestnut hair fell neatly onto her shoulders. Little button nose, pouty lips, and vibrant brown eyes. She thought her eyebrows were too thick, but she didn't have the courage to pluck them – that could make them even worse. Overall, she felt good about herself. Yes, she'd put on a few extra pounds over the years, but that's better than getting all wrinkly or having dry, earthy skin. For someone a tad over forty, she was quite attractive – she still had perky breasts, and a distinct waistline stood out between her midriff and buttocks (they were a little too wide, but whatcha gonna do?). If she could just shed ten pounds or so, she wouldn't be ashamed to go to the beach. It was a bummer Tys wasn't interested in her anymore.

'How much longer are you gonna slop around in there? Would ya get out already?!' she yelled, loud enough that Tys could hear her through the bathroom door.

'I just got in! How come you can never let me have a moment's peace? We have a crucial meeting today – it's our final one. I need to be prepared. I have to look like a brand-new penny!' he replied.

'I have places to be, too. One of my girlfriends is having a birthday party, I gotta get ready. But you've been in the tub all morning. Enough is enough!'

'Quit nagging me!'

'Get out this minute or I'll turn the light off on you!' Marichka threatened, still standing in front of the mirror and studying her chin.

'God, woman, just leave me alone, please! I'm almost done.'

'Do you realise that the tub isn't just yours?! You have to share! Just get clean and get out. You've been in there for over an hour. Are you going for a swim in the ocean or something? How long does it take you to wash that scrawny little body of yours? I have to wash and dry my hair and then run over to the party. And I don't even have a gift picked out yet! Alright, that's it. Get out of there! O-u-t, out!'

'I'm meeting with the organising committee today. The mayor and everyone else'll be there. We're unveiling the Fountain of Unity the day after tomorrow, and we're having our final session today. This is very important to me, don't you realise that? Your girlfriends can wait. Last thing I need today is those airheads messing up my plans. I'll be out in a few minutes anyway!'

'Couldn't you have started getting ready for your session a little earlier? Come on, let me in!' Marichka insisted.

'Oh, woman, you'll drive me to my grave! You know what you remind me of? The Hungarian Soviet Republic!'

'Huh? The Hungarian what?'

'The Hungarian Soviet Republic. The government took people's tubs away from them, so the workers could use them.'

'Huh?'

'In 1919, there was a communist revolution in Hungary. Bela Kun, Lenin's friend and a fanatical communist, orchestrated the whole thing. He established the Hungarian Soviet Republic. It didn't last long, a little less than six months, but it may have been the most absurd state in history.'

'But what does that have to do with me?' Marichka was at her wits' end.

'What do you mean? You're demanding I give up my tub! When the Magyar communists came to power, one of the first things they did was sort out the housing problem. It was barbaric – straight out of Bulgakov, worse even! First, they stripped the aristocracy of all their titles and nationalised their estates. Then they moved on to regular rich people. Think of it, Budapest, the city of pomp and wealth – and anyone who owned a large apartment was forced to share it with blue-collar trash. More than thirty thousand proletarians moved in with rich people. And you know what they did?! One businessman had to take in his former servant who'd stolen from him just a year before. And then that servant started bossing him around threatening him, too!' Tys said and cracked his knuckles loudly, as if to emphasise his point. 'A classy, sophisticated lady had to take in a prostitute who still had an active business going. One time, a drunk client mixed up their rooms on the way back from the bathroom and raped the old lady! But the history books are silent as to whether or not she liked it, he-he. Oh, about the bathtubs – now that's the best part. Anyone who owned their own tub – that was rare back then, a real luxury – was forced to share it with the plebs twice a week. A list of all the tubs in Budapest was compiled and then printed in newspapers and posted on building co-operative bulletin boards. Every Tuesday, anyone off the street could just come into your home and take a bath. And then on Fridays, those apartments were open to kids from local daycare centers and schools. The owners had to provide them with hot water, soap, and clean towels. There you go! So now do you see why your little hissy fit reminded me of the Hungarian Soviet Republic?'

'Listen up, you. I'm gonna say this for the last time – get out of the tub! And save your stories for the mayor and whoever else wants to listen to your nonsense! I'm already running late! Get out or I'll … !' Marichka's eyes bulged. She quickly glanced at herself in the mirror.

'Yep, you're sounding more and more like those bloodthirsty Hungarian communists! No sooner had they plopped down on their parliamentary seats than they began a bloody reign of terror. Magyars are just downright cruel. I mean they're Asians, former nomads. That's why they have the best meat dishes, though. Nobody can make salo like them, not even Ukrainians! And their sausages are delicious! They're conquerors who came to our neck of the woods on horseback. And you gotta have good food when you're on a long journey. They came up with the idea of putting fresh meat under their saddles. Their horses would gallop along and the salt in their sweat would turn it into jerky. To this day, their food is salty, spicy, and greasy, but it's just so delicious! Mmm!' Tys smacked his lips and then slipped under the water to rinse the shampoo out of his hair. He resurfaced and continued. 'They sure like fresh meat, they really do! The communist republic in Budapest only lasted 133 days, but thousands of people were killed, without trial – or even charges. I should know, I'm a historian. After all, communists in every country are just a bunch of bastards and murderers. But those Magyars were absolutely brutal with their victims. They gouged people's eyes out! They hung priests on crosses – that was their idea of an atheist joke. I guess shooting them just wasn't enough!'

'Screw you and your Magyars and your history lessons! Are you getting out or what?'

'I already told you, I'll be right out! Let me finish up. I take a bath maybe once a month, and all of a sudden you need to get in here! You're a damn commie, that's what you are. How didn't I pick up on that earlier?! Everyone told me – don't ever pick a sow from Sasovo! But I wouldn't listen. I got married anyway, and now I got a commie kicking me out of my own bathtub, in my own house! The house my parents built! You learned some bad things from your Magyar commie buddies. Yeah, they turned all the estates and palaces into spas for the proletariat, who came in and destroyed and plundered and shat on everything!'

'Alright, I've had enough of you!' Exhausted by now, Marichka waved her hand dismissively and went into the other room so she wouldn't have to listen to her wacky husband.

'Listen up,' the history teacher, who had no clue that his wife was no longer within earshot, continued enthusiastically. 'You're sure to get something out of this. History really does give us a lot to contemplate! Karl Popper was wrong when he said that history doesn't make any sense. It does! If we'd known about the Hungarian experience with communism in 1919 then we might have put up a stiffer fight against the Bolsheviks! Those antichrists! The Magyar communists promptly nationalized private enterprises and land, but the peasants were real surprised when they didn't get any of that land. The government decided to set up collective farms instead! The new managers were uneducated morons, so the whole economy collapsed like a house of cards within days, and famine broke out in the countryside. There was rationing – even in Budapest! Ever hear the joke about communists in the desert? What would happen if communism prevailed in the Sahara? There'd be a sand shortage before you knew it! That's no joke, though! In Bela Kun's Magyarland, utter economic collapse went hand in hand with censorship in the arts. Writers were divided into three categories and paid a salary according to their place in the pecking order. And, naturally, that was based on their loyalty to the government and ability to write ideologically sound books. The arts were turned into propaganda! They swapped their old flag for a red one, their coat of arms for a star, and their national anthem for 'The Internationale.'

Then a silly Karl Marx statue went up in downtown Budapest. That communist mess only lasted 133 days, but it managed to do irrevocable damage – and you'll never believe how it died! The Party banned alcohol and started shouting from the rooftops about how harmful it was, calling it a roadblock on the path to their commie paradise. Imagine that, in Magyarland, where there's a cult of wine and palinka, they banned alcohol. Completely banned it! The common man couldn't make himself a drink or buy one! All the while, the soldiers and Party members were traipsing around town drunk, murdering, raping, and pillaging. It was hell on earth! The alcohol ban was the last straw for the Magyars, though – that goes beyond good and evil. Boy, I know where they were coming from! So when Romanian forces rolled into Magyarland, the people rose up against the communists. If it hadn't been for Bela Kun's idiotic republic, Hungary would be twice the size it is today! The Triple Entente rewarded Romania with territory for quelling the communist threat in Europe. They got Transylvania and Máramaros County, which is right next to us. If it hadn't been for that communist regime, we might be living in Hungary right now! Ugh, I don't even want to think about that!' Tys made a wry face and went underwater again.

When he came out of the bathroom, Marichka made sure he noticed how coldly and wordlessly she darted inside. Then came the sound of the faucet turning and water pouring out. Our protagonist was in a fantastic mood. Towel wrapped around his waist, he trudged into the kitchen, opened the fridge, grabbed a cutlet off a plate, and plucked a pickle out of the jar. He plodded into his room, crunching happily and loudly, then sat down in his chair and began cutting his nails with large, rusty clippers. Once Tys had cut them very short, all the way down to the red skin, he went over to his wardrobe, his gait sprightly, and put on a pair of boxers. Thus attired, he migrated over to the opposite wall. A 2015 calendar hung next to a map of Europe. He sighed with delight and then crossed out the box for Saturday, August 22nd, with a marker. Lately, impatience had been eating away at him, and his idleness had been tormenting him so much that he'd decided to keep a countdown going until the longed-for day. There were only two boxes left or just one – Sunday – if you didn't count today. The formal unveiling of the Fountain of Unity would take place on Monday, and the first underground locomotive would set off for Hungary amid the celebratory frenzy.

Actually, everything was already in place. They could've started that very minute, but after much discussion, the partners decided it'd be better to send the first train to Hungary amid the fireworks and applause that would fill Peace Square when the fountain came on. That way, nobody would notice the racket coming from down below – that's if they could even hear it. Later on, if need be, they could chalk the underground noise up to the inner workings of the fountain. Every last detail had been considered, calculated, hashed, and rehashed! The tunnel had already reached the designated spot, and yesterday they'd been working on camouflaging the exit. The large hatch on the other side was in the woods, so they covered it with moss and grass. A road ran through the forest a few dozen yards away. Trucks would come in after dark to pick up product coming out of the underground corridor. The set-up on the Ukrainian side was even better; they could do as they pleased – the mayor had their backs.

Having a permanent entrance right under the fountain obviously didn't make much sense; it was right in the center of Vedmediv, way too exposed. The square was well-suited for digging and deepening the tunnel, but the actual entrance had to be somewhere else. A café right on the corner was the perfect choice. The building belonged to the city, so Zoltan Bartok terminated the previous owner's lease and let Icarus set up shop. There was a courtyard behind the café, big enough for trucks. They dug a side passageway to the fountain – a string of train cars was stationed there – from the basement. Now a truck hauling product could pull into the courtyard and unload – the cars were only about twenty-five yards away. Everything was flawlessly concealed, away from prying eyes. Even if someone were to see something, it wouldn't matter, because it'd be perfectly reasonable for people to be unloading a truck outside a café. Tys was especially proud of the fact that he'd finally convinced them to give the place a new name – the Café Danube. In his opinion, this name symbolised the deep ties between Transcarpathia and Central Europe. After all, the Danube ran through all the most important countries, as well as Germany and Austria, and Vedmediv's own Tysa River eventually joined it. The concept of disguising the gateway to Europe as an establishment called the Café Danube was tremendously satisfying for the teacher.

So, everything was ready to go. All they had to do was assemble the people of Vedmediv on Monday morning, cut the ribbon, and twist the valve. Then water from the municipal supply would surge into the Fountain of Unity, like Ukrainians into the European Union. Those bureaucrats in Brussels who claimed Ukraine's only path to the EU was through gradual reform, commitment to the rule of law, and years of hard work could never have imagined such a simple, yet brilliant solution, not in their wildest dreams! Actually, it was all supposed to happen immediately – a hole in the ground would be Ukraine's back door into Europe. Tys flashed his gold tooth in front of the mirror, poured some cologne on his open palms, and mercilessly slapped himself several times. After that, he rubbed his fragrant hands under his armpits. He had to look absolutely perfect today, like he was going to the dress rehearsal before the premiere on Monday!

Every detail was of the utmost importance, especially his hair, which was currently sticking up like the feathers on a plucked rooster. Tys ran into the kitchen, mixed some warm water with sugar, carefully wet his forelock with his concoction, and got to work, assiduously running his gap-toothed comb through dirty gray hair that had once been the colour of thick, greasy, spring manure. Then he opened his wardrobe and pulled out his very best suit, the white one, and a yellow dress shirt embroidered with palm trees and beach chairs. Sure, it was short-sleeved, but it's not like anybody would see that under his jacket. Tys was about to complete his outlandish getup with a brand-new pair of Zhytomyr-made socks, but they were just too perfect, so he decided to save them for Monday. Instead, he put yesterday's socks back on; after all, he wouldn't have to take off his shoes – the session was to take place in the mayor's office – so nobody would even notice. He grabbed his pointy dress shoes, spat on the tips one after the other, and meticulously rubbed them with an old sweater until he could see his dim reflection. Then he put his watch on his right wrist, took another good look at himself, and decided to head out.

Although it was just a little before noon and the meeting was set for one – that's what Icarus had told him over the phone, at least – Tys still figured he should get going. There was no point putzing around the house for another hour. Also, he had to walk there – it just isn't proper to ride your bike when you're wearing a fancy white suit. He strode out of the house without bothering to say goodbye to his wife. She was still splashing around in the tub. As he was leaving, he put on a pair of black sunglasses; one of the lenses was hanging on by a thread, and it kept falling out, so he had to cock his head way back when he was walking. Some passersby may have even thought that the teacher was holding his head high so he wouldn't have to look at anyone.

It was such a nice day. In its last moment, August ceased plaguing the Vedmedivites with its unbearable heat, and now there was a velvety, autumnal touch to the air; the grass and trees were gradually acquiring more pastel colors. The city froze, the streets were empty and dusty, men worn out from who knows what sat in front of cafés here and there, and a crow strutted down a cobblestone street. Tomorrow, once the bazaar opened, it would turn into a Babylon with shouting in many languages, colorful clothing, blaring car horns, and the neighing of Gypsies' horses, but today Vedmediv was drowning in a summertime daze: wives attended to their housework, washing windows and cooking meals, children played in their shady backyards, and men simply rested or stared off into space. The wheels would be set in motion tomorrow; they'd scurry around, spending more money than they had all summer long in preparation for the holiday – not Independence Day, though. They couldn't care less about that, actually. It was the Assumption of the Virgin Mary, the church holiday Vedmediv celebrated every year on August 28th, that always came with culinary splendor, new clothing, and festive haircuts.

Tys was slowly making his way downtown. He crossed Peace Square, amorously admired the Fountain of Unity, now covered with canvas in preparation for the unveiling, and walked up to city hall. His watch showed 12:15; he still had 45 minutes until the meeting. Tys saw Mirca's blue Toyota parked outside the building – and Icarus's car was there too – so he figured that his associates had already arrived. He went inside without hesitation, removed his sunglasses in the cool gloom, tucked them in his pocket, and then slowly headed up the stairs towards Mayor Zoltan Bartok's office.

It turned out it was open. Tys went in. Zoya, the secretary, was out – she had the day off. Plus, they couldn't have her listening to their confidential conversations anyway. Rosy-cheeked tomatoes floated in the fish tank, filling the room with the aroma of pickled joy. Only the ticking of the enormous clock, plated with fake gold and made to look like a wristwatch, disturbed the silence. The teacher went up to the office door, heard some voices, and then hesitated for a split second. The thought of the mayor bringing outsiders into his office made him uneasy.

'…but that doofus Chvak – I'm telling you, we've gotta do something about him. We're sunk if we don't,' came Mirca's voice through the door. Tys pricked up his ears when he heard the Genius of the Carpathians say his last name.

'I agree,' the Succubus seconded the Romanian. 'If a grown man goes around calling himself Tys, he clearly needs help. And if that clown insists on wearing that ridiculous white suit that looks like he picked it out of a dumpster, then I don't want him within a mile of me.'

That obnoxious, tasteless comment regarding his best suit offended Tys. By that point, he wanted to burst into the office and remind them that this whole project was his idea and they were a bunch of colourless, stupid, avaricious simpletons that didn't know the first thing about fashion. He was stopped by the voice of Icarus, who was apparently standing up for him.

'Nah, you've got it all wrong. I've known him since kindergarten. Yeah, maybe he's a little weird, and he looks like a slob. And he reeks.' Tys's eyes turned red with blood when he heard that. 'But he's a good, kind guy. He means well and he wouldn't hurt a fly.'

'Yeah, he's a good guy, but at some point, that moron's gonna demand that we start herding Ukrainians through the tunnel and into Europe. He won't even trouble himself to ask people if they want to cross the border, illegally or not. That clown's just obsessed! We need the tunnel for smuggling, but he needs it for his wacky ideas! He could wreck everything. He might start running his big mouth down at the bar and get us all thrown in jail!' the Succubus said.

'Cool it, cool it, cool it.' The mayor said, trying to dispel the tension. 'Yeah, I do agree that Chvak presents a certain danger, but what should we do about him? What should we do?'

'Gotta get rid of him. He's a threat,' the Succubus declared coldly.

'Last thing we need is another dead soul. Isn't having Ychi's death on our consciences enough?' Icarus replied indignantly.

'My dear, first off, let me remind you that we had no idea when Ychi would've come out of his coma and I was the one paying to keep him on life support,' the Succubus said, lifting her index finger. 'Secondly, we incurred some unforeseen expenses, but you didn't want to cover them. So, don't forget that selling Ychi's organs helped us solve our financial woes.'

Ihor and Yosif Lendian nodded in agreement, but Tys couldn't see that. The room went quiet for a moment. Absolutely stunned, the teacher just stood behind the door, too afraid to move a muscle.

'Alrighty then, so what are you suggesting, my esteemed colleagues? What are you suggesting?' The mayor of Vedmediv tried taking charge and facilitating a more constructive discussion.

'We've just gotta get rid of him, that's it. That'll put us all at ease,' said the Succubus.

'But his wife… what about her?' Icarus said, trying to tip the scales in his favor.

'Don't worry. Once our business gets off the ground, we'll find a way to thank her. It can't be easy living with a dope like him. She'll probably be glad to see him go,' the Genius of the Carpathians said.

'Thing is,' Ihor Lendian finally spoke up. 'We can't just pay him off or cut some sort of deal. He's completely delusional, he lives in his own deranged reality. He might do something off the wall once he realises that the tunnel won't ever be used for anything besides smuggling! So, we should just get rid of him now. Sure, it's sad, but we have to do it to make sure our project succeeds and we stay safe.'

'But how?' Zoltan Bartok inquired.

'We'll inject him with a sedative when he gets here. That'll be in another half hour. I already have everything ready,' the Succubus answered in a businesslike tone. 'Then we'll take him to my place. After dark, though, so we don't attract any undue attention. I'll take out his organs, so we'll even make some money off him. After all, he'll be doing something good for others, he'll be helping them live longer. He would like that idea.'

'Yeah, he'll euro-integrate himself. He'll go to the European Union, just like he dreamed of, piece by piece,' the Genius of the Carpathians said, roaring with laughter.

'Well then, let's do it. We can't endanger our project because of some bone-headed teacher,' the mayor said with a mournful sigh.

'I object!' Icarus said decisively.

'Boys, I've invested much more than any of you, ten times more. So consider this an ultimatum. We're getting rid of him, end of discussion,' Ulyana Kruk said in the metallic voice of a murderer. Nobody could come up with a counter argument.

Cold sweat dripped down Tys's collar and his knees trembled ever so slightly. Fear-stricken, he stepped out of the mayor's office as quietly as he could and then hightailed it down empty streets and back alleys to the outskirts of town. He kept looking back, afraid someone would be chasing him. Tys ran, knowing that death was breathing down his neck.

Chapter 16:

In Which Tys Saves Himself or Doesn't

'Woah! Woah!' hollered an old Gypsy, pulling on the reins. 'What's the rush, you little devil? Didn't you see my horses? You got a death wish? I hope ya—'

Tys just ignored him; he dodged the Gypsy's cart, running like a madman, and disappeared around the corner. Disheveled and drenched with sweat, he kept goading himself forward, yet wasn't fully conscious of where he was going. The right half of his shirt was still tucked into his pants, while the left half was sticking out. The lens had fallen out of his sunglasses a while back, so he was just holding it in his hand. He wasn't thinking about that at all, though. As a matter of fact, he wasn't thinking about anything – he'd turned into an animal driven by its fight-or-flight instincts. He ran, oblivious to the streets around him, not even consciously charting a course; it was as though some internal compass was steering him away from danger. He stopped – winded and sweaty – in a thicket at the foot of Black Mountain, on the edge of Vedmediv.

He caught his breath. He lay on the ground, arms splayed powerlessly, and looked at the sky hanging over the mountain, its clouds like greying lace. Face and chest burning, throat dry, he wheezed, and the hot air scratched his respiratory tract every time he inhaled. After a few minutes, he began to regain control; he removed his jacket and undid all the buttons of his shirt. A gentle breeze came up, cooling him down and gradually restoring his mental faculties and sense of reality. But his thoughts weren't exactly as uplifting and cheerful as they'd been just an hour ago, when he was heading towards city hall, anticipating his moment of triumph and eager to see his idea come to fruition.

'What should I do?' Tys pondered. His frantic thoughts staggered and collided, jumbled and interrupted one another. 'Do they really want to kill me? I was the one who came up with the whole thing! How will they unveil the fountain without me? Won't they feel any shame when they cut the ribbon? What will they tell my class and the school? Why are they so cruel? I shared the thing I cherished most – my dream. I guess that's what greed does to people! I'm getting in their way just because I'm a good person! A good person among wolves. A black sheep. And I thought they were my partners. More like murderers!'

'Do they actually want to kill me? Hmm. I mean, the Succubus said that she already had the syringe ready. They really would have killed me, there's no doubt about it. Just like they killed Ychi. And they would've carved me up like a pig. Just so some bastards in France or wherever could live a little longer. Who has the money to purchase transplant organs on the black market? People who've robbed and exploited others their whole lives, that's who! It's the cycle of human life… more like the cycle of human scum. The Succubus kills good people to help vampires, oligarchs, corrupt politicians, and mobsters – in short, people who benefit from the suffering and hardship of others – live a little longer. They already did away with Ychi, and now it's my turn. Those beasts will stop at nothing. And soon they'll run out of victims and start devouring each other. They're a pack of piranhas, not human beings!'

'Who can save me? Maybe I should go to the police and tell them the whole truth about the tunnel? I could save myself that way, couldn't I? The police won't protect me, though. Their function is to protect criminals and the government from honest people, not the other way around. They're all in cahoots. No police officer would ever take a stand against the mayor. They're all the sons of prosecutors and judges, and the judges are the children of mayors, and lawyers are the daughters of customs officers. They're all one big family, a prehistoric tribe that sticks together. And there's nothing an upstanding citizen can do about it. They'll hand me over to my loyal 'partners' as soon as I set foot in the police station. I mean, the mayor himself is a thief, a primitive criminal who got his start stealing toilet paper. The police won't look into the Succubus's dubious activities and illicit income, because she's on the city council. The law enforcement agencies didn't do a damn thing when Ychi disappeared. Icarus and the Genius of the Carpathians are big-time smugglers, everyone knows that, but it doesn't make any difference. It's because they give the security service, the border guards, and the mayor their cut. Dirty money, power, and the force of billy clubs are bound together so tightly that there's no hope of prying them apart anymore. At the top, everyone's related to everyone else, they're all links in one big chain. Even the hospital's part of it – they won't hire just anyone as a security guard. You gotta be the prosecutor's bone-headed nephew. So now you can take whatever medicine you want from their pharmacy. The prosecutor's nephew won't stop you; he's grateful you so magnanimously got him a job with decent pay.'

'And it's not just like that in Vedmediv. That's how things look across the whole region. Transcarpathia's representative in parliament is a well-known smuggler. His brother, who's even stupider than him, runs the regional government. And the stupidest of the brothers is the head of the traffic police. That's Darwin's hierarchy for you, in the 21st century. Ukraine's caught in a spider web of governance woven from mob money and backed by police sadists.

All the cogs in the machine wrap cocoons of security around themselves, often employing the methods of the medieval aristocracy – marrying the daughters of influential people, becoming each other's godparents, and joining the same hunting clubs.'

'I don't want to give up the tunnel, though. My big idea would be done for! Kaput! That's all she wrote! It's all ready to go, it's all set! Just go ahead and start taking people across the border – don't even need those train cars – they can walk the half-mile through the tube and pop out in the European Union. It's my idea, I, Tys, came up with it! It's mine! And it's all ready to go – should I really sacrifice it just to save my own skin? If they scrap the project now it won't ever come to fruition. But it's the most important thing I've ever done! Who am I without this project? Just a history teacher by the name of Mykhailo Chvak – not Tys, though, not someone who's changed Ukraine – and Europe – forever! The tunnel is more important than my life and that gang's avaricious aspirations. And I considered those criminals and murderers my trusted partners and associates! I can't just throw this idea away. I mean, the execution was just brilliant! It's like a metro, a real, international metro! So much money – more than I've made or ever will make – has already gone into it. No, the tunnel has to stay intact and start operating, no matter what, no matter the cost. I just have to get rid of my associates, and then everything'll be just great.'

'But for now, they're the ones trying to get rid of me. What should I do? For now, just stay away from them – that's the key. Hide, run from that deadly syringe, buy some time. After all, time is clearly on my side. I'm smarter than them, I should be able to trick them. Those dim-witted murderers aren't capable of using their grey matter. Well, they don't even have any brains, or hearts for that matter, just big dollar calculators instead of souls. So my job is to save the tunnel and my life and outplay those bloodthirsty gangsters. Seems like it'll be pretty hard, but you never know. Thing is, I never would've thought back in May when I came up with all this tunnel stuff that it'd be ready to go in August. Building a tunnel like this in secret – now that was beyond difficult, but it got done. Outplaying some small-town crooks will be much easier. I mean, this is me going up against them – me, Tys, a man with a mission of global significance!'

This line of thinking put the teacher in a more optimistic mood. He appeared to have bounced back from the initial shock and forgotten about the real danger facing him. His basic life functions awakened as well – he was suddenly hungry and thirsty. He'd decided to hide out for the time being, so he forged through a thicket towards the Tysa, skirting Black Mountain. Up there, above the river, there was a large apple orchard. It'd been around since the days of the Bear Empire. The teacher picked bunches of wild white grapes – they were very ripe and sweet in late August – as he walked along a path at the foot of the mountain. Once he reached the Tysa, he got undressed and went into the cool water. It washed all his anxiety, fear, and fatigue away. This rejuvenating water would be his salvation. Tys made a wry face and then took a few sips from the river. He knew that upstream, in Romania, they dumped chemical waste in the water, but he kept drinking because he'd worked up a merciless thirst galloping through town and eating those excessively sweet grapes. Water was his element and this river – the Tysa – was his homeland, because it was free, European, and capable of crossing any border, and because it had given him his name.

Once Tys, still in his boxers, had gotten out and hopped on each leg to shake the water out of his ears, he headed towards the orchard. It had once been part of a collective farm, but now it was severely overgrown, nearly wild. He picked some apples and went back to the riverbank, where he spread out his things in the shade of an old willow and then lay on his back. One question nagged him like a gnat – what should he do about Marichka? She might not be in any danger. His now ex-associates had said so. And she didn't know anything about the tunnel. It's a good thing he hadn't let the truth slip out. She was safe for now. What should he do, though? Who could he count on? How could he get out of this bind?

The sizzling sun was sending this year's last truly hot rays down to the Earth. Tys lay on the riverbank, absorbed in thought. His scrawny body, covered only by large boxers, was all he had to fend off this gang determined to kill him. For some reason, Tys was sure that he'd come out on top, that he'd pull it off, and that he'd get out of this trap alive. He had to hide for now, though. Nobody would find him here, in this forgotten orchard, but living here wasn't an option. What would he eat? How long could a person subsist on apples and grapes? Yes, he could fish, like he did a long time ago, as a kid, when he used to wade into shallow spring streams, dip a large basket into the deeper pockets, and then come home two hours later with a huge catch. He could try fishing now, too, using his jacket as a net, but what good would that do? Also, August nights are treacherous. It gets as cold as it does in autumn – too cold to sleep in the hills above the river. No, he had to escape. But where could he go? Not home – they'd find him there right away. Venturing into the city wasn't too smart either. He needed to remain unseen. Plus, he didn't have any money, so he couldn't go anywhere.

So, where should he go? The best and safest option would be to skip town and flee abroad, at least for a few days or weeks. He'd lay low until he developed a real plan of action. It'd be safe abroad; the gang's sticky tentacles wouldn't be able to reach him. They have the rule of law over there. And human rights. And a police force that protects you. It's safe there. An upstanding citizen will always be protected there. That's why Ukraine needs to get in there, into the European Union, legally or otherwise! But how could he, a poor, simple teacher, sneak in? Back in the day, in the early 90s, he'd gone abroad, to three different countries.

His first trip was to the former Yugoslavia, to the Serbian Autonomous Province of Vojvodina. In those days, you could sell just about anything there – alcohol, appliances, all kinds of manufactured goods – and bring back hard currency or something even more valuable – flashy clothing and real jeans, which were worth a fortune in bleak post-Soviet Ukraine. So, Tys and his aunt went to Yugoslavia several times – down to Subotica, the town closest to the border, where the bazaar was right next to the train station. They had to go through Hungary, too, so Tys added another country to his list, although he never did leave his train compartment and go out onto the platform at the Magyar stops; he was too afraid someone would snatch their product.

Another time, he and his enterprising aunt went to a big bazaar outside of Krakow. The teacher never saw the actual city, though; back then, nobody even considered heading into town to look at the architecture or just explore. Eating out was inconceivable for them, even at the cheapest joints in town. They'd bring bread, salo, and vegetables with them so they wouldn't have to spend any money. Not to mention, nobody even thought about paying to use a public bathroom. Opening your wallet every time nature calls? Yeah right! So, they'd run to the bushes or just go back to the bus. Entrepreneurs of that stripe would always bring a bucket – that way you wouldn't have to go too far away or embarrass yourself in front of your comrades in misery – plus it was cheaper. Basically, Tys had been to Poland, but he hadn't really seen it. He hadn't crossed the border since Hungary and Poland joined the European Union. That was because he didn't have a passport. What do you need a passport for if there's no chance you'll get a visa anyway? If you're an upstanding citizen with a college degree, work at a school, teach kids, don't steal, and don't break any laws, a visa is out of reach – applying for one is like trying to lick your elbow. You need money in the bank, an invitation, and forged documents – which you can't get without paying a bribe – so once the Schengen Area began sharing a border with Ukraine, travelling became impossible.

Those dim-witted European bureaucrats sitting in their fancy Brussels offices set everything up that way on purpose so only rich people could get visas and cross the border. And who's rich in a mafia state? Yep, that's right – politicians and other crooks, speculators, conmen, murderers, and the damn cops, of course. Upstanding citizens will never get visas, because they simply have no legal grounds to get them. That's why Tys didn't have a passport. For people like him, going to the European Union illegally was the only option. Like selling a kidney to some fiend and then buying a visa. Or crossing the sky-high Carpathian Mountains. But you have to know the way, like Mirca. He wouldn't find the trail by himself because nobody had told him where it was. So, he couldn't even sneak into the EU illegally.

But wait a second – he did know the way! He'd come up with the best and shortest passage to Europe! The tunnel! His own idea would save him! And it'd all play out like it did when they were choosing where to dig. If you want to hide something from people, just do it brazenly, right out in the open. If you're looking to build a secret tunnel, do it in the central square, not out in the sticks! That's exactly why the tunnel would save Tys today! That pack of dumbasses, headed by the mayor and the Succubus, would look for him at his house, at the bars, or even up in the hills beyond the river, but they would never think of looking for him in the tunnel! That was where he'd outplay them; that was his domain. He'd have home-field advantage down there, because it was his design, it was his own brainchild! He could trick those murderers. He'd slip past them, right under their noses!

Brilliant! The fountain's ready to go, all the machinery's gone, and now everything's been mothballed until the unveiling, so slipping into the tunnel right under the basin was a no go. It's a shame all of this hadn't happened earlier, like when the fence was up and Tys had his own set of keys. Everything would be just fine, though. He'd make his way downtown, sneak into the courtyard behind the Café Danube, crawl through the window into the basement, and then slip into the tunnel. The windows would be open because they'd just poured the concrete and they needed to make sure the place was well ventilated so it would set as quickly as possible. It'd be easy as pie. All he had to do was wait for nightfall, grope his way through the darkness back to town, head to the basement, walk through the tunnel, and then emerge in a free land, in safety, in the European Union!

It was decided – that's what he would do. Just make it to the European Union, get to the other side of the tunnel. Over there, with victory in the bag, the Succubus couldn't touch him. Nor could Bartok. Nobody could! And voila – everything would be inverted, just like a mirror. Nobody could threaten him. Actually, once he'd escaped, Tys would be able to blackmail his partners and checkmate them. Once he got far enough away, he could start threatening to expose them and wreck the project. So, his 'partners' would have no choice but to agree to his terms.

His terms would be simple – return to the initial plan. But now Tys would have two cars instead of one. Or maybe even three! He deserved it; he was the brains behind all this, but those traitors wanted to dupe him, hell, they wanted to murder him. So, four cars, yes, four of them, would belong to him, and the rest to those crooks.

He'd take Ukrainians across the border in his, and they could take whatever they pleased in theirs. So, that's what he had to do. It was a smart plan. A brilliant one. That way the tunnel would be preserved, which meant the dream of a lifetime would be realised. And Tys would save his own life, which was no less important. After all, he was still in his prime, still able to come up with countless other grand, monumental projects for Ukraine. So, Ukraine would euro-integrate itself and finally become a normal country, albeit illegally. Individuals with such lofty aims simply must utilise all possible methods. After all, he was out to restore historical justice to a great and magnificent country, once usurped by the Muscovite hordes, and return it to Europe, its historic fatherland.

Everything was just wonderful. It might even be better that everything had turned out the way it did, because if Tys hadn't heard his associates' bloodthirsty plans then they might have given him the runaround. They probably would've said they needed to test the tunnel and such, just so they wouldn't have to take people through. But now he would issue an ultimatum, and they'd be forced to accept his terms. Everything would go exactly as he'd conceived it. It's great being so much smarter than everyone else! Oh yeah!

Well, if it was going to be that easy, why not take Marichka along? She was safe for the time being, but those murderers could change their minds, you never know. They didn't seem to have an axe to grind with her… yet. But what about when they discovered that Tys wasn't at home, that he'd vanished into thin air, that he'd escaped from their clutches? They might start giving his wife a hard time: interrogating her, following her, haunting her, and keeping her up at night. And the poor woman would be all worked up over her husband's disappearance. He couldn't rule out the possibility that those scumbags would take her captive. Then Tys wouldn't be the

one doing the blackmailing – they would. Those subhuman creatures were capable of anything; they'd kill their own mothers for
a buck. No, the teacher couldn't leave them with any trump cards,
anything that could be used to put pressure on him. Those were
the only terms that'd make his victory a sure thing… or close to it.

Well, he loved her. He'd loved his Marichka tenderly and
fervently for over 20 years. Nobody understood him like she did.
Marichka had endured grief and hardship with him, but she'd never
experienced the happiness that should have been her reward. She
stuck by him when they were living in the dorm and all he could
give his pregnant wife was a single orange. She stood beside him
at the grave of their daughter, the light of their lives, Tremora. Yes,
after she died their relationship had soured, become almost unbearable, but Tys believed that their love was still alive, that he'd be
able to fix everything. Actually, deep down in his heart, he'd dedicated his tunnel to Marichka. He was wary of setting himself up
for embarrassment or ridicule; that's why he hadn't said anything
about it. He wanted to tell her once everything was up and running,
so she'd be impressed, so she'd regain her faith in him, admire
and adore him, and take pride in the fact that she was married to
a genuine historical figure.

Quite moved by his own musings, Tys made a firm decision –
his tunnel would be called 'Marichka,' for she had inspired him, for
she was the meaning and breath of his life. Ever since he saw her
outside the school that day holding a copy of *Kobzar*, she'd been
the meaning of his aimless existence. There was no doubt about
that. So, his brainchild – the tunnel – was hers as much as it was
his, it had to be, which meant he had to go get Marichka that very
instant, stay one step ahead of danger, tell her the whole truth, and
escape with her now that he had a plan. That would be the best solution, his way out. The two of them would escape to Hungary, and

soon enough that pack of smugglers would be dancing to their tune. Knowing that Tys had achieved something so important for all of Europe, Marichka would never permit herself to say a single nasty thing to him ever again. Their lives would be joyous and filled with love and mutual support, just like they'd dreamed about so many years ago. So, once night fell on Vedmediv, Tys would sneak home to get Marichka, and they'd run away together. It was the only way…

The darkness was as dense as silt when Tys stepped warily out of the thicket and began plodding towards the city. Every sound and shadow had him sweating bullets. First, he thought he'd wait until midnight, but then he realised it was still too early – after all, it was a summer weekend and a lot of people would still be out and about. He stayed up in the hills for another two hours; he was freezing his butt off, even though he was huddled behind a broad tree, protected from the wind. Waiting any longer wouldn't have made sense, because it would take him an hour to get home. Then he'd have to wake Marichka up and rush over to the Café Danube – all before the sun started coming up at around five. So, he began cautiously making his way towards the city.

He heard the intermittent roar of car engines coming from the road, but it did seem like the city was already sound asleep. Tys took back alleys and quiet streets. He kept kicking himself for wearing his white suit – not a great choice for trying to go unnoticed at night! Well, there was nothing he could do about it now. His shadow flitted into the backyard like a ghost. It was quiet and empty – no cars, no sign of his associates. None of the lights were on either. Nonetheless, Tys couldn't afford to take any chances; he still had to make sure those cunning murderers weren't lurking in the gloom of his house. He made a few cautious circles, peering into the windows. Then he climbed a cherry tree so he could see into the bedroom. There was Marichka, carefree and moonlit, sleeping soundly, arms splayed. Thank God! So none of those goons were in the house; the coast was clear.

Tys went inside without turning the lights on. He tiptoed into the bedroom, though he wasn't quite sure why, sat next to Marichka, and woke her up gently. She stretched, opened her eyes a little, and then saw her husband hovering over her, his white suit glowing in the moonlight. His face was happy and dreamy. He was smiling, his gold tooth glimmering dimly. He looked calm and inspired. Not like he usually did.

'Where have you been?' Marichka asked, softened by sleep and disarmed by her husband's unexpected affection. 'God, are you really drunk again? They came by the house earlier – Icarus twice, and then the mayor himself, real late. They were looking for you. I told them to comb all the dives in town.' She yawned.

'S-h-h-h, my darling.' Tys put his finger to her lips, but he did it so affectionately that she didn't even object. 'I'm sober. I was hiding by the Tysa, that's where I was. They weren't just looking for me, Marichka. They're coming to get me. They want to get rid of me, you know… kill me. Like they killed Ychi.'

'What the hell are you talkin' about?'

'I'm telling you the truth, the absolute truth. They killed Ychi. The thing is, that's not a fountain they're going to be unveiling on Monday. Well, it is, but that's just a front. There's going to be a tunnel underneath. Actually, there already is one – a half-mile-long tunnel that runs all the way to Hungary. I was the one who came up with the idea, and they helped make it happen. I thought that the tunnel would be Ukraine's road to Europe, like a way in for all Ukrainians, but they decided that they'd use it for smuggling, just to make a quick buck. And now I'm getting in their way. Yeah, me, the brains behind it all. They want to kill me like they killed Ychi – he was the guy who started digging the tunnel. That's why the mayor visited us in person. They're looking for me, they're following me. But I have a plan. We'll escape together. Through the tunnel, to Hungary. And then we'll really stick it to them once we get over to the European Union!'

Their conversation that night wasn't easy. They'd never really talked like that before. Marichka was stunned by her husband's story. First she made sure there was no alcohol on his breath, then she got very quiet and started looking at the moonlit ghost in the white suit, bewitched, at her husband who'd told her about the danger he was in and who'd come up with a plan to save her. Her husband was finally talking about something that mattered. He'd thought up something big. He'd taken a bold, dangerous step. And most importantly, he hadn't deserted her, which meant he loved her. He really did. Seemingly hypnotized, she wholly submitted to Tys, agreeing that they had to escape. They wouldn't need anything besides the clothes on their backs, their IDs, some water, a little food, and some backpacks to put it all in. She did take one more thing, but she didn't tell Tys about that.

A picture… of Tremora – she just looked so alive; she was having so much fun. They were making pierogis, and she had flour and dough all over her face. She looked like a little white cub with red cheeks. So alive and so happy. It seemed like that was the last time they'd looked like that – so alive and so happy.

At around four a.m., a couple of dark figures slipped out of the house and then scuttled from garden to garden towards Peace Square.

Chapter 17:

In Which the Part of the Story that Takes Place in the Best of All Possible Worlds Comes to an End

There was one day left until the unveiling of the Fountain of Unity. The key players were getting ready for the event.

The Mayor of Vedmediv, Zoltan Bartok, was the first to rise that Sunday. He wanted to get as much done as possible and keep everything under his vigilant eyes. The country's political situation was pretty shaky, and there was an election coming up, so even though building the Fountain of Unity was merely a front for the tunnel, it had turned into a grand project in its own right. The unveiling would be a crucial part of the mayor's campaign. He didn't intend to give up his position. So, tomorrow had to go perfectly. He would deliver a patriotic speech, say something about gifting Ukraine a Fountain of Unity – with Europe – on Independence Day, mention the Heavenly Hundred, and take his bombast so far that his constituents would be left without the slightest doubt that the heroes of the Euromaidan had, first and foremost, sacrificed their lives for this fountain in Vedmediv.

As every respectable politician knows – tomorrow's success begins today. So, Bartok got up at six a.m. and started completing the tasks on his to-do list (he'd written it up the day before). The first order of business was visiting an Orthodox priest; the mayor wanted to ask him to bless the fountain. Vedmedivites are pretty religious, so they'd like having him there, in addition to all the music, fireworks, food, and booze. The mayor would have to catch him before the morning service, though, so he could devote the rest of his day to checking off the other items on his list. There sure were a lot of them – choose the ribbon; purchase the largest scissors he could find to cut said ribbon; remind the employees at the House of Culture to bring the most powerful amplifiers – the music had to be so loud that not even a mouse would be able to hear the train rumbling under Peace Square – book a restaurant and select the menu for the banquet (he'd invited members of parliament and all the civil servants he knew – how could you pass up the opportunity to celebrate such a monumental event on the city's dime?); hire a team of pyrotechnicians; invite a dance team that would entertain the people of Vedmediv in Peace Square, as well as an orchestra and chorus from the local army post to perform the national anthem. He had to do all of that and a hundred thousand other little things, all of which would eventually turn into votes.

The Genius of the Carpathians had been up since the crack of dawn, too. He was an early riser. Sometimes he did want to sleep in and get fully recharged, but his eyes would open up all by themselves. Thing is, he would've been glad to just sleep all day, because there's nothing worse than those final hours of anticipation. They'd unveil the fountain tomorrow; everything would get going. But today was a day of anxiety, frantic glances at his watch, and empty time that he couldn't fill up with anything at all. And he'd struggle to fall asleep the night before, that's for sure. He'd toss and turn and count sheep, but sleep would resist him. That's how it'd always been; if he had to get up early, for a trip or something, his heart rate would rise, his breathing would become irregular, and thousands of thoughts, ideas, and memories would creep into his mind, instead of the calm he needed.

After he woke up, Mirca just lay still for a while, staring at the ceiling of his bedroom. He mulled over his plans for the day. Well, actually, he was just trying to think of something, anything really, that would keep him busy. He didn't have any plans except seeing his associates to bounce some ideas around at the post-project meeting slated for four p.m. He'd been entrusted with going to Hungary tomorrow and opening the tunnel on the other side. Good thing they'd picked him; he didn't really care for big celebrations anyway. He'd prefer to do something, like uncover the camouflaged hatch and prepare to accept the first convoy. For now, he'd probably just download a few movies, grab some beer, and hop in the tub, just to kill some time. An odd apathy enveloped his body. He just couldn't force himself to get up and make breakfast, let alone take a shower or turn on some music that would stir him from his lethargy. He lay there and stared into space, picturing the tunnel – tomorrow, it would start making him rich tomorrow. That went on for two hours, until his bladder finally forced him to get up and start the day.

Ulyana Kruk woke up a little later, and she was in a great mood. She took a shower, strolled out of the bathroom – in a soft robe with a towel twisted into a bizarre shape around her head – went to the kitchen, and made herself some coffee and toast with peach jam. Today would be a day of relaxation for her. The Succubus didn't have any important business to attend to, besides the meeting at four, so she'd decided to treat herself to a manicure, a wax, and some time at the tanning salon – she wanted to have a nice bronze glow for tomorrow, as if she, like most Vedmedivites, had spent every weekend that summer on the Tysa – and an evening massage and spa treatment. Time to soothe the soul and satisfy the body. She wouldn't be making any speeches or be involved in tomorrow's ceremony in any way. Although she'd contributed the most money, she flat out refused to even go on stage for the unveiling. She didn't want to be in the spotlight; she'd just watch with the rest of the crowd and try to gauge public opinion. This time around, the puppet master and main investor would stick to the shadows. That's always the safer option.

The Lendian brothers probably had the highest hopes for the unveiling. The whole city knew that they'd been doing construction work in Peace Square for nearly a month now, so they were guaranteed places of honour up on the stage. This would be their first public appearance, the first time Vedmediv would applaud the brothers and thank them for a job well done, so they were in high spirits. Seeking to soak up their 15 minutes of fame, they'd invited their whole family to tomorrow's festivities. Today, they planned to go to the bazaar to buy themselves new suits and dress shirts, get haircuts, and then whiz over to their photographer friend's place – he'd worked Yosif's wedding two years ago – and hire him to film the unveiling of the Fountain of Unity for their family archive. For them, the ceremony was just as important as the opening of the tunnel itself, if not more so. It was their big chance to improve their standing in the community. They also had to head over to the big hardware store in Mukachevo to pick up the elbow piece they'd ordered for the piping in the tunnel. The one they'd bought earlier wound up being too small. Actually, it had the same diameter as the pipes it was supposed to connect, but it needed to be slightly wider to fit around them. So, they had to get a new one and fit it that evening. Well, and they had to pick up some light bulbs; they'd laid the cable and even installed the sockets, but they hadn't put in the bulbs yet. Just those last two brushstrokes and their masterpiece would be complete.

The only one snoring away late that morning was Icarus. He had every right to, though; he'd gone to bed roughly when the mayor had gotten up. He had been taking care of some business the night before, not to mention looking for Tys, and then he went to see Miklos Svyscho, better known as 'the Fisherman.' The partners had decided to ask him to start up the fountain, since all of them wanted to be above ground on the stage for that moment. The Fisherman had to turn the knob and then press the button for the motor when the time came. So, Icarus went over to see Svyscho, and they ironed everything out, but when he was coming back, one of his bus drivers called. There were some problems at the border – the customs officers were insisting they file some new forms. In other words, they were asking for a bigger bribe. Icarus had to run over to the customs office, where he spent the whole night arguing, trying to reach a mutually beneficial agreement. At five a.m., he stopped by the Cafe Danube on his way home. The pipe that ran from the municipal water supply to the fountain was down there, in the basement. The Fisherman was supposed to come there the night before the ceremony to make the final preparations.

Before he did so, Icarus had to camouflage the large hatch that separated the actual tunnel from the basement. The hatch looked like an enormous cap with a turn wheel instead of a regular handle, just like the ones you see when they're breaking into a bank vault in an American movie. The partners had found it down there, in the basement, which had been a bomb shelter during the days of the Bear Empire. Icarus shut the hatch tightly and then moved two old wardrobes in front of it, so it wouldn't catch Svyscho's eye. When Icarus got home, absolutely exhausted, he just collapsed into bed. As he was falling asleep, he thought of Tys, who they still hadn't managed to track down. No biggie, they'd catch that drunkard after they unveiled the fountain.

None of the partners were concerned about the teacher's absence; they didn't find it the least bit odd or alarming. It merely reaffirmed their thinking – Tys had to go. If he could get that drunk two days before the unveiling and miss a crucial meeting – and if he was still roaming around at all hours of the night – he clearly wasn't fit to be their partner. His lack of discipline was a threat to the whole operation.

Meanwhile, Tys was jumping for joy, thanking God that he and Icarus had missed each other by a few minutes that morning. The teacher and his wife reached downtown just shy of five a.m. They warily scampered into the courtyard behind the Café Danube and then had to spend a good ten minutes struggling with the window before they could get into the basement. Tys tossed their backpacks inside and then crawled through. It was tough going for Marichka, though – she nearly got stuck. Once the couple finally made it into the basement, they saw headlights in the courtyard. Deathly scared, Tys grabbed the backpacks and ran towards the tunnel, Marichka in tow. It felt like the person following them was breathing right down their necks; they heard the lock on the basement door click open loudly. The only thing Tys could do was drag Marichka with him into the tunnel; they cowered behind the first cars.

Shortly thereafter, the light switched on in the basement. A split second later, they heard Icarus's voice.

'Hi there, sweetie pie, I'll be home in 10 minutes. Out with who? What tramps? I was alone! I'm telling you the truth. We just had a little misunderstanding at the border, but I cleared everything up. I'm already back in Vedmediv – I'm by myself. Come on, can you hear any voices? Just a few more minutes, and I'll be heading home!' Tys and Marichka huddled up in their hiding place, trying as hard as they could to shrink, evaporate, disappear. They weren't even breathing; they just listened to their hearts pounding and the voice of Icarus, Tys's buddy since their school days, once a family friend, now an enemy and possible murderer. Suddenly, metal screeched, and then a hollow sound, like a bag of flour falling to the floor, shot down the tunnel and the lights went out in the basement at the same moment. Then wheels started grinding monotonously, like a heavy-duty bearing was spinning right next to them. Tys leaned towards Marichka and whispered in her ear.

'Don't worry, my darling. We're safe now. That was Icarus dogging the tunnel hatch, so he has no clue we're inside.' For the next few minutes, there was the sound of wood scraping on the other side of the wall, like someone moving furniture around. Then everything went quiet and a deathly silence prevailed. Tys waited for a few minutes – just to make sure – and then hugged his wife wearily, yet tenderly. 'He's gone. We're in the clear!'

They hadn't been that affectionate with each other for a long while. Tys and his wife had become one as they snuck through the morning gloom. She held her husband's hand tightly, her trust in him absolute. For the first time in many years, she felt that Mykhailo loved her. He'd come back for her because he couldn't imagine his life without her, and now he was leading the way, laying out a plan for their future. Like a real man. That's what she was thinking about while the petrified Tys was keeping a lookout for anyone following them. His wife's hand, their intertwined fingers, helped assuage his anxiety. They were fleeing Vedmediv, but they were doing it as lovers.

'Time to go,' Tys said once he'd regained his composure. He turned on the flashlight on his phone, located the light switch on the wall next to the hatch and flipped it on, but the tunnel didn't get any brighter – there weren't any bulbs in the sockets. Tys spat and picked up their backpacks. Marichka saw that they were inside a concrete tube with tracks running along the bottom. The tube wasn't all that high, so you had to go forward bent double. Actually, crawling would've been their best option, but the cars were in the way. Tys gave Marichka his hand and then started pulling her along.

Getting around the train, which looked like a chain of mini box cars, proved pretty difficult – it was nearly as wide as the tube itself. They had to squeeze their way past; Marichka, the stockier of the two, had a particularly hard time. Their ordeal didn't last all that long, though. Within 10 minutes, Marichka and her husband had squeezed past the last car, which was probably the locomotive, since it had large headlights and no cargo compartment. The farther they advanced, the easier it was to move. At first, the couple was walking hunched over, their legs straight, but that proved to be unbearable for more than 20 yards, so they sat on their haunches and started inching forward. That wasn't too comfortable either – their legs were burning within a hundred yards, so the fugitives decided to take a breather. Then they began crawling on all fours, like dogs, their backpacks dangling off their chests. That way they were finally able to build up a little bit of speed.

Marichka was very impressed with the tunnel. It was a long, concrete tube, complete with tracks for train cars, and up at the top, there were sockets for bulbs every 15 yards. It's a shame that they hadn't been screwed in, though; the couple had to use the flashlight on Tys's phone instead. Nonetheless, it was quite the sight – a whole underground structure, built to the highest standards, the seams between the sections nearly invisible, the floor dry, and the air fresh. And who came up with all of this? Her husband! Just tremendous!

They covered the whole length of the tunnel within a half-hour, but a most unfortunate surprise awaited them at the far end – the exit was closed. A large aperture had been cut into the top of the tube, but it was covered by a rectangular, cast-iron hatch that looked more like a door lying on its side. This is clearly where they would unload their cargo, but it was shut tightly for the time being. Also, the lock and the handle were on the other side. Marichka got scared; she felt like this black, underground space was a trap they'd fallen into.

'What are we going to do?' she asked her husband, voice quivering.

'Don't worry, Marichka. Everything's gonna be alright.' He tried to calm his wife down as he frantically tried to think of a way to escape.

'Yeah, I know, but that's not what I was asking. I mean what are we going to do… you know, right now?'

'Well, the tunnel's locked. It'll be up and running tomorrow, on Independence Day, once the fountain starts working. So, we probably just have to wait it out. It's a good thing nobody knows we're down here. We're out of harm's way for now. Let's head back to the cars. We have water and some food. We'll just have to wait until tomorrow. Then we'll ride back here with the first batch of goods and slip through to freedom. Everything's gonna be alright!'

Marichka went quiet, her sense of alarm lingering. She'd been hoping that they'd be in the woods on the Hungarian side by now, that they'd be free, breathing fresh air, but now the tunnel was locked – on both sides, too. It's tough to keep your cool in a situation like this, because you can't help feeling like a corpse or an earthworm. There was nothing they could do about it, though; they'd just have to wait until tomorrow for this nightmare to end. Trying to rid herself of those gloomy thoughts, Marichka started crawling back towards the Ukrainian side of the tunnel. Then she stopped abruptly.

'Hey, there's water down here. My hands and knees are all wet,' she said, giving her husband a puzzled look.

'Yeah, you're right. That's nothing, though. Probably just some groundwater that seeped through. Just ignore it,' Tys replied with affected calm. He tensed up – the tunnel had been as dry as a desert when they were coming the other way. He knew that for sure, because he'd been stunned at how good a job they'd done. Now the whole floor was covered in water. He just kept crawling forward with an apathetic expression on his face so as not to alarm his wife.

While Tys and Marichka were crawling towards Hungary, Miklos Svyscho went down to the basement of the Café Danube. He had to go to an old army buddy's birthday in the next neighborhood over and he wasn't planning on getting back until really late, so he decided to test the fountain before the unveiling the next day. That would put him at ease. He went down to the basement, twisted the big knob, went up to the café, and then headed to the square. Everything was calm and quiet; the water wasn't leaking out of the fountain anywhere, which meant everything was hooked up just fine. All he had to do tomorrow morning was press a button that would open up a valve and start a motor that would send pressurised water into the fountain. That was it. The Fisherman went back down into the basement and suddenly pricked up his ears. He thought he'd heard water flowing. Surprised, he went up to the square again and took a look at the fountain but didn't spot anything out of the ordinary. Ychi's successor figured it was probably just the sewer. He turned around, closed the basement door, and then hobbled down Station Street to make the first train.

Tys crawled forward, realising that something was up. The water was rising, there was no doubt about that. Now it was about two inches above his hands. Also, he could feel a current coming from the end of the tunnel they were heading towards, from the Ukrainian side. He decided to start talking so Marichka, who was following him, wouldn't worry, so she'd think about something else.

'You know,' Tys began, his hands and knees slapping the cool water, 'there has to be some sort of grand design. Don't laugh now – I just think that this planet is the way it is for a reason. I got to thinking yesterday when I was lying on the bank of the Tysa, waiting for nightfall. How can people be so cruel? Where does that come from? Why do they want to kill and destroy each other? What compelled my friends, the people I shared my best idea with, my associates, who should've been grateful, to take that step? Even Icarus, who sat next to me in school all those years, agreed that it would be better to kill me and sell my organs. I thought about that for a long time yesterday, and then all the puzzle pieces came together in my head. I mean, I'm a historian, I know that throughout history people have mostly been fighting wars or killing each other just because. They couldn't stop. It was like some evil spirit was egging them on. All this time, century after century, just war and more war. After the horrors of the Second World War, everyone hoped that humanity – or at least our part of it, Western civilisation, that is – had grown wiser, that after the gas chambers at Auschwitz, systematic killing would never return to Europe, that we were wiser now. You know, we have all this technology, the Internet, international organisations, multiculturalism, and all that stuff. But no, in the early 90s, war broke out in Yugoslavia, and people started butchering each other en masse and burning down villages. Several thousand men from Srebrenica were murdered in just one day! That's in modern times, in Europe! And now there's this stupid, schizophrenic war with Russia...just why did Putin start all this up? What's it all for? Why did he want to kill thousands of people and sentence millions more to grave misfortune? What drove him to do that? I figured it out yesterday. He was driven by the same thing that drives the mayor, Icarus, the Succubus, Milosevic, and every other murderer. They're driven by human nature. Human beings aren't just good, they're evil, too. The murder and cruelty genes are inside every single one of us. It isn't eroded by culture and the progress of civilisation. It's inside every single one of us. The fur-covered Java

Man killed just like Putin's troops, though they have satellites up in space, ultra-precise weapons, and cell phones now... Just picture this – a soldier's walking around in Ukraine, and he has the Internet right there in his pocket, the whole world in his pocket, but he's killing everyone in his path, just for kicks. So, he's no different than his ape-like ancestors. Nah, he is different. He's worse than them, because he destroys much more, for no reason, and it only comes back to hurt him. So, there's something beautiful and something ugly about every person. But why is it that only the force of circumstances can squeeze out the beautiful, while the ugly comes out all on its own? I'll tell you why – it's all because of the planet, nature itself. It's just that there are too many people on this earth. Seven billion beings who gobble everything up and leave behind heaps of trash as high as Mount Everest. So the planet activates a mechanism that is deadly for us, a kind of defense mechanism, just so it can survive. It's the same mechanism the Sumerians or the people in the Bible described with the metaphor of the flood. The Earth comes up with incurable diseases – cancer, AIDS, viruses, and epidemics – to thin our ranks, to keep our count below seven billion, because wherever there are humans there's filth and grief, greed and ingratitude. We just don't appreciate our home, our planet. We can destroy the Earth with our unwise actions, so it has to protect itself. But no viruses or diseases can wipe out everyone. Only man himself can wipe out all of humanity. That's why he invented nuclear weapons. So, AIDS and all those wars are just like spring cleaning, a form of self-purification. The Earth doesn't need us, we've proven to be problem children, parasites on its body. So, it sends us an impulse that activates the bad, the belligerent, and the lethal inside all of us, and we go out and kill each other. That's why I don't have any ill will towards my ex-associates. They are merely tools in a game we didn't invent.'

Marichka didn't say anything in reply. She just kept crawling behind her husband, her breathing laboured and loud. Fear and alarm hung in the air. The water kept rising; it was nearly up to their elbows. And from far away, from where the tunnel began under the fountain, they could hear the sound of a waterfall. Every single one of Tys and Marichka's steps echoed inside the tube; their movements generated waves that crashed against the concrete walls. Tys went quiet. His wife wasn't talking either. They were paralysed by fear, and this feeling was intensified threefold by the darkness and cold of the enclosed underground space.

They eventually reached the head of the tunnel, where they saw that water was indeed falling from up above, from a pipe off to the right. Another pipe hung from the ceiling next to the first one. They were clearly supposed to be connected by an elbow piece, but they weren't. Tys tried shining his light on them, but he couldn't see anything because his battery was almost dead. He'd spent all of yesterday by the river and hadn't been able to charge his phone. Damn! It flickered several times and then turned off a few seconds later. Tys tried to plug the pipe – a thick stream of water was gushing out of it – with his jacket, but that attempt proved futile. The water pressure was so high that he couldn't even hold his jacket in the pipe with both hands. Terror sliced right through him. The water couldn't be stopped. Tys dashed towards the hatch; it was still shut tight.

'Give me your phone. We have to call the police or someone. They gotta save us. They sealed the hatch, it's air-tight, and the water's rising real fast. We'll get washed away within the hour, we'll drown in here. Don't care if they find us, to hell with it! We have to call the police, the fire department, they gotta get us out of here first. Then I'll deal with Bartok and the rest of them,' Tys yelled over the waterfall, turning around and facing the darkness behind him.

'Wait a second,' Marichka replied. Then came the sound of her backpack zipper opening, followed by about twenty seconds of nothing, except the sound of water.

'C'mon, what are you waitin' for? We're trapped!' Tys said, now panicking.

'We're in trouble,' Marichka said, her voice feeble with fright. 'Looks like my phone got all wet. I put it in the top pocket of my backpack. And when you said to put it on my chest, not my back… uh, that pocket was closest to the floor. Everything's wet now, my ID, too. My phone won't turn on… I'm not getting anything.'

'Damn!' Tys broke into a howl. They just sat there in the impenetrable gloom. Tys suddenly remembered his cheap watch. He pressed the backlight, not really hoping for anything, but the small, rectangular screen did light up. Guess they weren't lying at the store when they said it was waterproof. 7:42. 'Damn, damn! It's not even eight a.m. yet, but the water's already filled up a third of the tube! What should we do? Huh?' Tys pounded on the hatch madly, yelling as loud as he could. 'Save us! We're down here! Look, down here! Save us! Help!' That lasted for about 10 minutes, until he wore himself out. Then he slumped down onto the floor, his back resting against the wall of the tunnel. Marichka wasn't saying anything; he couldn't even see her. The water kept coming, roaring ferociously. Then Tys sprang to his feet so abruptly that he hit his head on the ceiling. He ignored the pain, though. He grabbed ahold of the pipe that led towards the fountain, and started screaming into it, begging for help and hoping that his screams would be heard above ground, under the oak in Peace Square. He kept screaming until he went hoarse. No answer.

Then Marichka started slamming her fists against the hatch. She'd finally snapped out of her daze. She pounded and pounded, cursed and cursed, but that, too, was all for naught. The tube was already half full. If the water kept coming that quickly they'd drown inside this giant jar within the next hour or hour and a half, tops.

'Let's go, follow me,' Tys said, yanking Marichka by the hair. He'd meant to grab her by the arm, but he miscalculated in the dark. 'Let's go. We have to get to the Hungarian side as quickly as possible, that's our only chance. This hatch used to be part of a bomb shelter; it can withstand a nuclear blast. But over there, in the woods, it'll be much easier to get out. Over there, we should be able to escape this hell. The two of us can do it – we'll bust that door open. C'mon, hurry up!'

Marichka complied unquestioningly. Her brain refused to accept this situation; it seemed as though all of this was just a dream, a nightmare, and she just couldn't wake up. Her husband had offered her a chance, a plan, a way out. Once again, she put all her trust in him. Now they left their backpacks; carrying them would only slow the couple down. Once they'd wormed their way past the cars – much faster this time around – they reached the less cramped part of the tube. As they crawled along, they had to cock their heads so their chins would stay above water and they wouldn't gulp down the waves when they were trying to breathe. The water was starting to feel cold, even icy. It may have been August, but water, especially in such abundance, was inevitably bone-chilling inside the concrete tunnel. Their clothing was soaked, heavy, which made it hard to move. Marichka first shed her jacket and then her shoes. The couple pushed forward, on the brink of exhaustion. The sound of the water under the fountain gradually faded away. Roughly halfway through the tunnel, Tys tried swimming, instead of crawling, and it turned out to be much easier and faster. Tys told his wife to let the current push her along and then swam ahead.

As Tys swam the last two hundred yards, he kept thinking about how he shouldn't have taken his wife along with him. He wanted to do something good, but it turned out like everything always did – just plain shitty. He didn't care about dying. He didn't feel sorry for himself, but why did this have to happen to his darling little Marichka? Why had he come into her life? She clearly deserved a better husband, didn't she? He brought her to this cursed town, where she languished for years on end. He ruined her life and robbed her of a future. He couldn't ever really support her or at least give her what other husbands gave their wives. They never had enough money to go to the sea, not even for one trip. After Tremora died, Marichka kept crying over how her daughter had never gotten to go to the sea, although she'd always dreamt about going. That's when Tys thought to himself, 'Marichka hasn't ever gone to the sea either, not once.' There was a time he felt that he was capable of rectifying that; he'd show his beloved the sea. Tremora never got a chance to go, but they would. Shortly thereafter, their relationship turned sour; they couldn't even have a civil conversation anymore, and Tys started hitting the bottle, retreating to sleazy bars. He was escaping from the tragedy, from the grief that flooded their house, plunging into drunken ramblings about the Kyivan counts. Now he and Marichka were in this tunnel, yet another product of his demented imagination. She'd never been to the sea, though. Why did he drag her here? Why couldn't he have left her at home and gone it alone?

'Because I loved her, because I still love her,' he thought, answering his own question as he swam through the underground darkness. He loved her, and now he would tell her that. That he really loved her, that he was lucky to have her, that he was grateful his Marichka had been standing outside the school that day, holding that Shevchenko cover, that she stayed by his side, that she ate the oranges he brought her after unloading boxes all night, that she went with him to Vedmediv, that she gave him a daughter, their greatest joy, that she didn't desert him during their darkest hour – after their child had died and their lives had fallen apart – that she stuck by him, no matter what, and that she put up with him coming home drunk. And that she never complained when he would lock himself in his study and freeze her out for days at a time. She was by his side this whole time, although she could've found herself a better man a long time ago. Maybe she just loved him. Loved him like he loved her. If she didn't, then she wouldn't have sprung out of bed in the middle of the night and followed her husband to an underground tunnel, to their way out, to the unknown. Marichka went with him, though. She put her faith in him, but he led her to her death. To the most horrid of deaths one can imagine – drowning in a concrete tunnel, as if inside someone's intestine. That's what he'd brought upon his beautiful little Marichka.

Tys no longer believed that they had any chance of saving themselves. The hatch on the Hungarian side was of the highest quality, just like the rest of the tunnel. They wouldn't be able to bust it open. They were doomed, but he didn't want to tell his wife that; he didn't want to scare her. Instead, he wanted to ask for forgiveness. For everything – for their dreams that never quite panned out, for being such a loser, for not being able to prevent their daughter's death, for not making her happy, for not showing her the sea, for disappointing her countless times, for bringing her, living and breathing, down here, underground ... Tys wanted to apologise and just say that he really did love Marichka. He hoped she'd forgive him, despite the fact that he had dragged her down to the tunnel; he simply had to be with her, he couldn't imagine his life without her. He loved her. That's why he dragged her down there. So, he hoped she'd forgive him or at least try to. Because he loved her. That's what Tys wanted to say to Marichka, but he couldn't muster up the courage.

The words got stuck in his throat. It's hardest to talk about love with the people you love the most, with the people you've loved so long and so deeply that it becomes self-evident. It's so obvious that you love them, so what's the point in saying it? People keep it in for years, too afraid of embarrassing themselves, of truly opening up, of feeling vulnerable. Because saying 'I love you' makes a person vulnerable, real. Tys just wanted to apologise and say that he loved her. There was nothing else to add. That way his dear Marichka, who'd suffered with him all through their lives, would know, at least in her last few minutes, that it wasn't all for naught; he really did love her, more than anything else. That's all Tys wanted to say; then their deaths wouldn't be so pointless. He wanted to say that to Marichka, but he couldn't.

Once they'd reached the end of the tunnel, they spent a good 15 minutes trying to bust open the rectangular hatch, to get out of this trap, to save themselves. They dug their feet into the floor and pushed against the hatch with their hands and shoulders. They drummed their fists on it and screamed for help, to no avail. They felt every inch of the hatch, trying to find some sort of hook, keyhole, handle, lever, or crack – nothing. They started pounding again, their blows growing weaker and more hopeless.

The water was rising. Now distraught, Tys and Marichka were kneeling in the cold water, in the darkness of the concrete tube that was soon to be their coffin. The backs of their necks were pressed firmly against the ceiling, and the water was already up to their chins. 'Is this it?' Marichka asked, sounding like a frightened child.

Tys turned towards her, took her hands in his underwater, moved closer to her face, which he couldn't see, and kept staring into the darkness, as if he were looking into Marichka's beautiful brown eyes. He knew what he wanted to say. He felt her next to him. In his mind, he thanked this dear woman for sticking it out with him until the end. He thanked her, yet wanted to apologise, because it was all his fault. He loved her; he just had to be with her.

That's what Tys wanted to say to his wife.

He held her hand in his, feeling her warmth, their kinship, despite the frigid water. It was as though this touch between Tys and Marichka had sent a pulsating current of love between them. Tys inhaled loudly, preparing himself to tell her just what he'd wanted to tell her for so long, yet couldn't find the courage and time for. They were the simplest words, the words Marichka had been waiting to hear from him for so long. Now was the time. Tys swallowed some saliva and tried to make out those beloved eyes in the dark. Now he'd tell her, his most cherished person, his celestial being.

The water rose, nearly reaching the cable meant to carry current to the absent light bulbs. A wave swayed and licked a socket – the charge shot across the water much faster than the speed of sound. The dry electrical crackle didn't reach the couple's ears quick enough. The water kept pouring in, but now it was silent. Silence prevailed in the cold tunnel. It was as dark as inside a coffin. Tys and Marichka were floating underwater, their bodies weightless. Their hands were still together, fingers interlocked. And their eyes were open; it was as if they'd decided they would just look at each other forever, like on that warm October night, ages ago, when Tys first saw Marichka in the glow of Uzhhorod's streetlights. God, she was just so beautiful that day.

Uzhhorod-Chernivtsi-Uzhhorod, 2014–2015

RECENT TITLES PUBLISHED BY JANTAR

Bellevue *by* IVANA DOBRAKOVOVÁ

Translated by Julia and Peter Sherwood

Blanka takes a summer job at a centre for people with physical disabilities in the French city of Marseille, where her encounter with their severe conditions ends badly. A novel about our inability to escape 'our own private cages', imprisoned by fear, anxiety and mistrust, no less than indifference to others.

-- ISBN: 978-0-9934467-7-1

In the Name of the Father *by* BALLA

Translated by Julia and Peter Sherwood

Balla's nameless narrator reflects upon his life filled with failures looking for someone else to blame. He completely fails to notice 'the thing' growing in the cellar. A hilarious satire poking fun at masculinity, the early years of the Slovak state and the author himself.

-- ISBN: 978-0-9933773-5-8

Big Love *by* BALLA

Translated by Julia and Peter Sherwood

Andrič and his girlfriend Laura have been seeing each other for a long time now but it isn't clear what each sees in the other. A critique of contemporary society, in which the triumph of liberal democracy has increased rather than diminished the Kafkaesque aspects of life.

-- ISBN: 978-0-9934467-8-8

For further news on new books and events, please visit
www.JantarPublishing.com